**Nothing in Chard's manner suggested that he thought he had met her before.**

'I trust that you are not finding my daughter too difficult a charge, Miss Lawrence. Her liveliness leads her into difficulties. Her tongue is a little long too.' For the first time he smiled at Emma.

That, too, had changed. It was a rueful smile, not one designed to charm. Emma found herself saying, with a rueful smile of her own, 'I know, and if I may say so without offence, she has used it to introduce me to you—frequently.'

The rueful smile grew broader. '"Papa says. . ."' He allowed his voice to trail off before adding, 'I can only hope that I have made a good impression.'

**Paula Marshall**, married with three children, has had a varied life. She began her career in a large library and ended it as a senior academic in charge of history in a Polytechnic. She has travelled widely, has been a swimming coach, and has appeared on *University Challenge* and *Mastermind*. She has always wanted to write, and likes her novels to be full of adventure and humour.

**Recent titles by the same author:**

A BIDDABLE GIRL?
THE LOST PRINCESS
NOT QUITE A GENTLEMAN
DEAR LADY DISDAIN
THE ASTROLOGER'S DAUGHTER
REASONS OF THE HEART
THE MOON SHINES BRIGHT
TOUCH THE FIRE
THE CAPTAIN'S LADY

# EMMA AND THE EARL

## Paula Marshall

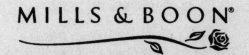

*MILLS & BOON and*
*MILLS & BOON with the Rose Device*
*are registered trademarks of the publisher.*

*First published in Great Britain 1996*
*Large Print edition 1997*
*Harlequin Mills & Boon Limited,*
*Eton House, 18–24 Paradise Road, Richmond,*
*Surrey TW9 1SR*

© Paula Marshall 1996

ISBN 0 263 14900 5

*Set in Plantin*
*42-9701-89668-14½-15¼*

*Printed and bound in Great Britain*
*by The Ipswich Book Company Limited, Ipswich*

# CHAPTER ONE

'HELL and damnation!' cried Mr Henry Gardiner as he staggered away on the backstairs landing of his London home. 'You have injured my foot, you bitch.' And, bent double, he massaged his damaged instep.

Miss Emma Lawrence, his two young daughters' governess, still calm and controlled, although her hair was dishevelled and the neck of her modest grey gown was awry, watched him as coolly as though she were attending some drama at Drury Lane. He had just seized her at the top of the stairs, muttered something unintelligible and begun to kiss and manhandle her as though she were a very doxy. The other servants had warned her of his nasty habits, but until today he had contented himself with watching her with lecherous eyes as she went about her business.

She had tried to fight him off without making too much ado, pulling her mouth away and protesting, 'No, I beg of you, no. Recollect who you are and who I am!'

All to no avail. He simply mumbled nonsense into her hair about her beauty having made him lose his head and what was a kiss among friends, redoubling his efforts to caress her so that there had been nothing for it but to bring down her foot on his with all her power. And if she had broken a bone, then so be it. At least she had made him release her, and his curses were more welcome than his kisses.

But her comfortable position in his household was at an end, and as she walked down the stairs he shouted after her, 'You miserable vixen. I'll have you out of here before the week's end, and without a character!'

Emma swung round and walked back to confront him on the landing, saying, still cool, 'I think not. You may turn me away, and I shall be happy to leave a place where I am to be treated as a trull, but it would be wise of you to allow me to leave without a fuss. Your wife would not be happy to learn of your behaviour to me.'

Now, Emma was not entirely certain that she was speaking the truth, but something which Mrs Gardiner had recently said had given her the notion that it was her family which supplied the Gardiners with their income and their comfortable life, Mr Gardiner having little fortune of his own. That being so, she might do what others in her case had done and leave him, taking the children with her, her money being settled on herself and them. Particularly as she had also, in her vague way, hinted that she was tired of enduring Mr Gardiner's wandering eye—to say nothing of his wandering hands! And particularly when they were wandering all over the servants; Mrs Gardiner found this humiliating.

At least if Emma had to leave—as she must—she would do so, she hoped, with the possibility of gaining another position.

'Bitch,' snarled Mr Gardiner over his shoulder, hopping back towards his room, knowing that Emma spoke more truly than she perhaps knew. His wife had already reproached him for his predatory behaviour towards the servants—and the indiscretion with which he carried it out.

All the same, Miss Lawrence would have to go—even if he could not attack her character when she left. He could not stand to be reminded by her presence that he had tried and failed with her so cruelly. Her predecessor had been only too flattered—which was, of course, why *she* had been turned away.

Nevertheless, when Mrs Gardiner sent for her later that day, Emma knew only too well the reason for her presence in her mistress's pretty boudoir.

Mrs Gardiner began in her usual vague and kindly manner. 'It grieves me to part with you, my dear Miss Lawrence, but alas, as you know, my husband is to be posted abroad to the British Embassy in Paris. He has a poor cousin there to whom he wishes to do a good turn, and she has said that she will be delighted to act as governess to dear Georgina and Selina when we arrive there. . . He will not hear of anything else. I am sure that you understand how I am placed.'

Oh, yes, Emma well understood how her employer was placed, and also that Mrs Gardiner knew how Emma was placed with regard to her husband's behaviour—although neither of them would admit it openly!

But Emma said nothing of any of this, and, as befitted a true lady, folded her hands on her lap as composedly as she could, bent her head submissively and waited for her employer to continue.

'Your conduct towards the girls, and your care and control of both of them has been exemplary. You seem to have a gift for controlling young children—such a pity that you are unlikely to be able to practise it on your own. Oh, dear. . .'

Mrs Gardiner was given to such verbal gaffes, and had suddenly realised that it was not exactly tactful to inform a penniless, familyless governess in her late twenties—past her last prayers, as the saying had it—that she was unlikely to marry.

Colouring a little, she ploughed desperately on. Miss Lawrence's expression had not changed, so she had probably not fully understood what had just been said to her.

'Fortunately, my dear, my cousin's wife, Lady Hampton, has asked me if I can recommend a governess for her brother's motherless little daughter. I gather that the last one proved most unsatisfactory. I told her that you would be leaving us through no fault of your own, and that I can recommend you without any reservations.'

She paused, a little out of breath, giving Emma the opportunity to ask, 'And this brother, madam, who is he? And where does he live?'

Flustered—she lived in a perpetual fluster, and no wonder, with the egregious Henry for a husband—Mrs Gardiner gabbled on distractedly.

'Oh, did I not tell you? Lady Hampton's brother is the Earl of Chard, and he lives at Loudwater in Northumbria. He married Isabella Beaumains. She was one of those Beaumains—the rich as Midas ones, or do I mean Croesus? I always muddle them up. . . Which was just as well, for Chard was as poor as a church mouse before he married her. His distant cousin—the previous Earl—had impoverished the estate by high living and gambling. . .so it was fortunate that Chard brought some wealth with him when he inherited Loudwater. . .'

Her voice petered out, which was also just as well, for Emma, on hearing the name of the Earl of Chard, had ceased to listen to her and had fallen into a trance where Mrs Gardiner's droning voice was all that remained to her of unkind reality.

Chard! Dominic Hastings—as he had been before he had unexpectedly succeeded to the title. To be a governess to Chard's child! Oh, no, fate could not be so unkind. She could never go there, never. God could not ask it of her.

But if she did not accept Mrs Gardiner's kind offer, where *could* she go? Homeless, with only one poor friend and no relatives—or rather none who wished to acknowledge her—and no money, she had no alternative but to consider the possibility that what she could never do, she *must* do. She would starve otherwise. And surely after ten years, with a different name and a completely changed appearance and station, Dominic Hastings would not know her.

'Miss Lawrence! Miss Lawrence!' It was Mrs Gardiner, looking most concerned. 'Are you well, Miss Lawrence? I thought that you were about to faint.'

'N-nothing,' stammered Emma. 'It is nothing.' She hesitated, then said, as impersonally as she could, 'Does the Earl, then, live at Loudwater?'

'So I understand. Since his wife has died Lady Hampton assists him in hiring and firing servants, and there is some sort of a poor relation who is Chard's chatelaine at Loudwater—in lieu of a wife, you understand—who has the care of the child, as well as the usual nursemaid. But I don't think you need trouble yourself about meeting Chard—if *that* is what troubles you. No, not at all. I believe that he was wild once, but no longer. He has some eccentric interests, Mr Gardiner says, but not the kind in which we ladies are interested or are likely to be involved. He has little to do with his neighbours and does not go at all into society, Lady Hampton says.'

Now, this did not sound at all like the Dominic Hastings Emma had once known, who had loved society, and it threw her into a little confusion— centred around the difficulty that, while it seemed madness to accept a position in his employ, it also seemed equal madness not to accept it!

To starve or not to starve, that was the question—to parody Hamlet, thought Emma wildly. And I don't wish to starve. After all, Emilia Lincoln, that stammering, fat girl of seventeen, was long gone, and ten years was also a long time. . . .

'I suppose Lady Hampton would wish to see me,' she said composedly. 'Yes, I will take advantage of her offer.'

'Then that is that, my dear. What a load off my mind.'

Mrs Gardiner was as kind as she was apparently silly, and Henry's insistence, when he had limped into nuncheon this morning, that she have Miss Lawrence out of the house as soon as possible—'I hate the sight of her churchyard face'—had distressed her a little. Few dependants were as trustworthy or as competent. But, knowing the true reason why Henry wished to be rid of her, it was as well for the poor young thing that she was found a new post as soon as possible.

Later Emma found herself unable to sleep for worrying over whether she ought to accept the post of Lady Letitia Hastings' governess. In the dark watches of the night the events of ten years ago, which she had thought long since dimmed by time, were as sharp and clear as though they had happened only yesterday.

She had told herself only a few days ago that that part of her life was over and forgotten, that its power to wound her had vanished, but the one word Chard—or rather the two words Dominic Hastings—had proved her wrong.

Sitting up in bed in the early hours, her mind in turmoil, she had almost decided against going to see Lady Hampton—who might also remember her—but the cold light of dawn brought her to a different decision. She would see Lady Hampton, listen to what she had to say, and make her decision then. Or Lady Hampton might make it for her, if she remembered that vanished past when she met Emma and recognised her. If so, she would be the last person whom she would choose to work for Dominic Hastings, fifth Earl of Chard!

All of this made it difficult for her to remain her usual calm self as she waited to be interviewed in an ante-room at Hampton House, off Piccadilly.

A pleasant woman opened the double doors which led to the library and told her that Lady Hampton was ready to see her.

She was seated at a table before a window which looked out onto a large garden. Her dress was comfortable rather than fashionable, and Emma recognised her at once though she, judging by her manner and speech, did not recognise Emma— which was what Emma had hoped, had, indeed, dared to expect.

Lady Hampton was a dominant, handsome creature rather than a pretty one, and was some ten years or so older than her brother Chard, which placed her in her early to middle forties. She turned a shrewd eye on the young woman who had come so highly recommended.

Miss Lawrence seemed a modest young thing. Her clothing was both neat and discreet, being a gown of some plain grey stuff with a linen collar edged with a thin line of lace. She wore no jewellery or ornament other than a small silver watch on a black moire ribbon which hung from her waist. She was dark with naturally curling hair, tidily strained back. Her complexion was good, and her most distinguishing feature was a pair of fine eyes.

Hardly the sort of would-be mermaid likely to attract Chard's attention—not that he made a habit of seducing plainish governesses these days, but one never knew what might take a man's idle fancy when other, more attractive women were not available!

All being well, this modest young woman might be the one to solve Chard's problem for him.

'You come well recommended, Miss Lawrence. Sit, I beg of you.'

Emma had remained standing, her hands folded before her, her head slightly bent, as though to catch every word that Lady Hampton might care to favour her with. This attitude, though charmingly submissive, bore no relationship to the inward Emma Lawrence, whose opinions of her superiors and employers would have surprised them greatly if they had been privy to them.

Well, Lady Hampton was a deal more courteous

than Mr Henry Gardiner, and a great deal more businesslike than his wife. She conducted the interview briskly, leaving Emma in no doubt that she knew exactly what she was doing.

'Lady Letitia Hastings is my brother Chard's only child,' she said, laying down Mrs Gardiner's letter, which she had been re-reading when Emma had been announced. 'She is eight years old, an old-fashioned little thing whose mother died when she was born. My brother is anxious that she should have as settled a life as possible, even though he does not, I understand, intend to remarry. Alas, however, the governesses whom we have employed so far have, for a variety of reasons, been unsatisfactory—which, as you may understand, has *not* led to a settled life for the poor child.

'Now, not only Mrs Gardiner but also your previous employer, Madame Dumaurier from the French Embassy, have informed me that you are, although comparatively young, remarkably steady and remarkably well educated. The young woman whom you are replacing vowed to us that she had no intention of marrying—and then promptly became betrothed to a visiting curate! Do I take it that *you* have no intention of marrying in the near future? If you do have such an intention, pray say so, and the interview will end.

'I may say that, having met you, I hope you can give me this assurance and end our current problems. Our wish is that you will see your way to remaining with Letitia until she reaches young ladyhood.'

Inside, Emma was burning with rage. Obviously, whatever else might have changed over the past ten years, Dominic Hastings remained the selfish and unfeeling person whom she had once had the misfortune to know. So he wished his little daughter to have a secure and settled life, did he? But the one thing which might ensure that—a second marriage—he was determined to avoid.

How like him! Her heart went out to his neglected child. If she had been in any doubt that she would accept this post, his callousness, and that of his sister, had swept them away.

Nothing showed. She said, in the coolest voice she could summon up, 'I have no desire whatsoever to marry. You need have no fears on that score. The mere idea is repulsive to me. I would starve, rather—something which your offer of this post will render unnecessary for at least ten years. If I prove satisfactory, that is.'

Lady Hampton looked up sharply. Emma's expression, her posture of subservient dependant had not changed, but there had been some note in her voice which troubled her a little. She shook her head—this was no time for whimwhams—said briskly, 'Madame Dumaurier has informed me that your command of French is that of a native, and Mrs Gardiner writes that in addition to all and more of the governess's usual accomplishments you are a mistress of the pianoforte. Nothing remains, therefore, but for me to inform you of your salary and set in train your journey to Loudwater—which you will, I hope, be able to undertake as soon as possible.'

'I understand,' Emma replied, 'that my replacement at the Gardiners' will be in post when they reach Paris and that Mrs Gardiner will manage without a governess until they reach there—thus enabling me to satisfy all your requirements.'

'Then that is that, Miss Lawrence.' Lady Hampton picked up a small bell in order to ring it and signify that the interview was at an end. She looked up rather more quickly than Emma had thought she would—to see on the governess's face an expression so strange that for a moment she halted, the bell held in mid-air.

The oddness about the governess's apparently modest and impeccably well-behaved person struck her all over again. She found herself saying, 'I have the strangest feeling that we have met before, Miss Lawrence. Can that be possible?'

There was nothing to do but lie. And what was it that had provoked *that*? Nothing about her could conceivably resemble the person whom Louisa Hampton had met once before—on Dominic Hastings' arm. It was true that as Lady Hampton had picked up the bell Emma had thought for a moment of that meeting, and had wondered ironically what Lady Hampton's response would be if she told her the real reason why the thought of marriage was so repulsive to her.

Instead, she said as calmly as she could, 'Oh, I think that most unlikely.' She put her head on one side and gazed at Lady Hampton thoughtfully. 'I'm sure that I should have remembered you, aren't you?'

If Lady Hampton thought that this statement was a little two-edged she gave no sign of it but rang the bell. The interview was at an end. For good or ill, the Lady Letitia Hastings had a new governess—and one who had promised to remain with her until she reached young ladyhood. That would be at least ten years, by which time Miss Emma Lawrence would be as resigned to spinsterhood as Lady Letitia would be to a grand marriage.

# CHAPTER TWO

MISS Emma Lawrence, however, was not resigned to anything, and the calm face which she had shown to Lady Hampton was a false one. In the middle of the sleepless night following her interview she sat up in bed and tried to drive from her mind the memories of almost ten years ago, which had invaded it and would not go away.

Useless—quite useless! They would not vanish. That which she had hoped—nay, believed—she had forgotten forever was as fresh as though it had happened yesterday. Perhaps it would be best not to try to forget but to let the memories come, and then, once experienced again, the past would go away. . .

She let it flow over her. . . Time turned in upon itself. . .

Emma was Emilia Lincoln, not quite eighteen, the only child and heiress of Henry Lincoln, a man of old family but of new-won great wealth. His late wife's family was even older. She had been exquisitely beautiful, slim, blonde and fragile, but Emilia, alas, took after her father and was unfashionably dark. Worse, she was plump, and growing plumper by the year. Her governess called it puppy fat and said that she was a late developer and would soon become as slim as her lovely mother had been.

But time passed by and Emilia began to despair. Worse, though, than her heavy body was the stammer, which had begun to afflict her shortly after she had put on weight when she had reached adolescence. The harder she tried to lose it, the worse it got.

Her father loved her dearly—she was all that he had left of his wife—and, like the governess, hoped that both stammer and fat were part of a passing phase. The only consolation was that his daughter's mind was as acute as his own—although the stammer unfortunately disguised that fact.

Or was it fortunate? For it was inconvenient for a woman to possess a good mind; it often stood in the way of marriage. Not that that was a drawback for Emilia. Being a great heiress, there was no shortage of suitors for her hand. That being so, Henry Lincoln gave her the education of the son whom he would never have, since he could not bear to marry again.

Some of the suitors were rich, some poor, some had titles, others had none, and all were members of the cousinry—the nobility and gentry who ruled England and were all distantly related to one another. Henry Lincoln put no pressure on her to accept any particular one.

'You may choose whom you please,' he told her, 'other than anyone whom I know to be a scoundrel, or to whom I would not trust you, knowing that they might ill-treat you.'

At first Emilia thought that even to gain a fortune a man would not wish to marry a stammering fat girl, but she soon came to understand that most men would propose to a crippled hunchback to get at the fortune which she was sure to inherit. The difficulty was in deciding which one of her many suitors really cared for her. Shrewd in many ways, she soon learned to detect falsity, and stammered her refusal at pretty young fellows and hardened middle-aged men whom she was sure held her in contempt. Few of them ever cared to look behind the shy façade to discover what Emilia Lincoln was truly like.

Nor did she make any friends among the confident and pretty young ladies who were led into the ballrooms and drawing rooms of the *ton* to compete with her for a husband during her first and only season. She shared none of their interests and many of them looked down on the plain-seeming heiress and despised her because her father, though of good family, had made his wealth in trade. She was well aware that they giggled behind her back at her lack of looks and her lumpish figure.

And then, midway through the 1804 season, she met Dominic Hastings, as he then was. The first sight of him dazzled her. She was at a ball given by Lady Melbourne, who brought him over to where she sat with Miss Dacre, once her governess and now her duenna. She was a poor young lady of good family—a clergyman's daughter thrown upon the world to earn her living after her father had died at a comparatively early age.

'My dear Miss Lincoln,' Lady Melbourne said in the self-assured manner which went with the beauty which had remained with her until middle-age. 'Pray allow me to bring to your notice a young kinsman of mine, Dominic Hastings, who has just come to town but has long desired to meet you.'

Lady Melbourne was noted for her cultivation of youthful male protégés, and she was of the opinion that young Mr Hastings—he had just reached twenty-four—deserved his chance to win the Lincoln fortune.

Emilia was immediately overset. She had seen the beautiful young man enter the room a little earlier and had thought that he was the image of all the princes in the books of fairy tales which she had loved as a child, and all the heroes in the Minerva Press novels which she was currently reading!

He was tall and blond, broad-shouldered and long-legged. His face was as handsome as that of the statue of the Apollo Belvedere—a copy of which stood in the hall of Emma's home in Piccadilly. Better still, he was a very tulip of fashion in his black silk knee-breeches, his black and silver striped waistcoat, his black silk jacket and his snowy white cravat tied in the most elegant bow. Emma had learned later that Beau Brummell, that supreme arbiter of fashion, had taught him how to tie a cravat. His voice was beautiful too—a caressing baritone.

An older woman would have detected the faint touch of conceit which he carried around with him, and seen that he was used to both masculine and feminine admiration, but Emilia saw only perfection.

He was a noted athlete, sparred with Gentleman Jackson, played real tennis well and could ride and shoot with the best. His body was as finely tuned as his face was handsome. And this was the young man who was bowing low over her hand, looking up into her eyes as he straightened up and assuring her of his pleasure at meeting *her*.

Emilia's stammer as she assured him of her pleasure at meeting *him* was worse than it usually was. Excitement at having him by her side, at listening to him as he asked her how she was enjoying her first season was so great that her gaucheness had never been so apparent. Nevertheless, he did not allow it to trouble him. He asked her a series of questions tactfully designed to draw a young girl out—such as what did she think of Kemble, had she been to Astley's, to Vauxhall—so that at last her manner with him grew a little easier, although her stammer still troubled her.

But it did not seem to trouble him; he appeared not to be aware of it. He bent his beautiful head, listened gravely to her as she stuttered her answers, and led her onto the floor in the quadrille. He danced like an angel, having the light, fleet foot of an athlete, but Emilia, stumbling and turning through the convolutions of the dance, had seldom felt less fairylike.

She was astonished when, after the quadrille was over, he turned to her and said, still with that exquisitely charming gravity which appeared to be his hallmark, 'You will do me the honour of dancing the minuet with me later, Miss Lincoln, I trust,' before he led her back to Miss Dacre.

Miss Dacre was all of a twitter.

'What a piece of luck for you, Emilia! He is recognised to be the most handsome young man in the *beau monde*, and, although he is as poor as a church mouse, there is only one life between him and the Earldom of Chard. He wanted to be a soldier, but his widowed mother, who died just over a year ago, absolutely forbade it. He was all she had left, she said, and he must not desert her. And in her last illness she made him promise that he would never join the Army. Not very likely now, one supposes. He could hardly afford to.'

The only sensible thought that Emma had about him in the whole time that she knew him when she was Emilia Lincoln was in response to that. Well, he can hardly be so very poor, judging by his clothes and his horses and curricle. But that small piece of cynicism disappeared when his attentions continued even after the disaster of the minuet, when, in her excitement, she turned her ankle and he had to lead her from the floor.

In the end that was extremely fortunate for her,

since he refused to dance with anyone else for the remainder of the evening, preferring, he said, 'To sit by you, and entertain you.'

Which he did, telling her amusing stories about the other people present, and introducing her to George Brummell when that gentleman arrived and greeted him with great friendliness.

'And who is the charmer who is keeping you from the dance-floor, Hastings?' asked Mr Brummell, bowing to Emilia. 'Pray introduce me.' Mr Brummell had also been absent from town in the earlier part of Emilia's season.

Charmer! In the delightful haze in which she was living Emilia's stammer grew worse and worse and her plump cheeks more and more florid. Neither gentleman seemed to notice, and presently Dominic—he refused to allow her to call him Mr Hastings—departed to fetch her lemonade and sweet biscuits. 'To mend her ankle,' he said, cascading charm all over her.

Once he had gone Mr Brummell looked thoughtfully and somewhat drily at the flushed Emilia, and said, 'Do I collect that this is your first season, Miss Lincoln? Have you known Hastings long?'

'No, and no—although the season seems as though it has gone on for ever, like most things one experiences for the first time,' returned Emilia, recovering her wits now that the distracting Dominic had gone. Alone with Mr Brummell—who seemed a pleasantly mild gentleman despite his reputation as a dandy given to putting fools down—she had lost her stammer. Something of which Mr Brummell made private note.

'Ah, I thought by the fashion after which you were conversing that you were old friends.'

'Well, he seems to be my old friend now,' said Emilia. 'Even though Lady Melbourne only introduced him to me earlier this evening. He has been so very kind to me—missing the dancing which he has come to enjoy in order to sit here entertaining me, since I unfortunately ricked my ankle performing the minuet with him.'

If Mr Brummell thought that young Dominic Hastings' kindness was not so remarkable, having regard to his own poverty and the Lincoln heiress's great wealth, there to be won by a fortunate young man, he did not say so.

They talked for a little, and Mr Brummell's shrewdness soon told him that behind Miss Lincoln's unfortunate looks there was a good brain. His intuition and his experience of life also told him that Miss Lincoln was, as her governess also thought, a late developer, and would not necessarily remain fat and plain for ever. He doubted, however, that the pretenders to her fortune who danced around her—one or two of whom approached her whilst they sat talking— cared very much about her or her looks, only her money. He hoped that young Hastings would be kind to her if he won her. Something told him that Miss Lincoln could easily be hurt.

But Miss Lincoln was not thinking of being hurt. When Dominic returned with her lemonade and biscuits, all grave solicitude, she gave him her most dazzling smile, which transformed her face for a moment. Her shyness almost overwhelming her, she found herself eating her biscuits so greedily that Mr Brummell privately wondered whether he ought to advise Miss Lincoln to cut down on the fodder, but he decided that he did not yet know her well enough.

All in all, the evening was by far the happiest which Emilia had spent since the season began, and so she told Miss Dacre in the carriage on the way home, before she began to enlarge on Dominic Hastings' charm and kindness. Miss Dacre was only too happy to agree. How lucky for her charge to meet at last a pleasant and handsome young man who was sensible enough to realise that Emilia possessed virtues hidden from the many.

Duenna and charge alike took him at face value—and his face was worth valuing.

The rest of the season passed like a dream. Emilia was seen everywhere with him, and she refused the proposals of other suitors on an average of two a week, until one day her father sent for her and said kindly, 'Do I understand from your behaviour, my dear, that you are refusing so many eligible offers—including a duke—because you are hoping that young Hastings will propose?'

Emilia flushed and stammered. 'Y-y-yes, Papa. Do you mind?'

'Not at all, my dear. He is as empty-headed as most young men, but I do not think him vicious or unkind. He has no money but he is near to a title, and, should he propose to you—why, I should make no objections. Unlike many of your other suitors, he is not so very much older than you are.'

Empty-headed! Her Dominic—for so she had begun to think of him—how could her father say so? Her stammer disappeared and she spoke to him clearly and sensibly—as she always did to Mr Brummel but as she had never done to Mr Dominic Hastings. 'Oh, no, Papa, I don't think him empty-headed. Not at all.'

Later she was to think ruefully how correct her judgement of the apparently easy and carefree young man had been. No, he was not empty-headed. Dominic Hastings knew exactly what he was doing as he squired the young heiress around society. More, by holding back from proposing to her at once, he was allaying any suspicion that he was over-hasty in purusing a fortune. His modesty was put down by Miss Dacre and the Lincolns to a fond lover's decorum.

Not long before the season ended, Emilia and Miss Dacre took the carriage to Hyde Park one afternoon in the hope of seeing him there, riding the great black which few men, however skilled, could control as easily as he could.

There he was! Coming towards them! Emilia's heart began to thump as it always did when she saw him. He looked so absolutely splendid in his blue coat, his buckskin breeches and his highly polished boots with their golden tassels. He was always so *à point* that he made poor Emilia feel more dowdy than ever. Her heart beat so hard that she felt quite dizzy, and the mere idea that she might soon be his wife—for she was sure that he would propose before the season ended—had her going hot all over.

So besotted with adoration for him was she, that it never occurred to her that in all their time together he had never spoken to her of anything serious—had always treated her as though she were a charming but backward child. The Emilia Lincoln whom she had been before she met him would have resented what she would have seen as patronage, but, so bedazzled was she by his bright beauty and her own good luck in attracting him, that she never once questioned the basis on which he was so assiduously courting her. She took his apparent admiration as her due.

Recollecting her behaviour all these years later had her blushing for very shame at the naïve child she had been. But then her eyes on him had been adoring as he'd reached her carriage. He had leaned over to speak to them—his manners as beautiful as he was—and said, 'I am happy to see you both. My dear Miss Lincoln, I need to speak to you privately. Not here, you understand. May I hope that you will allow me to visit you tomorrow afternoon? And, after that, may I have the honour of speaking to your father? I know that it is the wrong way round, but I believe that you and I already understand one another.'

Emilia's heart began to beat so loudly on hearing this declaration that she wondered that he could not hear it. Unlovely crimson flooded into her face, and her stammer was at its worst as she struggled over her answer, 'O-o-of c-c-c-c-c—' and she finally got the word out '—course, Mr Hastings. I shall be m-m-most p-p-p-leased to see you.'

What a fool he must think her! But no, the tender blue eyes which went so well with his blond curls were tender for her, and for no one else.

'So pleased to hear you say so. And shall you be at Lady Corbridge's ball this evening?'

'No, I think not, alas,' replied Emilia slowly. 'Papa has guests and I must stay to entertain them. I doubt that they will leave in time for me to attend.' Then, greatly daring, the stammer for some reason absent this time, she added, 'But I must not repine. We shall be seeing one another tomorrow.'

'To my delight,' he murmured softly. 'To my eternal delight. Do carry that thought with you, Miss Lincoln.'

Oh, she did, she did. And when she told her father what her lover had said—for Dominic had at last made it plain that he *was* her lover—he replied, 'Then you must go to Lady Corbridge's ball this evening.'

'Your guests. . .?' she faltered.

'No, my love. Your life and your happiness must

come first at all times. Tell Miss Dacre that you may dine in your room, and I shall order the coachman to be ready for you whatever time you choose to go.'

Oh, delight! To see her beautiful lover again before tomorrow. Emilia ran upstairs and told Miss Dacre, and ordered her maid Nancy to put out her blue gown and be sure that all the trimmings which went with it were ready for her. She wished to look her best for her golden Apollo.

Afterwards she was to ask herself what folly, what *naïveté* could have made her believe that the handsome young man who demanded perfection in all his possessions could conceivably think that dowdy and plain Emilia Lincoln was someone for whom he could care. But at the time Cupid, the little god of love, had stripped her of sense, and, love being blind, Emilia Lincoln could not see the truth.

To be with him again so soon! She was late in arriving at the Corbridges', for at the last moment her dress had needed a small repair, and, all impatience, she had allowed her maid to mend it. She must look her best for him. For once she glowed a little, and the promise of a delicate beauty which lay behind her present lack of looks was there for those who had eyes to see.

George Brummell was one who had eyes, and he knew what the glow meant. But he also knew something else which Emilia had yet to discover. He was looking around for young Hastings, who had earlier thrown a half-drunken arm around Brummell's shoulders and spluttered, 'She won't be coming tonight, Brummell. One last night of freedom for me, thank God! Let's go to Laura Knight's to have some fun as soon as the rest of the fellows arrive!' Laura had been London's leading Cyprian at the time.

Yes, he needed to find Hastings quickly, to warn him to be wary. His heiress was unexpectedly present, after all, and he must be careful in what he said and did.

Emilia knew nothing of this, neither then nor later. She did not know why Brummell came up to engage her in his usual bantering style and then, a trifle officiously, to involve her in a lengthy conversation with pretty and flighty little Caro Ponsonby, Lady Bessborough's daughter, before bowing his farewells.

All this prevented her from going to find Dominic, but after as little time as politeness allowed she made her excuses to Lady Caro and, dodging Miss Dacre—after all, she would soon not be needing a duenna—set off to look for him.

But the house was large and the rooms were full. He was not on the dance-floor, nor in any of the adjoining ante-rooms. For some reason Emilia began to worry a little, and almost went back to Miss Dacre and the flighty Caro, but stubbornness kept her searching for him. The determination which lay behind her lumpish exterior even drove her to wander alone down a dimly lit corridor because she could hear male voices coming from a room at the end.

She half ran towards it in her relief, because she thought she could hear him. Yes, it was him—no doubt of it. Her haste had made her hot and disarranged her toilette, so before she entered the room she began to rearrange herself—and those few seconds of delay were to cost her everything.

Putting her hair to rights—it was slipping from the bandeau which Nancy had so carefully arranged—she heard her own name on Dominic's lips. He was speaking in a strange, slurred fashion, but mockery was plain in his voice. 'Of course I shall go with you to Laura Knight's. It is, when all is said and done, my last night of freedom.'

Another voice she did not recognise said, 'Oh, cease to bam us, Hastings, you lucky dog. Think what you are losing your freedom for. A fortune.'

'Oh, yes,' came Dominic's voice, mocking still. 'But look what I have to take with it! A fat piece with a distressing stammer, a taste in dress like a housemaid's and no conversation to speak of! Think of having to sit opposite to *that* at breakfast. One needs a fortune to reconcile one's self, do admit.'

Emilia stood there, stunned, her face going slowly white as for the first time she heard her lover's true opinion of her. Then a great blush of shame passed over her whole body, leaving her trembling. Could it really be her Dominic speaking of her so cruelly?

For a moment the shock was so great that she was on the verge of fainting. Surely she must be wrong. It could not be Dominic speaking such cruel words. She recovered herself, saw that there was no one about and moved forward to peer through the half-opened door into a room which Lady Corbridge had provided for her son Jack and his rowdy friends. She knew that they would stay long enough to do their duty by making an appearance at her ball before they went on to other, more dubious pleasures.

Alas, it *was* Dominic. But it was a Dominic whom Emma had never seen before. His image of careful perfection was quite gone. He was sprawled back in a big armchair, one foot on a small occasional table laden with empty bottles. His cravat was undone and his shirt was unbuttoned to the waist, revealing dark curling hair. She had never seen a man overset by drink before, but she knew at once that that was his condition.

*In vino veritas*, the saying went—a drunken man speaks the truth. And Emilia was sadly certain that for the first time in their acquaintance Dominic Hastings was speaking the truth about her.

'And besides,' he went on callously, 'she is getting a bargain too—something to which she could not aspire without a fortune—a title, no less. For who would marry such a fright otherwise, since it seems that my cousin Chard's heir is slowly dying.' His voice was lost in his fellow's guffaws.

She had told her father that he was no fool. Nor

was he. He was something worse—a greedy knave who had used his charm to fool her into marrying a man who found her contemptible. But chance had caused him to be found out. When he called on her in the morning, instead of a gullible girl hanging on his every word and eagerly ready to hand over herself and her father's money, he would find Miss Emilia Lincoln, the scales having dropped from her eyes, only too ready to refuse him.

He would have to start heiress-hunting all over again!

But, oh, how sick and sorry she felt. For had she not truly loved him, her handsome god with the feet of clay? She overheard a little more, which merely confirmed her determination to hurt him as he was hurting her. Emma felt as though she had lost her skin, had been flayed alive, and wondered how it would be possible for her to return to the ballroom, certain, as she now was, that she was the unlovely object of pity and contempt.

Listeners never ever heard any good of themselves, so it served her right for eavesdropping. Emilia was not sure that she was glad or sorry that she had. And, thinking this, she understood that she must vanish before she was caught.

Her head ringing, her eyes smarting, her whole body racked with shame and disappointment, she made her way back to the ballroom, stopping for a moment at a glass door which led onto a terrace overlooking London. She opened it and walked to the balustrade, to grip it tightly as she tried to compose herself. No one must ever know what she had found out. Pride forbade it.

Below her and stretching into the distance were the lights of the town. They were fuelled by the new gas which had caused such a commotion, and in which her father had invested money. The night air was cool on her hot, flushed cheeks. Her heart ceased to beat so violently and her hands slowly unclenched. She moved back into the house.

Miss Dacre looked curiously at her as she made her way to where she sat with a group of other duennas.

'Oh, there you are, my dear. I wondered where you had got to. Did you find Mr Hastings?'

Emilia shook her head. 'No. Someone said that he and Jack Corbridge and a party of other young men were off to look for excitement. After all, I did tell him that I wasn't coming.'

She was proud of the cool way in which this came out. Only, something must have shown, because Miss Dacre stared at her closley and said, 'Are you well, Emilia? You look a trifle pale.'

'Oh,' she answered, as carelessly as she could, 'I think the heat is oversetting me. Since Dominic is not here we may as well return home—that is, if you don't mind leaving early.'

And since Miss Dacre was only too ready to quit the hot ballroom she eagerly agreed, and Emilia journeyed home in a state of mind far removed from the one in which she had arrived at the Corbridges.

And there was still the long night and the next morning and Dominic Hastings' proposal to endure.

Somehow she slept, and was still a little pale when Dominic was announced. Miss Dacre, who thought her charge a trifle subdued, but concluded that that was probably because Emilia was so excited at the notion of marrying her admirer, left them alone together.

If Dominic thought that Emma looked a trifle pale, and also that her toilette was even more unbecoming to a fat girl than usual, he did not say so.

Instead he bowed gravely over her hand, straightening up to find her gazing hard at him with the most direct stare she had ever given him. Usually she blushed an unbecoming reddish purple, and hung her head when she spoke to him. But not this morning. Her manner had changed dramatically.

Emilia thought that her faithless lover had never looked so handsome. He had evidently dressed with the utmost care to come and ask her to marry him. He was not to know how useless all his valet's devoted attentions had been! Such a shame, was it not, that his beautiful coat of the deepest Lincoln green, his cream breeches, his shining black boots, his fine silk shirt and his cravat tied in an elegant butterfly—surely a work of art—were all wasted?

Wasted, too, were his beautifully brushed golden locks and his close-shaven jaw; not for

Dominic Hastings the careless stubble of lesser men. He was always *à point*, and particularly so on this propitious morning—for so he thought it—when he would finally net his heiress.

So, confident of success, he gazed deeply into Emilia's eyes, after exchanging the usual politenesses and saying, 'I am sure that you know why I have come, my dear Miss Lincoln—Emilia.'

'No,' she said coolly. 'No, I don't, Mr Hastings.'

She could see that this took him aback a little. It was not the answer or the manner which he had expected. The other character in his private drama was reciting the wrong lines, and now he was not quite sure how to utter his correct ones.

'You must,' he said, determined to get them out, 'be aware of how much I have come to respect and admire you this season, and, therefore, what I am about to say should come as no surprise to you. You intimated as much to me yesterday afternoon. My dear Miss Lincoln,' he went on, determined to see her refusal to understand him as mere maidenly modesty, only to be expected of a young girl, particularly a plain one, 'I am here to ask you to do me the honour of becoming my wife.'

He spoke as though there was no doubt of what her answer must be. He was so very sure of her. After all, had she not been his adoring admirer for so many weeks, his constant companion at all the great events of the season? The whole of society was waiting for him to ask her this inevitable question, and all society had no doubt as to what her answer would be.

Emilia was seeing him as though for the first time. She saw that behind its pretty boy's façade his face was strong, not weak. She saw the golden hairs on his powerful jaw, and the evidence of last night's debauchery in the pale mauve shadows beneath his eyes. And, when she answered him, she also saw his shock and bewilderment at the nature of that answer, however much he tried to hide them.

'You do me a great honour,' she said, bowing her head, 'in asking for my hand. Alas, I fear that I cannot accept that honour. My answer must be, regretfully, no.'

She had nonplussed him. That was plain. But his composure, like hers, never faltered.

'Oh, come, my dear Emilia, this is no time for false modesty. We have spent the whole summer being happy together. Let us spend our life being the same. I know that a well brought up young lady must be modest, but you and I have come to know one another too well to pretend that we do not understand one another.'

Alas, she understood him too well—but until last night she had never known him, nor did he know her, or the steely intelligence which lay beneath her outer awkwardness. Had she not heard him the night before she would have believed him, so sincere he seemed.

Instead, she murmured as gently as she could,

'No false modesty, sir. None at all. Yes, we have been happy together this summer—but as friends. I have never thought of you as a husband, no, not once—and I do not do so now.'

By his expression he did not believe her, so, before he could speak, she said, again with the utmost composure, 'I am sorry, most sorry, if I have in any way deceived you as to my interest in you, and caused you to waste your season by paying me attentions which I can never return.'

Dominic's face at last betrayed his agitation. 'Yesterday. . .' he began. 'Yesterday, I thought by your manner when I spoke to you in the park that you understood why I asked to speak to you this morning, and then to your father—that you knew it could only mean a proposal of marriage. You gave me no word of discouragement—not one. On the contrary. I would not have approached you today without your implicit encouragement.'

Now it was he who was almost stammering and not she. He who was discomposed and she who was cool.

'Alas, you must put that down to my lack of knowledge of the polite world. Had I understood fully what you meant when you spoke to me, then I would have tried to save you—and myself— embarrassment. Pray, sir, let us forget this unfortunate circumstance and remain good friends.'

Emilia had never been so much in command of herself, and if every word was a blow to him then it was an even greater one to her. For he had not loved her but she had loved him—or rather she had loved the Dominic Hastings she'd thought she knew, who had deceived her so cruelly. But she was determined that in this interview at least, cost what it might, for the first time she would be the one to dictate the terms on which they met.

Strong within her was the distressing realisation that if he had proposed to her without her having heard him speak so slightingly of her, of his intention to marry her solely for her money, she would have accepted him with stammering joy. Instead, he was responding to her refusal with stammering distress.

'I beg of you—' he began. He had been so sure of her, she knew. Adoration of him had been so plainly written on her face throughout the whole season that it was almost beyond him to believe what she was saying.

'Pray do not beg me, for it will make no difference. Accept that friendship with you is all I wish, not marriage.' Each harsh word which Emilia spoke to him broke her heart, for it was so different from the manner in which she would once have received him.

And now, for very shame, for decency's sake, he must give way. The prize of which he had been so sure had slipped from his grasp at the very last moment, and he had no notion as to how or why it could have happened.

He could see that Emilia was adamant, that she would not give way. She offered him a smile so sweet that it almost stunned him. For a moment he saw in her the promise which Brummell had already detected—and then it was gone.

In any case, it was of no moment. She was not for him.

He bowed his head. 'There is no hope for me, then? You do not intend to reconsider, to give yourself time to think on my offer?'

Emilia shook her head gravely. 'I have already considered, and you have my answer.'

He bowed to her and took her hand in his, to kiss the back of it.

'Then you will give me leave to go. We shall meet again—in friendship, if nothing else, I trust.'

'Oh, indeed.' Emilia retrieved her hand and gave him another blinding smile. 'It was as I said. Friendship. I wish you well.'

'And I you.'

He was gone, without a backward look, and as he walked through the door, to close it gently, the slow tears of bitter regret ran down Emilia's face.

It was only when his footsteps had finally died away that Emilia, in some surprise, realised that she had not stammered once since she had over-heard his slighting remarks about her the previous night. From whence she had summoned the inward strength which had sustained her since that terrible moment she did not know. Nor did she know, then, that it would sustain her long after Dominic Hastings had passed from her life.

It sustained her when her father came in to her

not long after Dominic had left. There was concern written on his kind face. 'I thought that he had come to propose to you, Emilia. Did he not do so?'

'Oh, yes, Papa,' returned Emilia brightly. 'He did, but I refused him.'

'Refused him?' Her father was surprised. 'I had thought that you and he dealt well together. You seemed so happy in each other's company. So much so that I was sure that you would be husband and wife by Christmas.'

A lie was necessary to deceive him. 'Oh, no, Papa, I never thought of marriage. Friendship, merely, I do assure you.'

If her father thought that there was something strange in this unlikely answer, he did not say so. He loved his daughter, so he would not press her too strongly, she knew. There would be other suitable men to propose to her, and she would doubtless accept one of them.

So he said no more, but he thought that there was more to this than his daughter would tell him now—although she might later.

But she never did. Emilia was never to tell anyone why she had refused the handsome young man of whom she had been so enamoured during her first and only season. Shortly after the season ended, and they returned to their big country house at Mistley in Surrey, she asked her father whether she need take part in the season again. 'At least not for two or three years, Papa. I don't think that I am ready for it yet.'

He gave way, partly because as time went by the fat melted away from her, and in the doing revealed beneath it a piquant face and a graceful body. The distressing stammer disappeared for good as the self-confidence which Emilia had gained on the morning after that distressful night grew stronger and stronger. When after a few years she returned to London society, he thought, she would take it by storm. . .

But there was never to be a new season. . . She returned to London the following year, but to rivate, not public life. The only person from her previous season who visited her was George Brummell, and he came on the day after Dominic Hastings married the great heiress Isabella Beaumains.

He showed no surprise when he was admitted to her presence, although she had changed completely—as he had expected. Slim and straight, the delicately classical face now plain for all to see, not lost in fat, she impressed him by her cool control of herself and those about her.

'I had heard that you were receiving no one, but I took the liberty of calling in the hope that you might receive me.'

Emilia smiled. She was radiant in white with a pale blue sash, her dark curls carefully arranged around her shapely head, and she was aware of Mr Brummell's admiring eyes.

'You were always kind to me,' she told him gravely. 'And for that you deserve a reward.'

'Nor was it difficult to be kind,' he replied. 'May I tell you that I am not surprised by your. . . transformation—only surprised that you did not embark immediately on another season.'

'Oh, I did not enjoy the first so much that I wished to repeat it immediately. Pray tell me, did you attend Mr Hastings' wedding yesterday? I understand that it is like to be this season's great event—he having married rank as well as wealth.'

This came out so clearly and coolly that Mr Brummell could only admire her *savoir faire*.

'I had thought—' he began, and then, 'No, I should be wrong to say so.'

'To say what, Mr Brummell? You intrigue me. Do not hesitate to speak your mind.'

'Very well. That you and young Hastings would have been in church together long before yesterday.'

'Oh, no.' And if Emilia's heart was bleeding, there was nothing to show. 'By no means, Mr Brummell.' She said this as firmly as she could, for if she were ever to return to society she did not wish the shadow of Dominic Hastings to lie over her.

One of Mr Brummell's great virtues was that he knew when to keep quiet and when to speak, so he said no more and they talked only of inconsequential matters.

Later that night the tears came again, as they

had not done for over a year, and Emilia wondered how she would be able to see *him* with his wife without a pang for what might have been when she entered society again.

But the season never materialised, because before it arrived there came the débâcle of her father's end. . .

Time came back to the present. She would not think of that lost past again. It had been hard enough to remember the pains of her first love, and the inexperienced young girl who had seen a selfish and careless young man as a handsome demigod. And if it were foolish of her to put herself in his way again, then so be it.

She had to live, and she could not afford to turn down a splendid offer because of something which had happened so long ago. There was one thing she must do to exorcise the memory of her love for him. She must always try to think of him as 'm'lord', as his other dependants did, never as Dominic Hastings. Only then would the past be truly dead.

At last, she slept. To dream of him again in his glory, with herself the adoring young girl she had once been. . .

# CHAPTER THREE

ALL the way to Loudwater Emma wondered whether she had taken leave of her senses in having put herself in the way of meeting Dominic Hastings again.

She had spent a morning with his solicitors in Lincoln's Inn, signing various papers and being given her ticket for the coach and precise instructions as to her journey north. Lady Hampton had arranged for her to leave the Gardiners' home as soon as Emma could pack her bags, and Mrs Gardiner had wished her luck in her new post before a Hackney cab whisked her away to the coach station in the Strand.

For one brief moment, immediately before she had finally committed herself to being Lady Letitia's governess, Emma had considered withdrawing on the spot, pleading ill-health or some family brouhaha, but the thought had died aborning. It was as though what had happened ten years ago was unfinished business, and to decline this opportunity which had so unexpectedly come her way would leave her always with the feeling of 'What if?' Would she always worry over what might have happened if she had met him again?

Ten years ago such a 'What if?' would have frightened the timid girl she had once been, but time, chance and the suffering and hardships of earning her own living had transformed Emma in many ways—not least in turning her into a strong-minded woman who was willing to take risks.

She had said goodbye to her old friend Mrs Gore, her father's one-time housekeeper and the one person who had stood by her when her world had collapsed about her after her father's suicide. She had provided her with a home and refuge, saying, 'Your father was always good to me, and I cannot see his daughter turned out onto the street with no one to care for her.'

She had kissed Emma goodbye when the cab had come to take her to the inn from which the northern stage-coach started, and had wept a little before bidding Emma, 'Write to me, mind, and tell me what Loudwater and the little girl are like.'

Emma had kissed her back and promised to do so—feeling a little uneasy because she was deceiving her old friend about the family for whom she was to work. She had not told her that the Earl of Chard had been Dominic Hastings, for she knew that had she done so Mrs Gore would have advised her against going to work for him.

The memory of him as he had been ten years ago had stayed resolutely with Emma as she travelled from the soft south to the harsh north, the scenery growing wilder with each passing mile. And now, seated alone—for few were taking passage on the Great North Road that day—she began to regret her decision to re-open a chapter in her life which she had thought closed.

But it was too late to go back. The die, as Julius Caesar had once said, was cast, her decision made. She was crossing her personal Rubicon, as Caesar had done, and must face the consequences. So, stifling her fears, she changed coaches at York, taking one which made for Alnwick where she knew that arrangements had been made for her to be picked up by a carriage sent from Loudwater, which was situated only a few miles away.

Even before Emma reached Alnwick she arrived in a landscape which was new to her. The late spring, blossoming all around her, could not disguise its savage beauty, and enhanced the pleasant order of the little town. Standing in the stableyard of The White Swan, the big coaching inn on Alnwick's main road, she watched her few boxes being loaded into a smart chaise with the arms of Hastings of Chard on its side: a golden leopard ramping across a black shield.

'Miss Lawrence, the new governess?' John Coachman had enquired of her as she had emerged from the stage-coach *Northumbrian Flyer*, its only passenger. Once she had agreed that she was indeed Miss Lawrence, he had ordered the brisk young footman with him to 'pick up the young lady's bags, instanter.'

John was a burly, middle-aged man with a kind face, and he immediately asked her in a worried voice whether she would like to enter the inn's parlour and order Mrs Stout, the landlady, to bring her a dish of tea and some good northern currant loaf, before she undertook the last stage of her long journey.

He thought that the new governess looked 'a bit peaky like', as he later told Cook, but Emma shook her head, replying simply, 'Thank you for your kindness, but I would prefer to go straight to Loudwater.'

It seemed to her of all things essential that she reach her destination as soon as possible, before she decided to bolt back to London—and safety—on the next coach south. She thought that she must be mad to be climbing into the chaise, assisted by the footman, and preparing to meet Dominic Hastings again—if not immediately, then almost certainly at some time in the near future.

She did not look mad. Quite the contrary. Both John and the footman, Tom, thought that she looked a nice, quiet young gentlewoman, who could make her mind up quickly and without fuss, just the right sort to keep Lady Letty in order.

The road to Loudwater was rough, but not rough enough to make her journey too uncomfortable. Emma was so busy admiring the trees, the green, sheep-filled fields, the stone walls around them and the occasional stream, that she temporarily forgot her misgivings—until the sight of Loudwater itself drove everything from her head except admiration for its size and its classic beauty.

Golden in the late afternoon sun, it was a copy

of a Greek temple. Three giant Doric pillars were mounted in its front, their noble proportions dwarfed by the size of the house itself, and on either side of the porch supported by the pillars were four large windows.

Emma was later to discover that each side of the house was similarly arranged—the back of it facing magnificent gardens sloping down to a river with a noisy waterfall from which the house took its name. It had been designed and built by the present Earl's grandfather after he had been on his Grand Tour, and had been intended to display to all the world the taste as well as the wealth of the Hastingses, Earls of Chard—although maintaining it had long ago destroyed that wealth!

It stood on a slight hill at the end of a drive entered through a magnificent stone arch just off the road. Beside the arch was a lodge, whose keeper came out to signal to John when the carriage passed through, John raising his whip in reply. As the drive twisted and turned the house disappeared and reappeared in Emma's view, emphasising to her each time that she saw it the immense social distance between the owner of Loudwater and the humble governess who was arriving to look after his daughter.

No servants were waiting on the front steps to greet her. Instead John drove through another noble arch to the stables at the side, where he came to a stop before an entrance distinctly less grand than that at the front, where the nobility and gentry entered. Tom put down the small steps to the chaise door, opened it and helped Emma down, handing her to the groom who ushered her through the entrance into a small hall with two flights of stone stairs leading out of it.

Behind her Tom lifted out her luggage to carry it in; before her was a small woman in a fine black silk gown, high-waisted and with a delicate lace collar. She wore a widow's cap on her silver hair, and the lace on the cap was as expensive as that on her collar.

'Miss Lawrence,' said the groom to the woman, and, to Emma, 'Mrs Morton, m'lord's cousin who looks after the house for him.' This apparently was to serve as an introduction before he gave them both a small bow and disappeared.

Mrs Morton smiled and put out a hand to Emma. 'Most pleased to see you, my dear Miss Lawrence. I hope that your journey has not been too exhausting. It is cold for the time of year, and even colder here in the North than you are doubtless accustomed to. The late spring has made it worse than usual. I have ordered tea and a small collation to be served to you in your room. I hope that you will allow me to join you—in drinking the tea, at least. I have but recently partaken of luncheon. Come! You shall see your charge when you have rested.'

This friendly greeting had Emma's eyes filling with tears of gratitude. Few people had been kind to her since her father's death, and she could not have expected such a warm welcome from a stranger as she was now being given—especially after Lady Hampton's coldness.

'This is most good of you,' she replied gratefully.

Mrs Morton shook her head. 'By no means. It is what Chard would have expected of me, had he been here. He is visiting Newcastle-upon-Tyne at the moment, and we are not certain exactly when he will return.'

And what a relief that is, thought Emma. For I am too tired at the moment to feel equal to meeting Dominic Hastings again. A few days' grace is a blessing I had not expected.

She allowed Mrs Morton to lead her in, and they mounted not the stone backstairs but the grand front ones, to reach the second floor where her small suite of rooms, the schoolroom and the nursery were situated. She drank tea and ate food which tasted like manna while talking to a congenial companion, and she felt that in some sort she had reached haven.

'Miss Lawrence, I wish that you might call me Tish, or Tishy. My first governess called me that. It was my second governess, Miss Pont, who nicknamed me Letty, and everyone else since has copied her. But I do not know myself as Letty.'

Emma and Lady Letitia Hastings were sitting in the schoolroom. Emma had ruled a sheet of blank paper with even lines and the little girl—'a brown wisp of a thing', as Mrs Morton had named her to

Emma on her first day a fortnight ago—was busy practising her pothooks on it.

'Do you think that your papa would approve?' Emma was cautious. She had learned caution in a hard school.

Tongue protruding with the effort of producing a perfect script, Letty looked up at Emma. 'Papa is here so seldom,' she told her new friend, 'that I am not sure that he knows what I am being called when I am not Lady Letitia. So I cannot answer you. He is often away on business,' she added, before admiring the page which she had just completed.

Unseen by the little girl, whose head was now bent again over her work, adding one last penman's flourish, Emma's lip curled. Knowing Dominic Hastings of old she could guess what his 'business' consisted of! Eating, drinking, women and gambling, no doubt! Poor child—to have such a father, neglecting her for all the wrong reasons. But, from what Tish had said so far, she worshipped him. Papa, to Emma's slight discomfort, was frequently present in her conversation.

She gave her new charge an answer which would please them both, and hopefully would satisfy Papa and Mrs Morton.

'Suppose I were to say that you might be Tish when we are alone, but in public you must be Lady Letitia or Letitia? What then?'

The little girl considered for a moment before looking up and saying, 'What a splendid notion!

Then everyone will be happy—and it shall be our secret! Yes. As Papa says when he agrees to something which solves a difficult problem, "Yes, it will do! Most definitely, it will do!"'

Her imitation of a grown man's slight pomposity was perfect, and had Emma giving a small, secret smile whilst Tish took another sheet of ruled paper from her and began to copy the sentence written at the top of it: 'All that glitters is not gold'.

The sentence copied, she said, eyes shining, 'Papa promised to be home before the month was out when he left just before you came. I wonder what he will bring me this time. Last time he gave me Mirabelle, my best doll—the one you admired so much, whose eyes shut when I put her to bed.'

'One would hope that he does not always bring you a present when he goes away,' said Emma, busy ruling another page and writing at the head of it in her own beautiful hand. 'Go to the ant, thou sluggard. Consider her ways and be wise'.

'Oh, why is that, Miss Lawrence? I like it when Papa brings me presents.'

'It is bad for one's character—and besides, you should value your papa for himself when he returns, not for what he gives you.'

Even to herself Emma thought this statement sounded extremely priggish and prosy, and Tish obviously agreed, for she lifted her head again, making an inkblot as she did so, to announce solemnly, 'Oh, but I love Papa even when he doesn't bring me presents. Perhaps next time when he goes away I ought to ask him to bring one back for you instead of me. I like you much better than my previous governess. *She* never made my lessons interesting.'

Emma sanded the maxim she had just written. 'Oh, no, that would not be proper. And governesses do not expect presents. Besides, in another week you might not care for me so much. After all, I have only been here for a short time.'

'Quite long enough to know that "Miss Lawrence is not like that hoity-toity and idle Miss Sandeman".'

This came out in a quaint imitation of Cook. Tish, being lonely, had spent rather more time than she should have in the kitchens, and she had a fund of overheard servants' gossip as well as her unexpected gift for mimicry.

'I am hoping that you will be more conscientious than your predecessors,' Mrs Morton had told Emma soon after she had arrived at Loudwater. 'I found that Miss Sandeman was leaving Lady Letitia in the kitchens whilst she sneaked out to visit her curate.'

'I can safely promise you that I shall not sneak out to visit anyone—particularly curates,' Emma had informed her solemnly.

'No, indeed. One sees that.' Mrs Eleanor Morton, Lord Chard's poor and widowed cousin, had been approving.

Miss Lawrence was undoubtedly a real lady. Quiet but firm. And it was plain that she and

Letitia were getting along splendidly. Why, the Sandeman woman had even made eyes at Chard, but, his loose days being long gone, he had not responded at all, and she had had to make do with the curate—who had departed the living for another at Chard's arrangment.

'Chard told his sister to find him a quiet, plain governess next time—who didn't hope to be his next Countess.'

Which tells me why I so attracted her ladyship, Emma had thought, not at all put out that her biggest recommendation had been her lack of obvious looks, showy or otherwise.

'Not, my dear, that *I* think you plain,' Mrs Morton had remarked agitatedly, realising, like Mrs Gardiner before her, that she had been tactless. 'On the contrary. Well bred, and tasteful. The perfect governess.'

And that, Mrs Morton had thought ruefully, is perhaps not too tactful, either—perfect governesses not being notable for their looks or anything but being unobtrusive and keeping out of everyone's way. Which Miss Lawrence did.

But on the other hand there was something a little strange about her. Something which Mrs Morton could not put a finger on. Occasionally Miss Lawrence said things which, if one thought about them afterwards, frequently held a double meaning. The question was, was she aware of what she was doing? And what did it signify if she did? She was a very poised young woman, very composed. Too composed, perhaps. . . Mrs Morton had given up.

We really must count our blessings, she had finally summed up to herself. For, if Miss Lawrence is truly the paragon which she seems, then all our troubles are over. . . But perhaps I ought not to make that judgement too hastily—before she has met Chard. I wonder when he will return—he did say he would not be away too long this time. After all, he has only gone to Newcastle-upon-Tyne, which is not so far away. . .

She had a soft spot for her cousin, who was twenty years younger than she was, and would have liked to mother him. But mothering Chard, she had ruefully decided not long after meeting him for the first time, would be rather like mothering a large tiger, with blue not yellow eyes!

Every governess they had ever hired for poor little Letty had either fancied themselves in love with him when they had first met him, or had been frightened to death of him. There seemed little other reaction to him between these two extremes.

And how would Miss Lawrence behave when she met him? That was the question. Probably as she had been doing while this conversation had rambled on. Sitting quietly stitching at the tapestry which she had brought with her, displaying every sign of the extreme good breeding which one hoped that she would pass on to her poor little charge, whose idea of good breeding was imitating Cook or the youngest stable lad!

Kettie, Tish's nursemaid, who bustled in with the teaboard just as Tish finished copying out her maxims, also approved of Miss Lawrence. The kitchen and house staff were all agreed that she seemed a much better proposition than any of those who had gone before her, being considerate towards everyone as well as being kind but firm to poor Lady Letty, that motherless child.

Her mouth crammed with shortbread, Tish thought it expedient to mumble through it inelegantly, 'I expect Papa will want to interview you in order to see whether he approves of you. Though he need not trouble to do so. I am sure Aunt Morton will tell him "what a treasure you are like to prove".'

Emma stifled her amusement at this exact rendering of Mrs Morton's gentle tones to say coolly, 'Tish, I must inform you that it is neither ladylike nor proper for you to imitate all those to whom you speak, or to repeat their every word. The maxim that little children should be seen and not heard is a harsh one, I know, but you would do well to heed it. Neither should you speak with your mouth full. Apart from everything else, the sight of crumbs flying in all directions is neither edifying nor attractive.'

This had the effect of reducing Tish to giggles before, having emptied her mouth, she said, 'Oh, it amuses Papa to hear me imitate people. He says that I am a proper little parrot. Of course, I don't imitate *him*—or not very often.'

'Indeed not,' replied Emma, wishing that Papa would walk out of the conversation. She felt that she had heard quite enough of Dominic Hastings for one day, and, contrary to Tish's wishes, hoped that it would be some time before he again set foot in Loudwater.

She had begun to enjoy herself in Mrs Morton's company. The house was well run, the servants hard-working and cheerful but unobtrusive, and Tish was a lively and interesting child. Fortunately for Emma's peace of mind she did not resemble her absent father, but neither did she resemble her mother, whose portrait hung in the drawing room. The late Lady Chard had been a large and showy blonde, and the painting by Lawrence showed her in the elaborate court dress in which she had been presented to the Prince Regent when he was the Prince of Wales.

Emma had asked if Tish took after her mother, but Mrs Morton had shaken her head. 'Oh, no. Lady Letty is a Hastings through and through so far as her character is concerned. She does not take after her mother in any way, which is perhaps as well. . . .' And she had let her sentence die away— one of her habits, Emma had found—which had left Emma to wonder exactly why it was as well that Tish did not take after her mother. Good manners had prevented her from quizzing Mrs Morton further on the matter.

Whether or not it was the number of times that Tish's papa had arrived in the conversation that day which had disturbed Emma, or whether it was something else which had distressed her, she could not decide, but that night she found herself unable to sleep. Shortly after midnight, when she was still wide awake, there was a great noise in the stable-yard beneath her window. The sound of horses, carriages, and of men running and shouting roused her curiosity. She rose from her bed and walked over to the window to discover the cause of all the excitement.

A large travelling coach, followed by two post chaises, was drawn up in the yard below. Grooms were unharnessing the spent horses on the carriages and leading them away. Footmen stood about carrying flambeaux. Several men were dismounting from the chaises whilst Outhwaite, the head groom in charge of the stables, was opening the door of the travelling coach to allow its occupant to climb down from it.

Dominic Hastings, fifth Earl of Chard, had arrived home in the middle of the night! For there was no doubt that it was he who was now standing before Outhwaite, being bowed to and apparently giving orders to the various footmen and flunkies who were unloading the carriages.

One of the flambeaux-carrying footmen ran forward to give m'lord light and to escort him into the house. She could not see his face—that was in shadow as he bent his head to speak briefly to the footman—so she could not tell what the passing years had done to him. She had forgotten how tall he was, and how broad his shoulders were. Otherwise her best view of him was of his long greatcoat and his polished boots.

Suddenly, as though he was aware that he was being watched, he swung around, away from all the flambeaux, and looked up towards the window where Emma stood, his face white in the moonlight. Immediately she moved back, and saw him shake his head and turn again to walk into the house by the side door through which she had entered a fortnight ago.

And after that Emma could not sleep at all, until dawn broke and in its pale light she at last found oblivion.

M'lord slept little better than his new governess did. He had left Newcastle-upon-Tyne late at night, declining to join in the mild debauchery at a local inn which his business companions had arranged as an end to more than a fortnight of work and bargaining. He had returned to the house he rented there, woken up his servants and ordered them to make the journey back to Loudwater as soon as they decently could.

He had arrived home in a divided state of mind: half pleased to see the place whose beauty always compelled his love and admiration, half annoyed that it hung around his neck like a millstone. Its size, splendour and cost of upkeep threatened to bankrupt him unless he were careful, despite the fortune which his late wife had brought to him.

So tired was he after his hard work and the journey, that on climbing out of the coach he had felt a little light-headed. It had almost been as though some presence awaited him there, had been calling him back. So strong had the feeling been that he had looked up at the line of bedroom windows above him—to see a frail ghost peering out of one of them, staring at him.

He had blinked at it in surprise—and as he had done so the ghost had disappeared, leaving behind a blank window pane.

I run mad, he had thought. To behave like a cowardly fool, seeing bushes as bears and believing that ghosts are waiting for me in an inhabited house. I must be tired. Yes, that is it.

But he had not been so tired that he could sleep, so that in the end he rose earlier than he had intended and, without ringing for his valet, dressed himself in his oldest riding clothes—those in which he felt most comfortable—and went downstairs to take a walk in the clear morning air and so cleanse his brain of the megrims which afflicted it.

He wanted to be alone, and, of all annoying things, as he walked into the great square black and white flagged hall, surrounded by Doric pillars similar to those on the outside of the house, he found that there was someone already there.

In the centre of the hall was a statue of the head and shoulders of the Apollo Belvedere mounted on a plinth. Before it stood a young woman in a plain morning gown of dark blue. She was leaning forward to stroke Apollo's beautiful face, one graceful white hand trailing from forehead to chin. She was so rapt that she did not hear him coming, and thus gave him the benefit of her profile.

It was one of great purity, of severity almost. She possessed a high brow, a delicate straight nose and a mouth both firm and shapely, the whole intriguing a man who was tired of conventional beauties.

M'lord wondered who she could be. A relative of Mrs Morton's, perhaps? He also wanted to see the rest of her, so he gave a short 'Hmm' and a cough, which had her swinging round to face him.

A delicate creamy complexion flooded scarlet at the sight of him. Her face, though not conventionally pretty, had a classic cast, so that for her to admire Apollo was to admire someone of equivalent character to herself. He could have sworn that he had never seen her before—and yet there was something disturbingly familiar about her.

Of course! She was the ghost at the window last night—awoken by his arrival, no doubt. That must be it. And, his errant common sense told him, she must be the new governess, installed in the rooms so recently occupied by Miss Sandeman.

He must not stand there staring at her. She would think him mad—or presumptuous—or seeking female prey. Which was not his intention at all, so he favoured her with a distant bow, which she returned, her natural pallor now restored.

'Forgive me, madam,' he began. 'I must have

surprised you. I am Chard, of course—and you are my daughter's new governess, I suppose.'

Emma bowed again. 'Indeed, m'lord,' she said, and fell silent trying to master herself. Yes, he was Chard, no doubt of that. But he was so unlike the man he had once been that the sight of him overset her, even though she had recognised him immediately.

Ten years ago he had been a pretty boy, blond and bland, his blue eyes warm and ingenuous, not hard and shrewd. Never less than immaculately dressed, he had been slender and graceful, and the young Emma had fallen immediately and wildly in love with this paragon, this double of the Apollo Belvedere, the most beautiful of all the Greek gods.

But how he had changed! This man still had the body and stance of an athlete, although he was broader and more powerful than he had been, but the pretty boy was long gone. Life had written its mark on him. Oh, Apollo could still be dimly seen through the ravages time had wrought on his face, but the effects of pain and passion were there as well.

The tender mouth had gone too; its new harshness was accentuated by two lines, one on each side of it, giving him an appearance of stark and uncompromising command. He was Jupiter now, the master of the gods, not his youthful son. The once warm eyes were cold and knowing, and his long and curling blond hair had been trimmed into a severe cut which emphasised the stern lines of the face which had once been so invitingly soft.

And his clothes! There was nothing of the dandy left in him. He was dressed for the field in workaday garments chosen for their durability and comfort, not to dazzle the eyes and senses of those around him. His manner had changed too. It was cool, not charming and ardent. It was the manner of a man carelessly used to command, who kept people at a distance when as a boy he had been gregarious, hating to be alone.

Emma could not help but wonder what had changed him so.

And if she could still recognise the young man he had once been, changed though he was, the question must be, could he, would he, still recognise her?

Apparently not. Nothing in his manner suggested that he thought he had met her before. Surprisingly, he was lingering. Emma had been prepared for him to walk unthinkingly away from her once the proprieties had been observed, but no, he was speaking again.

'I trust that you are not finding my daughter too difficult a charge, Miss Lawrence. It is not so much that she is naughty, but that her liveliness leads her into difficulties. Her tongue is a little long too.' For the first time he smiled at Emma.

That, too, had changed. It was a rueful smile, not one designed to charm. Emma found herself saying, with a rueful smile of her own, 'I know, and if I may say so without offence, she has used it to introduce me to you—frequently.'

The rueful smile grew broader. '"Papa says. . ."' He allowed his voice to trail off a little before adding, 'I can only hope that I have made a good impression.'

Now, why was he troubling himself with so inconsiderable a person as herself? Unless, of course, he was bored and had decided that a governess who was after all not so very plain, and was a lady, might be more attractive to him than the late Miss Sandeman had been. He was not so much flirting with her as being a little particular. She would answer him in similar vein.

'Oh, the best, I assure you, m'lord. Papa appears to be a cross between the Prime Minister and the Primate!'

M'lord—for so she was determined to think of him—gave a great shout of laughter almost despite himself.

'Continue in that vein, Miss Lawrence, and I shall be persuaded that my sister did us all a great favour when she sent you to us. And, having said that, I shall have a deal of trouble in living up to such a description, I assure *you*. The Prime Minister I might allow—but the Archbishop of Canterbury? No, I cannot aspire to his office!'

It was not only his face which had changed, but his intellect! The boy she had known had been easygoing, and would have been quite unwilling as well as unable to joust with her after such a knowing fashion. His humour had been that of a young man used only to conversing with the idle dandies of the *ton*. This change in him so overset Emma that she felt she needed to leave him to come to terms with what the years had brought about.

So she smiled, bowed, and said as deferentially as she could, 'I must not detain you, m'lord,' and made to pass him.

M'lord surprised himself by sidestepping a little so that she was unable to do so. 'Oh, you are not detaining me, Miss Lawrence. I have no immediate duties to perform at such an early hour. I was merely about to embark on a morning walk. I was surprised to see a young lady in the hall. I had forgotten that you would have arrived here before my return.'

'Of course.' Emma bowed again, and made to pass him again.

Why, on this very first glance, did she intrigue him so that he did not want to let her go? She was quite different from the women he knew—either the elegants of the world of society, or the more obvious beauties of the *demi-monde*. He had long since failed to be attracted by the charms of either group, so why was he instantly attracted by a cool young woman, drably dressed, who had neither cringed before him nor tried to attract him in any of the ways to which he was accustomed? Perhaps it was because her beauty was as subtle as theirs was showy, designed to lure him.

'Mrs Morton has ensured that you have all that you require to do justice to your teaching of your charge?'

Now, this was making conversation with a vengeance.

Emma bowed. She was the very picture of mannerly deference. Inwardly she was seething— not with rage, but with having to suppress a series of questions which she wished to ask of him but could not. Such as, What has changed you so? And, Is the change for the better? Or, Are you merely selfish in a different way?

'I have no complaints on that or any other score, m'lord.'

'Excellent, Miss Lawrence. Do not fail to approach me if there is anything you require about which Mrs Morton may be doubtful. I wish only the best for my daughter. Motherless she may be, but I always endeavour to try to make up for that in every way I can.'

The devil got into Emma. 'Oh, I will be sure to remember what you say, m'lord. Except. . .' And then she hesitated. Could she really speak to him so boldly? After all, she was no more than a servant.

M'lord noted her hesitation. He was aware that he was noticing everything about her. There was a small mole beside her left eye which acted as a beauty spot. Something tugged at his memory, then was gone.

'Except, Miss Lawrence? Except what? Pray

what am I to conclude from that? Or have you not finished?'

In for a penny, in for a pound. The devil demanded it—and what had happened ten years ago.

'It is not for me to advise you, m'lord, but I would have thought that a—' Could she say it? She could '—a second marriage would supply Lady Letitia with all and more that she might require. A governess and the best of books and globes are but a poor substitute.'

He stared at her as she finished, bent her head and folded her hands submissively. No servant could have looked more humbly respectful than Miss Emma Lawrence did.

He spoke at last, and whether he was angry or amused Emma could not tell.

'You say that it is not for you to advise me—and then you do! Let me answer you as plainly as I may. The second marriages which I have known have not necessarily been to the benefit of the offspring of the first. Besides, I have no wish to marry again. Do your duty well, and I shall be eternally obliged to you. I cannot say more.' He bowed, and turned away.

She had angered him! And yet he had answered her.

Then he turned back again to say, 'And may I add that if you are as forthright and honest with Letitia as you are with me, then the curse which has lain upon all the governesses we have employed so far may, at last, be lifted!

'And, Miss Lawrence, to further the education of your charge and yourself, I wish you both to be present at dinner with me. Except. . .' He paused to smile at her. 'My "except" is a mild one—unlike yours. Except when I entertain those gentlemen with whom I do business. My secretary, John Bassett, will also dine with us, and Mrs Morton— plus my librarian, Mr Cross—so there should be a sufficiency of good conversation.

'Thus Letitia will learn to conduct herself properly, and you may assist her. I hope to see you with her at—' he pulled out his watch '—four of the clock. Until then, *au revoir*.' He bowed again and was gone, striding across the hall and through the door, finally to take his walk.

Good God! Could a man change so much? Was she dreaming him? To have Letitia at his dinner table! That alone was so unlike the conduct of any of the gentlemen and noblemen Emma had ever known, who hardly knew that their young children existed, never mind ate their meals with them. And it was plain that her impudence in querying him about a wife had amused rather than annoyed him.

Emma made her way up the grand staircase to find her charge and to start the work of the day. The business of the house had already begun, and footmen were on duty to open and to close doors for her. Unlike most governesses, she had already become a favourite of the staff—a rarity, as she knew only too well from her contemptuous treatment by them in the other families for whom she had worked.

She must wait until her busy day was over to ponder over how much Dominic Hastings, Earl of Chard, differed from plain Dominic Hastings. . .

# CHAPTER FOUR

DINNER on that first afternoon initiated Emma into the pattern of life at Loudwater when its owner was in residence.

Shortly after a light luncheon, taken by Tish and Emma in the schoolroom just before twelve of the clock, Mr Ben Blackburn, a knowing-looking man and a local landowner, arrived from his own neglected mansion to stay at Loudwater. He spoke in the accents of the North-East, and claimed to be a great authority on coalmines and iron-founding. He joined the party at dinner, together with m'lord's land agent, Jemson, who had been overseeing the running of his master's estates in Bedfordshire. They were, it seemed, in a bad way, for the agricultural depression which had followed the late wars had hit the tenant farmers hard.

Emma had already discovered that, contrary to usual custom, m'lord ran the home farm himself, instead of putting yet another tenant in it, and, judging by the conversation at the dinner table, he was knowledgeable about agricultural matters as well as coalmining! This was yet another surprise for Emma. She doubted whether the young Dominic Hastings could have told a turnip from a tulip—he had probably thought that coal came down from God in a scuttle!

Tish behaved herself beautifully; she sat by Emma and ate her food with a solemn expression, determined not to let Papa down. Her presence, Emma suspected, kept table talk both dull and respectable—except for a few lapses frowned at by m'lord. She wondered how much it would change when Tish, Mrs Morton and herself retired to the Egyptian drawing room, leaving the men to their drink.

M'lord watched them go. Miss Lawrence, he had noted idly, had beautiful hands as well as beautiful eyes and beautiful manners, and the change she had already brought about in Letitia was evident in her improved behaviour. There were hidden depths there, he thought, and smiled a little at his interest in such an ordinary young woman.

Perhaps Ben Blackburn had been right when he had told him bluntly the other night when they had dined together in Newcastle that he needed either a woman or a wife. 'T'aint right to live like a monk,' he had said into his ale. 'Does a man in, not to get his oats.'

M'lord, who had not been drinking—he rarely did—had shrugged his shoulders. Lately little had interested him but the task of restoring Loudwater's fortunes, and even Miss Sandeman's freely offered and obvious charms had failed to rouse him. Since his late wife's death he had frequently agreed with Hamlet in the play—'man delights me not; no, nor woman neither'.

So what was he doing mooning after Miss Lawrence as she left the dining room, shapely head erect, one hand in his daughter's, the very picture of modesty and virtue?

Ben Blackburn must have been watching him, for as he poured out his port, holding it to the light and complimenting m'lord on his cellar, he said knowingly, 'Nice bit of skirt, your governess, Chard. Though a little too close to home for a wise man to indulge one's self, one supposes.'

'Not to mention monks,' m'lord returned. 'Nothing out of the ordinary there, Blackburn, surely?'

Ben considered his port again. 'If you say so, but I thought. . .' He hesitated.

'Thought what?' enquired m'lord, wondering how on earth he had come to find himself discussing his daughter's governess's charms at the dinner table. He could see the look of disapproval at the turn the conversation had taken on the faces of several of the party round the table, but damn that—he was curious to hear what Ben Blackburn thought he had discovered about Miss Emma Lawrence.

'I thought—nay, I *think*—that there is more to Miss Lawrence than meets the eye. She suppressed a smile when Cross, there, your learned gentleman, quoted a line or two from Horace, so as not to discommode the child, Mrs Morton and the young lady by saying what he shouldn't in plain English before them. She not only understood the

Latin, but she also understood the somewhat shady implications in it!'

Before m'lord could reply, his secretary threw himself into the fray, saying sturdily and indignantly, 'Steady on, Blackburn! That's no way to speak of a quiet and modest young lady. You have no evidence, no evidence at all, to suggest any such thing on such a short acquaintance.'

From staring at Ben Blackburn, the company now turned its attention to John Bassett. Ben gave a sneering laugh, and said in his usual brash fashion, 'Oh, so she has netted you as well, has she? All in one short dinner-hour. I compliment the lady and drink to her.'

Before John Bassett, his face crimson, could protest further, m'lord spoke in as bored a voice as he could summon up.

'And that is enough of that,' he commanded, drawing on his rank to dominate everyone at table. 'I should never have said what I did—and nor should you, Blackburn. A lady's honour is at stake here, and we have all been quite wrong to blow upon it lightly. Blackburn, I shall wish your company when I visit Geordie Stephenson at Killingworth. If his engine and trams work as rumour says, then my coalmines, too, must have an interest in acquiring them. We in the North-East must show the way to the rest of the world. Tell me, is his reputation overblown? Or are you one of those who take it at face value?'

After that the drink and the bottle circulated

until, shortly before everyone became completely
overset—including himself, for he was unused
either to company or to drinking overmuch—
m'lord rose abruptly to make his way into the
drawing room to have another and a better look at
Miss Lawrence.

Only to find that she and Tish had already left
for the nursery suite, so that Tish might retire and
Miss Lawrence rest.

Later, not drunk, but tired to the bone as he often
was these days, his responsibilities heavy upon
him, m'lord mounted the main staircase and,
instead of making for his bedroom, took the first
turning which led to the nursery. He caught a
glimpse of himself in a floor-length mirror just
before he arrived at the nursery door. He could not
help noticing how dishevelled he looked, how
white his face was. For a moment he stood hesitant
before the door, wondering what he was doing
there.

After all, he could not apologise to Miss
Lawrence for what had been said or hinted of her
in her absence, and of which she did not know.
Even as he thought this he saw his hand rise to
knock at the stout oak panel, and heard her call to
him to enter.

He opened the door to see her sitting before the
fire, a piece of sewing in her hand and an
occasional table by her side. On it was a small pile
of books, plainly from the library downstairs, since

all of them had the Hastings arms gilded on the back or side. As she saw him she rose, a slight querying smile on her face.

'M'lord? You have something to say to me?'

Outwardly she was demure, her manners perfect. So why did he feel that Ben Blackburn was right? That there was something odd, or deep about her? Was she inwardly laughing at them all? And, if so, why?

But he had to say something, and quickly, or look a fool. She had her hands clasped in front of her, her head bent. Yes, he must say something—for why else was he here?

Inspiration struck. 'Your charge, Miss Lawrence. What did you think of her behaviour this evening? Only eight years old and to be thrown into adult company. Was it too much for her, do you think?'

And do you think, Miss Lawrence, that I have taken leave of my senses to pursue you with such banalities? he added silently.

'Why, m'lord, I thought that she behaved extremely well, but. . .' Emma paused.

'But, Miss Lawrence? Pray continue—or do you intend to make a habit of constantly modifying or qualifying every remark which you make to me?'

Emma's head dropped ever more submissively. 'Oh, no, m'lord. It is only that I think it might be rather too much to expect a small girl of eight to attend your dinner table every evening. It is hard on her—and on your companions.'

He could not stop himself. All he could see of her was the top of her head.

M'lord put out a long finger, placed it under Miss Emma Lawrence's chin and tipped it up so that he could examine her delicate, grave face.

'Pray look at me, Miss Lawrence. I am moved by your consideration for everyone. Do you never consider yourself? Do you wish to be condemned to nursery meals every day and all day?'

'It is the common habit of governesses, m'lord. Did you invite Miss Sandeman to your table?'

'No, indeed, and do not think me ungentlemanly if I say that it is not such as Miss Sandeman whom I wish to sit at my table.'

'You have no need to be a gentleman. You are, after all, a nobleman—and you have no peers here, so your word is your law. But I think it best that you do not exercise it by compelling Tish—I mean, Lady Letitia—to sit at your table every day.'

'Suppose I wished to see *you* sit there?'

There, it was out! And he had first seen the woman only eight or nine hours ago, and really knew nothing of her at all except that she intrigued him. Perhaps Ben Blackburn was right. Living like a monk did bad things to you, and you ended up admiring your daughter's new governess for no reason at all!

'No, m'lord, you cannot wish that, and nor can I. You keep a gentleman's table and wish to speak on topics which entertain gentlemen. Neither Lady Letitia nor I are fit persons to be there often.'

'Are you arguing with me, Miss Lawrence? A moment ago you said that my word was law. Whatever happened to that maxim that you challenge it so quickly?'

'Maxims, like rules, are also subject to exceptions—which, the copybooks inform us, prove the rule!'

Her face was animated now, her eyes glowing, and she was challenging him after a fashion which no woman had ever done before.

What m'lord did not know was that Emma Lawrence was asking herself again and again whether she could be mistaken. Was this man really Dominic Hastings, the careless, flighty boy whom she had once known? And why was she speaking to him so boldly, as she had never done when he had been Dominic Hastings, and she had been fat Emilia Lincoln? And why was he responding to her? For there was no doubt that he was. More to the point, what was he doing in her room? Was she already marked down as prey? From what Mrs Morton had said, he had shown no interest in Letitia's previous governesses—not even the young, pretty and flighty Miss Sandeman—so why was he pursuing Miss Emma Lawrence?

She had thought that he had looked ill when he came in, but now his face was glowing, as hers was. He gave a stifled laugh, and said, 'Oh, a woman always has the last word, I am told, and you are determined to have yours. Very well, I note what you say. It shall not be every night that you bring

Letitia to dinner, but occasionally, when I feel the need of gentler company. It is true that I have grown used to a dining table surrounded by men and men's affairs, but do me the favour of believing that I wish for something a little less like the camp every now and then.'

Emma bent her head again, and this time he made no effort to lift it.

'Very well, m'lord. I hear you and obey.'

She was roasting him again. He was sure of it. He bowed, a low bow, and she bowed back—but not quite so low. He did not want to leave her, but he must. She was suddenly temptation itself. He fought against it, won, and turned to leave.

His hand was on the doorknob when she spoke again, and what she said had him marvelling at Ben Blackburn—and at himself.

'Speaking of the camp, m'lord, a word to the wise. It might be as well to inform Mr Cross that I have a good command of Latin—and of Greek too. Goodnight!'

If Emma had told herself on that evening that she must keep her wits about her, go carefully at Loudwater and try to avoid its owner, she found living up to such a sensible resolution difficult.

It was not that he pursued her, but that Loudwater with its owner present was a very different place from when he was absent. Everyone and everything deferred to him. Even if her meals were taken in the schoolroom with Tish, she could

not help running into him on her way round the
mansion, large though it was.

He took an interest in Tish's education, and
judging by Tish and Mrs Morton's behaviour this
had been his habit in the past; he was not simply
haunting the schoolroom to speak to the governess!

Several days after the dinner party he walked
into the schoolroom where Emma was instructing
Tish in the use of the globe. His entry was so quiet
that neither Tish nor Emma heard him, so
interested were they both in the lesson.

Emma found Tish a willing pupil, and they were
laughing together as Tish put a finger on the north
of England, saying happily, 'That is where we live.'
She leaned forward to peer more closely at the
globe. 'Do you think, if we looked very hard, we
might see Papa on Pompey?'

Before Emma could answer, m'lord gave a
short, 'Ahem,' adding, 'You hardly need to look
closely at the world, Letitia, to see Papa. He is
before you, though not on Pompey.'

Tish gave a delighted squeal. 'Indeed not, Papa.
You could hardly ride Pompey up to the schoolroom—could he, Miss Lawrence?'

'Certainly not,' said her father, pulling out a
chair and straddling it, his chin on its back.
'Although I am told that a bold, bad ancestor of
yours and mine made a habit of riding his war
horse into the castle which stood here before your

great-grandpapa pulled it down in order to build the present mansion.'

Tish's eyes widened at this piece of information, and Emma said, before she could stop herself, 'That would be the wicked Baron, would it not? The one who was King John's friend.'

The deep blue eyes surveyed her steadily. 'I see that your governess has been using the library to good advantage. Mr Cross tells me that Miss Lawrence spends a considerable amount of time there when not about her duties.'

Emma decided to be perverse. His very presence excited her. The contrast between past and present was creating a kind of tension in her attitude to him, which was only paralleled by the tension created in her employer by the enigma which the governess presented.

He had become aware that she was greatly liked by all members of his staff, from high to low. John Bassett was obviously taken by her and Ben Blackburn was constantly twitting m'lord about her. Ben was also seeking Emma out to speak to her himself. What was there about her which was creating such a brouhaha?

M'lord was considering this, his eyes shuttered, when Emma replied challengingly, 'Some might say, m'lord, that it was part of my duties to work in the library, and learn as much as possible about the place where I live. For example, until Mr Cross showed me the maps of the region I had no idea that Loudwater was quite so close to Hadrian's Wall.'

M'lord's fine black brows, intriguingly at odds with his blond hair, lifted a little. 'And you have never visited Northumbria before? Never visited the Wall? Shall we escort Miss Lawrence there, Letitia, and introduce her to it?' he asked of his daughter.

'And have a picnic?' she replied eagerly. 'Oh, do let us have a picnic at the Wall, Papa.'

'When I return from Alnwick,' her father told her gravely. He always spoke to Tish, Emma noticed, with the same polite deference which he would have used to a person of his own age. This consideration had Emma marvelling at him all over again. She remembered only too well how careless Dominic Hastings had been with everyone.

'Oh!' Tish was plainly disappointed. 'Do you have to leave us so soon, Papa? I thought that we might have our picnic tomorrow.'

'Time and tide wait for no man when business calls, as Miss Lawrence will doubtless instruct you.' He had risen while Tish was speaking and had picked up her copybook, full of wise saws and sayings, and was leafing through it approvingly.

'I must say, Letitia, that I wish that when I was your age I had had a tutor who was half as strict with me as Miss Lawrence is with you in the matter of your writing hand and your moral guidance. It would have saved me a deal of sorrow in later life. I was left to my own devices—and exceeding poor they were.'

M'lord came out with this very lightly, but Emma could not but sense that there was very deep feeling behind this outwardly calm speech. He laid the book down on the table and said slowly, 'I am pleased that you use the library, Miss Lawrence, and would encourage you to use Mr Cross's learning as well. He would like to feel that he serves the interest of others as well as himself.'

'He does not serve yours, then?' Emma could not help saying.

The eyes on her were sharp. 'Oh, he finds me blue books and Board of Agriculture papers on scientific farming, and he has brought Arthur Young's treatise home for me from London to read, but he would rather that I studied Bishop Butler on theology and Mr Hume on philosophy— his pet interests.'

He saw that Emma was looking a trifle puzzled as to who Mr Arthur Young was, and added, still lightly, 'Mr Young writes well on agriculture, and I am making up for my misspent youth by reading him and as much else as I have time for. The owner of so many acres should not be ignorant of the use to which they are put. My agent tells me that sheep are the best crop here, but I need to know that for myself. My own belief is that coal is the best crop of all!'

'Coal and sheep are not crops, Papa,' interposed Tish, puzzlement on *her* face now. 'Miss Lawrence has made me list the main crops of the Northern counties, and coal and sheep are not among them.'

Her elders smiled at this, and m'lord said, still light, 'One finds them both in a field, Letitia, as one finds wheat or barley. Shall we ask Miss Lawrence whether or no we may call them crops?' He turned his blue eyes, now slightly mocking, on her.

Emma, amused, but putting on what she always thought of as her schoolmistress's face and voice, said solemnly, 'Crops grow and sheep grow—that at least is true. But, unlike crops, sheep move about. One supposes that they *might* be thought of as a sort of crop. But coal? No, I do not think that Tish and I may admit that.' Then she went on, daring again, 'Perhaps Papa would not have called them crops if he had had the benefit of my teaching when he was young!'

'Oh, Papa might have done many things very differently with a proper teacher,' announced m'lord gaily, wondering why he felt it necessary to challenge Miss Lawrence, and for her to challenge him back. Well, at least they were providing entertainment as well as education for Tish—and where had that nickname come from? The universally admired Miss Lawrence, no doubt.

It was time for him to go. His interest in the governess was sure to be remarked on sooner or later if he overdid things—and what, precisely, did he mean by that? Well, he could not 'overdo things' whilst he was at Alnwick, meeting Lord

Lufton and Ben Blackburn at The White Swan and discussing George Stephenson with them.

Lord Lufton positively refused to visit Loudwater, not because he had anything against the house or its owner, but because he never visited anyone anywhere, nor invited them to his own home either. Inns and the offices of the lawyer he was hiring at the time were his preferred places of entertainment for his superiors, equals and inferiors.

I wonder how Lord Lufton would fare with Miss Lawrence? was m'lord's last thought, before he boarded his coach for Alnwick and forgot about her for the time being. Or tried to.

He was still thinking about her when he arrived home a week later—not, this time, in the middle of the night, but in the middle of the morning. He took John Bassett upstairs with him to his room, to dictate a letter arranging for a visit to Killingworth to meet George Stephenson at last.

He, Blackburn and Lufton had agreed to meet Sir Thomas Liddell, Sir John Boyd and Mr Damian Holdsworth, all good men with coalmines and lands around the Wall, to discuss with them Stephenson's plans for a new tramway system. It had been agreed that they should be the ones to meet Sir Thomas, the leader of the enterprise. They had the capital; Stephenson had the know-how.

This last word had come from Mr Holdsworth,

who had recently spent some time in the United States where innovation and knowhow were inextricably linked and men of substance did not think it demeaning to soil their hands in order to make money, or, as in m'lord's case, to save their estates.

His dictation finished, m'lord looked out of the window to see Tish running across the park away from the ha-ha, with a kite in her hand and Miss Lawrence, Kettie the nursemaid and Jack the footman, who always accompanied them on their walks, trailing behind her.

How graceful Miss Lawrence was! Even in her demure dress of the palest blue and her small straw chip bonnet with its deep blue ribbons, completely unfashionable though they both were, she carried with her an aura of elegance and quiet control. She paused to take her parasol from Jack before sitting down on one of the rustic benches which were dotted about the park.

A moment later a little procession came into view. At its front was Mrs Morton, also carrying a parasol to protect her against the midday sun, behind her were footmen carrying a small table, and behind *them* came another little troop holding high plates of food and the silver and china necessary for a cold collation.

'Forgive me, old fellow,' m'lord said hastily, examining himself in a mirror to check that his journey had left him presentable, 'but there seems to be a luncheon taking place on the back lawn. The footmen have just carried out the tea things and a fresh dish of tea would be most acceptable. Come and join us when you have finished your work.' And he was gone, striding out of the room as though he had been summoned to an audience by the Prince Regent himself.

John Bassett raised his eyebrows, wondering what had interested his usually phlegmatic master. Taking luncheon on the lawn, indeed! And this from a man who spoke as little as possible to anyone and to whom he would have thought a luncheon with others in the open would be anathema—something to be avoided at all costs.

He walked over to the window in time to see m'lord arrive on the lawn and bow to Miss Lawrence. She had removed her bonnet, and put down her parasol now that she was seated in the shade of a large stand of cedars. Another flotilla of footmen had brought out chairs, and m'lord sat down on one of them and accepted his tea from Mrs Morton. Meantime Tish, trailing her kite, had come over and was greeting her father with what—could John but have heard them—were excited squeaks of joy.

So, sat the wind in that quarter? He was willing to bet that Miss Lawrence was the attraction for his employer, not the dish of tea! John sat down and finished the letter in his best hand as quickly as he could before making his way down to join the party on the lawn. If his expression was rather rueful it was because his opinion at first sight of Miss Emma Lawrence, and confirmed by subsequent conversations with her, had been that here was someone who might make Mr John Bassett a useful wife.

Now, whatever plans m'lord, the Earl of Chard, had for her, it could hardly be to make her his wife—useful or otherwise. He wondered what in the world m'lord could be finding to say to her. The man whom John Bassett knew was not exactly a master of small talk—or the art of flirting, for that matter.

'The weather seems a little warmer inland than it is near the coast, Miss Lawrence,' was what m'lord was saying—which was hardly the wittiest sentence a man could offer to a woman who attracted him. Although why she did so, m'lord still did not know.

Tish saved him by saying happily, 'You have come back sooner than you said, Papa. You said that you would be away more than a week.'

'Did I so? Well, my business went well and we finished early, so here I am eating my luncheon with you. Whose idea was luncheon on the lawn? Yours, Mrs Morton?'

Mrs Morton, who had been astonished to see m'lord arrive to eat with them in the open, a thing which he had never done before, took a moment to answer him.

'Why, m'lord, I think that Miss Lawrence and I were both agreed on the matter. Tish wanted to fly her kite, the day is warm, and outdoors seemed more attractive than indoors.'

Now, all this was banal in the extreme, and still Miss Emma Lawrence had not said a word, but sat there, a demure sphinx whose home was in the wild countryside of Northumbria, not the wide sands of Egypt.

'And you, Miss Lawrence. Do you care for *al fresco* meals?' Now she would be compelled to answer him, to turn those great dark eyes on him. He would lose that perfect profile, but gain by hearing her measured voice.

'I have partaken of few in my life, m'lord, but this one seems pleasant enough.' If he could talk in banalities, so, too, could she.

'Miss Lawrence, in our previous conversations you have been quick to offer me a qualifying word after what seemed to be a definite statement. This time you have not offered me a qualifying word, but I fear that I detect a qualifying tone in your voice. Am I correct?'

He was so engaged in teasing Emma that he did not see Mrs Morton's sharp glance in his direction, nor did he notice that John Bassett had also arrived, and was displaying an expression which was quizzical to say the least.

'You are sharp, m'lord,' she said gravely. 'I admit that I was wondering whether the hard work which our little party has caused to so many of your staff was worth the pleasure we are taking in it.'

Such considerations had never occurred to Emma in her old life, but the eight years she had spent as a governess, suspended between the servants and the gentry and nobility whom she served—an alien in either group—had taught her how much back-breaking effort went into ensuring her employers' pleasant lives.

Brought up hard against this cool offering, m'lord replied gently, 'But you must admit, Miss Lawrence, that hard though the labour of Loudwater's servants may be, they are better off doing it than being thrown upon the parish to starve—as so many less fortunate are.'

Well, such a measured answer was difficult to rebuff, Emma knew, so she simply said, 'But that is no reason why they should be driven like cattle. Although, to be fair to you, m'lord, you are kinder to your staff than any of my previous masters.'

M'lord bowed his head, and John Bassett, who had just accepted a cup of tea from Mrs Morton—who had sat open-mouthed whilst Miss Lawrence came out with such Jacobinical heresies, and to his lordship's face too—said eagerly, 'And that I also know to be true. And I also know that the kitchen staff will probably be eating their food in the open, as well. Although I grant you not in such luxury as ourselves.'

Both men smiled at her, not unkind smiles, nor serious ones, but such as they might have offered to one of their own sex after a pleasant discussion. For no reason at all Emma's heart swelled within her. She looked steadily across at m'lord, and for the first time smiled back at him.

It had the strangest effect on him. First of all her face was transformed, as though a candle had been lit in a dark room, and secondly, for a moment, he had the oddest sense of *déjà vu*. It was as though she had smiled so at him before. Something tugged at the corner of his mind, some memory long lost—and even as he tried to retrieve it it was gone. She was the unknown Miss Lawrence again.

He could not stop himself. Watched, as he knew he was, by both John Bassett and Mrs Morton, he could not refrain from saying, 'You should smile more often, Miss Lawrence. It becomes you.'

And that overset Emma too. It was a personal remark for m'lord to make such as no gentleman ever made to a lady—either in company or out of it. It was sure to be remarked on by their hearers.

'You must thank the fairness of the day for my pleasure, m'lord,' she said, again as simply as she could—for she must say something.

'And the company, Miss Lawrence? Surely you must credit the company for a little of your happiness as well?'

His bantering tone was so unlike m'lord's usual one that both his secretary and his housekeeper could scarce forbear to stare at him.

'Oh, yes, the company. And Tish—I beg your pardon. I mean Lady Letitia.'

'No pardon needed. I prefer Tish myself. The other mode of address is a horrendous mouthful for such a small child.'

And now at last he was rising. For if he did not

go soon, who knew how much he might reveal of the inner self which he had always kept hidden from the world? An inner self which was finding the composed young woman beside him more and more attractive.

And who was it she reminded him off?

Trailed by Tish, who had taken up her kite again, he walked towards the house, golden in the afternoon sun.

Watching him go, John Bassett thought glumly that if m'lord had decided on luring Miss Lawrence into his toils—a melodramatic phrase, but he could surely have no serious interest in her—what chance did poor John Bassett possess?

Miss Lawrence was also exciting interest elsewhere. Ben Blackburn and Lord Lufton were spending the day drinking together at the inn which m'lord had earlier left for home.

'Dour fellow, Chard,' offered Lord Lufton, holding his glass to the light and admiring the port in it—a drink for men as wine was a drink for boys, or so he was fond of saying. 'Should get himself a woman. Proper monk, or so they say. Never heard of his being with one since that wife of his died.'

Ben, already half-cut, gave a careless laugh. 'Might be about to mend his ways, Lufton. Who knows?'

Lufton set down his glass of port with exaggerated care.

'Any evidence of that, old fellow?'

'Why, his daughter has a new governess. A demure creature. Hidden depths there, though. At least Chard looks at her as if he thinks so.'

'Does he so, indeed? And are you serious?'

'Very. . .serious. . .very. . .' The port was getting to Blackburn. 'Tell you what—I've been thinking about having a go there m'self.'

'Want to bet on it? I bet that he won't bed the little governess—or you either. How about that?'

'Why not? Twenty guineas that I do before he does,' said Blackburn, taking another swig.

'Fifty, rather,' returned Lufton, who was a great deal richer than his crony.

'Steep, but done.' Ben thought a moment, then said owlishly, 'I'd be a widgeon not to take you on even at such a price. Of course one of us will bed her. Let's shake hands on it and write it down before we forget—or get too drunk to remember.'

So they did, and killed the rest of the bottle, and the one after that, before driving to their respective homes the next day—with raving headaches and an equally raving desire not to lose their bets.

This was so strong in the case of Lord Lufton, who, like so many enormously wealthy men, was very mean with his money and did not wish to lose even such a meagre sum as fifty guineas, that he decided that a plot he had been hatching for some time might as well be started on its way.

His heiress was his much younger sister, the Lady Clara, and now, he thought, was the time to break the habit of a lifetime and propose a long visit to Loudwater. The prospect of Lady Clara as a rich wife might turn Chard's eyes away from his little governess towards someone more suitable—and more marriageable—of his own class.

And, to add to the fun, when he wrote to Chard he would propose to add Ben Blackburn to the party as well. May the best man win! Who exactly was the best man, and what exactly he would win, Lord Lufton was not quite sure.

Why, he might even take a long look at the little governess himself.

# CHAPTER FIVE

ALL unaware that she had already made her mark on Northumbria, albeit not quite after the fashion she might have desired, Emma went her composed way about Loudwater.

Mrs Morton had once begun to say something about m'lord to her along the lines that it was unwise for Emma to encourage him, but Emma had affected not to hear her. Mrs Morton was not the first to discover that for all her gentle ways and perfect manners Miss Lawrence had a will of iron. She parried Mrs Morton's attempts to warn her in the same cool fashion with which she spoke to John Bassett, who had taken, she thought, to tracking her around Loudwater.

Two days later she entered the library after lunch to find him sitting at a table in the window, thick ledgers in front of him. He gave a loud sigh as she passed him on her way to the shelves where tall folios lay on their sides; she was drawing a detailed map of Asia for Tish, who had expressed a desire to know exactly where the East Indies were.

So loud, indeed, was his sigh that Emma took compassion on him and smiled at him, whereat he said sadly, 'You do well to pity me, Miss Lawrence. This is the worst part of my task. Figuring was never an accomplishment of mine, as

I told m'lord. But writing, now, that is quite another thing.'

Emma walked to his side and looked at the column of accounts from m'lord's coalpits which John was trying to add up. Judging by the ink he had spent and the blots he had created, he was failing.

Something in her look alerted him. 'You do not fear them, unless I misjudge you, Miss Lawrence?'

Emma rewarded him with a smile again, and replied gently, 'My father, for some reason, insisted that I knew my numbers as well as my letters. No, I do not fear them. Would you like me to sum this column for you? Once you have found it to be difficult it becomes hard to sum it correctly. If I do this one for you, starting a new one might be easier.'

She had become aware of John Bassett's interest in her, and had concluded that one way of deterring him from his pursuit might be to show herself a knowledgeable bluestocking. She had never found that gentlemen liked women who seemed to know more than they did.

John Bassett stared at her in amazement. A female who could add up. What next! He decided to test her—after all, he could always check her work later.

'Why not?' he said, and swung the ledger towards her, handing over his quill pen and the piece of paper on which he had been making notes.

Swiftly and surely Emma added up the column

before her. It appeared that the Earl of Chard was doing well at this pit, at least, and probably at his other ones too. Equally swiftly and surely she wrote in the correct figure at the bottom of the column after she had done a double-check.

She swung the ledger back towards John Bassett, who stared at it and her, saying dolefully, 'Yes, I thought that was the answer, but every time I checked it, I came up with a different one. You should be keeping m'lord's books, not me. Or he should—he's good at figuring too.'

Now, this *was* a surprise. Emma could have sworn that the man whom she had once known would not have been aware of the difference between a plus or a minus. But she said nothing, simply watched poor John check her sums and acknowledge that she was not mistaken.

But she had been mistaken if she had thought that her attraction for him would dim if she showed off her mathematical as well as her book-learning prowess, for it was plain from then on that he had become even more besotted with her.

Which was unfortunate, for, whilst Emma wanted him for a friend, she by no means wanted him—or any man—as a lover or as a husband.

She had hardly handed the ledger back to John and sat down at the big map table and begun to examine the folio showing the continents of the world, when the library door opened and m'lord came in. Mr Cross, seated at his desk in the far corner of the room, looked up, a trifle bemused at the sight of three visitors where the library rarely saw more than one at a time.

M'lord was dressed more punctiliously than was usual. There was little of the careless gamekeeper about him today. He was wearing a bottle-green coat, white pantaloons, highly polished black boots and a spotless shirt. His cravat, instead of being carelessly knotted about his neck 'any old how', as his valet, Louis White, was wont to grieve, was artfully arranged in that gentleman's most artistic waterfall.

He had recently allowed his hair to grow again, and it had been brushed and arranged *à l'Apollo* until it was as burnished as it had been when he was the boy whom Emma had known. But his face was unchanged: granite-hard where it had once been soft.

The three already in the library stared at this rare vision of a town dandy. He stared back at them, a trifle haughtily for him, and said brusquely, 'I am informed by a letter which only arrived this morning that Lord Lufton is visiting me today with his sister Lady Clara and her companion Miss Straight, with Ben Blackburn in tow for yet another conference before we meet Geordie Stephenson. They should be arriving—' he pulled out a superb gold hunter to check the time '—in about half an hour.

'I propose to offer them tea and, seeing that Mrs Morton is visiting the vicar's wife at Loudwater village today, I would be most grateful if you, Miss

Lawrence, would do the honours as my hostess in her absence. I have told Kettie to look after Lady Letitia this afternoon.

'I shall expect you all to be in the grand salon as soon as possible, ready to receive them with me. I shall also expect you to be present at the dinner table at six o'clock sharp.'

Both his hearers stared even harder at him as he finished. He ignored them and looked over at Mr Cross to say, 'I think that you ought to be present at dinner too. Lord Lufton has asked to examine the old maps of the district which my grandfather collected. Apparently some new-come fellow from London who has purchased Granger's Hall is challenging ownership of one of his coalpits. I dare say we have a few which might help him in the matter.'

He bowed in everyone's direction and left the room. John Bassett's expression was dazed. 'We have had more excitement at Loudwater since you arrived, Miss Lawrence, than I can remember in the five years I have been here. Is not that so, Cross?'

Mr Cross nodded a bemused assent.

'Well, you can hardly give me the credit for Lord Lufton and Mr Blackburn's visit,' Emma exclaimed reasonably, unaware that she was wrong. Lufton was making his visit precisely to discover how Lord Chard stood in relation to his daughter's new governess, and to prevent Ben Blackburn from winning his bet!

'No, indeed,' agreed John, who had no idea that he was not the only promising young fellow in hot pursuit of Miss Lawrence. 'But things have grown livelier recently, I assure you. And now we had better make ourselves presentable, ready to obey our master's summons.'

He paused, and added, 'And furthermore, in all the time that I have known him, I have never seen m'lord in such splendid fig.'

But Emma had seen him in even more splendid fig, and for a moment, when he had come in, she thought that time had turned backwards. She had, however, no wish at all to sit at table with m'lord's grand visitors—and so she would tell him.

With a rapid, 'Excuse me,' to John, she followed in the path which m'lord had taken—she was sure he was adjourning to his study, his favourite room, and she would confront him there.

Yes, he was there, and called, 'Come,' after she had rapped on the door. He looked at her in surprise, eyebrows raised as she entered and bowed to him. He was standing behind his desk, some papers in his hand.

'Yes, Miss Lawrence. What is it?'

This was going to be harder than Emma had thought; he looked so much more daunting, so much more 'the Earl of Creation and the Lord of All' in his fine clothes than he had ever done in his everyday ones. Nevertheless, it must be said.

She swallowed and began. 'M'lord, I fear that I

must decline your kind invitation to dinner this evening.'

His eyebrows rose even higher. 'Indeed not! It is imperative that you attend.'

'But I have nothing fit to wear for such an occasion.'

'Nonsense!' He was being more autocratic than she had ever known him. 'Absolute bosh! You look charming in whatever you wear!'

There was no answer to that, other than to say feebly, 'I fear that Lady Clara and her companion may not approve of my presence.'

How high could his eyebrows rise? He had put his papers down and come from behind his desk to confront her.

'*That* consideration does not trouble me at all. *I* do not approve of their presence—it was forced upon me; they invited themselves—but I shall not say so. I require you to be present for two reasons: firstly, to make up the correct number of women to balance the presence of two female visitors, and secondly, I wish to have at least one of your sex at table who appears able to converse reasonably on reasonable subjects.

'Lady Clara is an accomplished fine lady who is as vapid as most of them are, and Mrs Morton is a good soul who has no conversation—as you well know. Of Miss Straight I know nothing, and wish to know less! Your presence is necessary to save *my* soul. And if you do not obey me I shall come upstairs to the schoolroom and fetch you down—

whatever you are wearing. Do I make myself plain?'

He had moved dangerously close to her, so that she could feel the warmth of him, the power of his presence, the strength of him—all turned on her humble self.

'Yes, m'lord. Very plain. I shall come down to dinner—under protest.'

As if suddenly aware of how close they were, he now stepped back a little, turned those ravishing blue eyes on her—they were all that was left of the Dominic Hastings she had once known—and said with a little laugh, 'You may come down under a parasol or a punkah with a servant working it, for all I care, so long as you come down. And if anyone objects to your presence and is foolish enough to protest—why, they may leave the table!'

This would not do, was Emma's dazed response. This would very much not do. Where would all this lead—and did she wish to follow?

'Consider what will be thought by others, m'lord, if you are so particular to me.'

'No, Miss Lawrence. I will not have that. There will be several of my staff at table, and your presence at it will be no more remarkable than theirs. That you are a female is of no import. You will also be present to lend Mrs Morton support. And now be off with you. I insist that you be with me in the grand salon when Lufton's benighted party arrives, and I am sure that you will wish to array yourself in something more splendid than the grey gown and the brown holland apron which you are at present sporting.'

Emma, who had by now reached the door, could not resist a parting shot. She paused before leaving to say sweetly, 'You confuse me, m'lord. A moment ago you informed me that what I wore was of no consequence. Have you changed your mind?'

His only answer to that, as she closed the door behind her, was to throw in her direction a half-whispered, 'Hussy!'

Now she must go to make herself 'presentable', as John had said, and stand in for Mrs Morton. She was still wondering what Lord Lufton's party would make of that. She decided to wear her best summer afternoon gown—a modest cream muslin with a lemon stripe and a pale lemon sash.

M'lord nodded his approval of it when she arrived, and John Bassett made eager eyes at her. Indeed, so charming did she look that when Lord Lufton and Mr Blackburn were announced, Lord Lufton thought at once that Mr Ben Blackburn had known whereof he spoke when he had drunkenly insisted on the governess's attractions.

Not only that, Lord Chard was arrayed as none of his visitors had ever seen him before, and whether or no it was the governess who had inspired him to achieve such heights of sartorial perfection had yet to be discovered.

Emma did not care for the way in which Lord

Lufton, a gross man, verging on middle-age and still unmarried, looked at her. He reminded her of Mr Henry Gardiner. He spoke to her as Mr Gardiner had done, in that slightly patronising, droll fashion which some men used towards women whom they thought of as prey. He held her hand a little too long when m'lord introduced Miss Lawrence as his deputy for Mrs Morton, who was out visiting, and told him she had consented to welcome the two ladies Lord Lufton had brought with him, as was only proper.

The Lufton heiress was indeed a fine lady. She bowed stiffly at Emma and then offered her two fingers, looking not at her, but over her shoulder. To be welcomed by the governess! Even in lieu of the absent Mrs Morton this was indeed unfortunate.

It was the reaction which Emma had expected, and if Lady Clara refused to look at Emma, then Emma took a good look at both her and her duenna, and did not like what she saw.

Lady Clara, short in stature, and with little in the way of address, was decked out in pastels: a mixture of pale blue and pale pink. It was an unfortunate combination seeing that she possessed a high colour and a petulant expression. She resembled an inexpensive doll ready to be laid out on the counter of a backstreet toy shop. Her manner, though, was that of a pampered beauty.

Passing on from Emma, she gave her whole attention to m'lord, ignoring Mr Cross, John

Bassett and Ben Blackburn, whom she thought of as one of her brother's rustic friends. Chard, now, was quite different. What had her brother meant by speaking of him as always being dressed like a small squire or a yokel? He was quite splendid. A positive tulip of fashion.

Miss Straight, Lady Clara's friend, also thought of herself as a cut above a governess. She was a woman of good, if obscure family, who had attached herself to the Lufton household so as to make her entrée to the highest society secure. She had not come to Loudwater to chat to someone who was little better than a servant.

She found it surprising that Chard had seen fit to promote her into the company of ladies. Driven to it, one supposed, by the unfortunate absence of his cousin, the only lady in the household. All that would change if Chard married Lady Clara. A consummation devoutly to be wished since it might provoke Lord Lufton into offering for Miss Straight, to replace his sister as the Lufton hostess.

She looked vinegar at poor Emma, particularly as her own lack of attractions was exposed by Emma's possession of them. She had, being dark with a strong, if slightly mannish face, often congratulated herself that she outshone the milk pudding charms of her charge, but no such consolation was offered to her by the governess.

Nevertheless, since no one else appeared to be willing to speak with her, she sank onto a sofa, patted the empty seat beside her and drawled,

'Pray sit by me, Miss Lawrence. Tell me, are you one of the Shropshire Lawrences? They are friends of mine at home—when I am not in town, you understand.'

'Not to my knowledge,' replied Emma coolly. After all, since she had gifted herself with the name, she was not a Lawrence of anywhere at all. But she was not about to tell Miss Straight so.

'Ah, perhaps the Derbyshire family, then? I met Miss Persephone Lawrence at Lady Cowper's last ball of the season nigh on a year ago. A most distinguished female. Poetically inclined. Are you poetically inclined, Miss Lawrence?'

'Alas,' said Emma who, perversely, was beginning to enjoy herself as she suffered this artless patronage, 'I am not related to them either, or to any well-known family of Lawrences. And, I fear, I am far from being poetically inclined. On the contrary, I am most prosaic.'

Miss Straight fanned herself, as though such a downright declaration made her feel positively faint.

'Indeed. How unfortunate. Lady Clara, now, is most poetically inclined. She wrote the sweetest lines on her pet canary when it died.'

Emma felt it her duty to offer sympathy on the canary's demise, ending by asking how it had come by its unfortunate end.

'Alas, poor Clara forgot to shut the cage door, and the cat got at it. Dear Clara, indeed, was so overset that we had to have the cat put down.'

Miss Straight heaved a sigh and put a handkerchief to her eyes.

Emma nobly refrained from commenting that, given the story as told, justice would have been better served by having Lady Clara put down for her carelessness. She was suddenly aware that m'lord had walked over to where they were, and was listening to them. Behind him came footmen carrying the teaboards, on which teacups, plates, silverware and a selection of sandwiches, cakes, biscuits and teabreads were displayed.

His arrival saved her from further badgering by Miss Straight. After all, why should she continue to converse with the humble governess when her noble employer was at hand?

M'lord dragged up a chair and listened again to the sad story of the canary—which he had already overheard, but could not say so. His internal reaction was the same as Emma's, and his nobility consisted of trying not to catch Emma's eye as Miss Straight embellished the poor canary's death even more in order to emphasise her charge's sensitivity. She and her patron, Lord Lufton, were at one in wishing to snare Chard and Loudwater for Lady Clara.

Emma decided to move on. She was fearful that she might lose her fine control as Miss Straight's account of her life with Lady Clara grew more and more moving. Her charge appeared to have an unfortunate effect on the dumb animals who surrounded her. Her pug dog had also met a distressing end—occasioning a lengthy ode from her pen which Miss Straight insisted on reciting to m'lord.

At this point Emma rose, bowed, and made her way to where Lady Clara was reluctantly speaking to John Bassett and Ben Blackburn, m'lord having deserted her. Lord Lufton was talking to Mr Cross about maps and coalmines. Emma naughtily thought that he ought not to take his sister to visit any of them if he wished to retain the health of all his pit ponies.

On seeing Emma approach, Lady Clara said in an autocratic voice, 'You will forgive me, but I must rejoin my dear Miss Straight and our host.' Not deigning to acknowledge Emma's presence, she put her fan before her face and strolled over to sit beside m'lord.

What a blessed relief, was Emma's only thought. Now he and his two guests could discuss the sad fate of Lady Clara's pets and Miss Straight's many and aristocratic relations to their heart's content.

Mr John Bassett was making his way over to her eagerly, having found Lady Clara heavy weather, but, alas, he was cut out by the big guns of Lord Lufton, who abandoned Mr Cross the moment the governess arrived among them lest Ben Blackburn reach her before him.

'Miss Lawrence, is it? Any relation to my old friend "Salamanca" Lawrence of the Light Bobs and Seely Sussex? I suppose I ought to refer to him as Henry, but his prowess in the Peninsula will always stick to his name.'

Emma began the litany which had her disclaiming all knowledge of any Lawrences, whether of Shropshire, Sussex or Derbyshire—or anywhere else.

'Pity, that. You have the look of his sister Honoria. She married Lord Tenterden. Of South Yorkshire.'

Perhaps she ought to have claimed that she belonged to a distant branch and made the man before her happy. But no, the truth was always the best—except, of course, that if she were truthful she would not call herself Lawrence at all!

'You find Lady Letitia a pleasant child? Biddable, is she?'

'Very,' replied Emma, a trifle bemused, wondering why such a powerful magnate should be troubling with her at all. She supposed that small talk about small girls was hardly Lord Lufton's usual line.

'You have been in Northumbria long, Miss Lawrence? How does it strike you, eh?'

'Very wild and beautiful,' she replied, which was no less than the truth. 'But I have had small opportunity to see much of it yet. I hope to visit Hadrian's Wall ere long—and see the Upper Tyne, of course.'

'Oh, indeed. Yes, you must. Very wild, the Wall. Very fine, the Upper Tyne. I should like Miss Straight to see them too.'

He swung round on one heel and called over to m'lord in an imperious bellow which had the whole room listening to him. 'I say, Chard, Miss Lawrence tells me that she has not seen the Wall yet. Bad business that. While we are here we must all go over to it—and if the good weather holds we must eat *al fresco*. With your permission, of course.'

Released from the clutches of Lady Clara and Miss Straight, who had passed from the topics of pets, poetry and Lord Byron's wicked ways to the pleasures of Almack's and the London season, in none of which m'lord possessed the slightest interest, he rose, excusing himself to the ladies for breaking off his delightful conversation. He would, he said, be pleased to organise such a party as Lord Lufton had suggested, and would set matters in train at once.

'My daughter will be on her highest ropes,' he added. 'I have promised her such a treat, but have not yet found the time to accomodate her.'

'You work too hard, old fellow,' Lord Lufton bellowed. 'Take heed of your copybook. All work and no play makes Jack a dull boy. Isn't that so, Miss Lawrence?'

His hearers reacted to this unaccountable favouring of the new governess each in their own fashion. M'lord thought savagely that he ought to warn Miss Lawrence of Lufton's reputation as a rake; Ben Blackburn seethed as he began to realise that Lufton was trying to win his bet by cutting out the governess for himself, now that he had seen that she was as delicately attractive as he had claimed; John Bassett suffered even further agonies of jealousy and Mr Cross, like his master, decided that a few warning words to poor Miss Lawrence might not come amiss.

As for Lady Clara and Miss Straight, they were both aghast. Miss Straight at the prospect of losing Lord Lufton's hand—of which she had always had vague hopes—and Lady Clara at the thought of acquiring a low-born sister-in-law, whose offspring might cut her off from the promise of most of the Lufton wealth.

Both separately comforted themselves with the further thought that, given Lord Lufton's amorous record, he was more likely to make Miss Lawrence his mistress than his wife. Neither of them considered for a moment that Emma would have the bad taste to be other than flattered at his attentions—legitimate or otherwise.

Emma herself was astonished at being the centre of such attention. For nearly eight years she had lived on the edges of fashionable life, sitting unacknowledged in corners, hardly spoken to, unconsidered and abandoned, finding companionship only when with her young charges. She could quite understand the dismay of Lady Clara and Miss Straight when they found themselves no longer the leading ladies in the circle which they graced.

She would have liked to quit the company, but

with m'lord's bright blue eyes on her, defying her to do any such thing, she could not do so.

What he did do was rescue her, by coming over to Lord Lufton and suggesting that he and Ben Blackburn might like to visit the stables where his head groom, Outhwaite, was busy training the latest pair of chestnuts which he had bought for his curricle. 'I think,' he offered, 'that the ladies might wish to retire to their rooms to rest after their arduous journey and before they come down to dinner.'

Emma, with difficulty, suppressed the giggles which were afflicting her—brought on by the unlikely situation, where every man in the room seemed bent on pursuing her, from Lord Lufton downwards, and by the realisation that the bridling Lady Clara had no intention of being sent to her room.

'By no means,' she declaimed. 'If my dear Calypso Straight wishes to rest—or Miss Lawrence, for that matter—by all means let them do so. I have no intention of retiring. I, too, would wish to visit the stables and examine Lord Chard's latest acquisitions. I believe that you were a famous whip, m'lord, when you were a member of the *ton* before your marriage.'

'My dear Clara,' exclaimed her brother hastily, 'you must do no such thing. The stables are not a proper place for a young lady.'

'Now, there, brother, I must contradict you. What possible harm can there be if you are my escort? You know that I wish to set up my own carriage, and I should be grateful to Lord Chard if he would offer me the benefit of his advice.'

M'lord bowed. Emma watched him, fascinated. He had reverted to the young man she had once known, all suave charm.

'I fear that you flatter me, Lady Clara. Outhwaite is the man to advise you, and, although I understand your brother's reservations, let me assure you that if you give me a quarter of an hour to arrange matters I will ensure that when you visit the yard you will not see or hear anything untoward to distress you. You will allow, Lufton?'

Oh, neatly done, was Emma's inward and amused response when Lord Lufton reluctantly agreed to m'lord's suggestion. Then m'lord turned to her and said, in exactly the kind of aloof voice which an employer ought to use to his daughter's governess, 'You have my permission to retire, Miss Lawrence. We shall meet again at dinner.' She could not but savour his *sang froid*.

Lady Clara was not savouring anything. So! The governess was to be inflicted on them at dinner, was she? What in the world were things coming to? First her brother fawned on Miss Nobody from Nowhere, and now Lord Chard was taking up where he had left off. And was not Ben Blackburn bowing far too low to her as she passed him on leaving the room? Had everyone run mad? What a bore it was to be the only sane person left in the world. Except for Calypso Straight, that was.

M'lord was offering her his arm, to move onto the terrace to wait there with the others until all was ready for her in the yard. Well, there, at least, she would not have to share him with one of the servants.

The servants were eating their luncheon in the kitchen—they always took it after their masters had finished theirs. The conversation—inevitably—revolved around the doings of those said masters. Mr Louis White, m'lord's valet, was being particularly noisy in answer to a query from Blount, the butler, asking whether he had any notion as to why m'lord had suddenly reverted to the style of dress which had been commonplace to him years ago but not lately.

Mr White, a cockney despite his elegant manner of speech, which he had copied from m'lord, was busy finishing his beef sandwich which he had liberally spread with horseradish sauce, and he mumbled indistinctly through it. 'It's her, isn't it? Stands to reason.'

'Her, Mr White?' queried the housekeeper, who had just arrived, as custom had it, in time for the dessert; she was usually served her meals in her room—rank was as important in the servants' hall as it was in m'lord's drawing room. 'You mean Lady Clara?' she finished.

'Nah,' replied Louis, his mouth empty now, putting a finger to the side of his nose, winking as he did so, and reverting to his original cockney. 'Not 'er. The governess, a 'course.'

'The Governess!' echoed half a dozen voices.

'You're bamming us, man,' came from the butler.

'Not I.' Louis was elegantly spoken again. 'You don't see as much of him as I do. Watches out for her, he does, and stops her on any excuse. Haunts the schoolroom—insisted on her meeting Lord L. and that plain pudding his sister, didn't he? Some excuse about having a proper lady present. Never bothered him before, did it? And Ben Blackburn's sniffing round her as well—and Lufton, too, when he gets his eye in. I know the looks of the gentry on the prowl.'

'Lor', Mr White, you are a one,' tittered Mrs Morton's maid. 'But it's true that m'lord has visited the schoolroom much more often since the governess arrived.'

The butler said, 'I don't believe a word of it. A nice quiet proper young lady is Miss Lawrence. Not like the Sandeman woman. Now, if he were going to come to terms with anyone, it would have been her.'

'Very quiet, true,' observed Louis, now scoffing syllabub as though he hadn't eaten for a week. 'But still waters run deep, they say, and m'lord was a plunger when he was young. Been steady now for a long time, though. Probably feels ready for a change. There's a look in Miss Lawrence's eye sometimes. . .'

'Don't believe a word of it,' repeated the butler, who liked Miss Lawrence. 'She's a real lady—not like the previous governesses, who all dangled after m'lord.'

'Thought of having a go there myself,' continued Louis remorselessly, 'but probably don't stand much of a chance against m'lord.'

He looked around the table. 'Want to bet on it, anyone? Put your money where your mouth is? I say he's interested, and that madam's not averse to him for all her prim ways. Money on the table.' He threw down a guinea to the oohs and aahs of all the women around the table. 'Match that. Odds two to one that m'lord has her before the summer's end.'

The butler reluctantly fished out a guinea. Not to accept Louis's challenge—not the first, by any means—would brand him skinflint and miser. 'That says you're wrong,' he muttered dismally, thinking of all the times he had bet against Louis and lost.

Louis picked up the guineas—a small fortune for both of them, but never mind that—and tossed them to the housekeeper. 'Hold them for us, dearie, until Michaelmas Day—and then we'll find out who's the goose. Me or Blountie, here. May the best man win.'

Above stairs, below stairs, drawing room or kitchen, it was all the same. Only the language differed, and the quantity wagered. And the governess, quiet, prim and reserved, new-come among them, was the innocent focus of attention. . .

# CHAPTER SIX

SHOULD she, or shouldn't she? Emma had lifted from a trunk which stood in the corner of her bedroom a dress carefully wrapped in tissue paper. It was the last link with her life as Emilia Lincoln, the rich heiress. It was a high-waisted apricot silk creation trimmed with delicate ivory-coloured lace, which dated back to the last days of her father's wealth. She had been a little plumper then than she was now, but some years ago, with the help of Mrs Gore, she had altered it to fit her newly slender figure.

Alas, beautiful though the dress was, she had never found an occasion for its use. It shrieked of the expensive dressmaker who had originally created it, and was not at all the sort of toilette in which a humble governess ought to deck herself.

Emma also pulled out of the trunk a small fan of chicken feathers, dyed apricot with silver and ivory sticks, long apricot-coloured silk gloves and a reticule so dainty that it barely held a lacy cobweb of a handkerchief. Ivory-coloured kid pumps and a shawl to match the handkerchief completed the ensemble.

Gone, alas, were the rope of pearls, the small pearl tiara and the bracelet which her father had given her to wear with it in the week before he had shot himself. All that was left of her once full jewel box was a small seed pearl necklace—a modest trifle given to her when she had been a child.

But the insolent scrutiny of Lady Clara Lufton and Miss Straight had awoken something defiant in Emma—that and the avid manner in which all of the men had looked at her. There was no mistaking the intentions of any of them; even poor John Bassett's mouth visibly watered whenever she walked into his line of sight.

So, they might as well have something to stare at, and whether the reason for their outrageous behaviour was her own attraction, the lack of suitable women for a gentleman to pursue or simply the fact that she was a new female face in the county was immaterial. She would rise to the challenge.

More than that. Something inside herself was whispering, Years ago *he—m'lord*—insulted and hurt you. Never mind that he was unaware that you heard him doing so. What a splendid thing it would be if you could pay him back after some fashion! Suppose that you could make him hanker and moon after you, as you once hankered and mooned after him! Even better if you could remain as cold towards him as he was to you—what then?

Revenge, they say, is a dish best eaten cold. Why should not you, went on the voice insistently, eat that cold dish and pay m'lord back in kind for the suffering he caused you when he described you so unkindly and revealed that he was simply a vicious fortune-hunter?

Emma did not ask herself whether she ought to be eating it at all. Nor did she ask herself whether she was still indifferent to m'lord, for she would not have liked the answer. She had long told herself that she was, and she pushed to the back of her mind the uncomfortable fact that she was still drawn to the man he had become.

Impulsively Emma laid out all her beautiful belongings on her bed. The dress had been made with a classic elegance which would overcome the eight years since it had been created. She could drape it slightly differently, and why should she not dress her hair fashionably and discard the small lace cap which she had been wearing as a dutiful governess should?

Eyes glowing, lips slightly parted, Emma began to dress herself. Not in her usual dull brown velvet, but in the clothes which her father had intended she should wear on her nineteenth birthday. . .

She walked downstairs to meet Mrs Morton in the stone-flagged hall, with the busts of Apollo and all the early Roman Emperors standing on tall stone pillars, their blind eyes staring at her as she met that lady's startled gaze. Mrs Morton was dressed in her best black silk and looked a picture of elderly rectitude.

'My dear Miss Lawrence, I was troubled lest you had nothing fit to wear at m'lord's table when all his fine guests were present. I see that I should not have been concerned for you. As usual, you are completely *comme il faut*.'

Emma bowed her thanks for this compliment, and the pair of them entered the great drawing room to find that m'lord, Lord Lufton and his sister were already present. Miss Straight had not yet arrived, and m'lord thus had the pleasure of all Lady Clara's attention.

Until, that was, she turned—and saw Emma.

'Good God,' she drawled rudely, after surveying her up and down. 'It's the governess!' And, turning her back on both Emma and Mrs Morton, she said to m'lord in the sweetest voice she could summon, 'It is very good of you to supply us with a full complement of. . .ladies, but you really need not have troubled yourself. My good Miss Straight is really all the female company I ever need, I do assure you.'

M'lord treated this sublime piece of rudeness by saying in his most charming manner—a manner which took Emma back ten years—'Oh, my dear Lady Clara, such independence of spirit does you credit, I am sure, but since my cousin, Mrs Morton—whom I now present to you—and Miss Lawrence are accustomed to sit at table with me, I could not in decency pass one of them over. Knowing that, I am sure that you will welcome them both—as I do.'

Now, here's a thing, thought Emma, highly entertained by the spectacle of Lady Clara reeling and writhing in coils like a bitten snake in an effort to recover ground with m'lord after his tactful snub. She wriggled so hard that Emma unkindly thought that one more twist would have her low-cut dress off her shoulders and displaying more of her to the world than was modest.

'Oh, of course, Chard, of course. Your eccentricities are delightful, and your kindness verges on the sublime, isn't that so, brother?' The over-vigorous tap of her fan on Lord Lufton's shoulder was one which she would sooner have given m'lord, but did not dare. There was something a little formidable about his harsh face and big body.

'What's that, Clara?' exclaimed Lord Lufton, turning himself about so that his slightly goggle eyes fell on Emma for the first time. 'Oh, it's Miss Lawrence? Happy to see you, madam. Your joining us will keep Clara in countenance, I'm sure. Wouldn't want to be the only young filly among us, would you, m'dear?'

How she kept a straight face as Lord Lufton, unaware of what his sister had been saying, came out with this improbable statement, Emma never knew. Only the knowledge that m'lord's eye was on her, and that he, too, like Lord Lufton was reacting favourably to her new splendours, kept her from disgracing herself. She thought that his mouth twitched at the notion that Lady Clara needed a governess to keep her in countenance, but otherwise he kept a stone face. They were all saved from further unintentional *faux pas* by the arrival of Calypso Straight and the other men in the party.

After that dinner was an anti-climax. Lady Clara, perhaps put on her guard a little by what had already occurred, confined herself to trivialities, determinedly ignoring the two upstarts—as she privately thought Mrs Morton and Emma.

Neither lady was overset by being omitted from the delights of her conversation. Mrs Morton was too good-natured to care what Lady Clara thought of her presence, and Emma was too busy being entertained by Lady Clara's pursuit of m'lord and fending off the unwanted attentions of Lord Lufton who sat on her left, and his rival, Ben Blackburn, who sat on her right.

She was only too aware that Lady Clara was bursting with fury to find that the governess's toilette was superior to her own, and that the female whom all the men were obviously attracted to was that same humble governess and not herself.

Fortunately m'lord appeared to be immune to the wretched creature's charms, but occasionally even *his* attentions to her faltered as bursts of laughter came floating up the table from where the governess was seated. Really, the wretched woman seemed to possess no understanding of what was seemly in good society!

Emma was surprised to find that she was enjoying the new sensation of fending off male admiration, and doing it after such a fashion that her admireres were not offended. Her change of appearance had come too late for her to go into society to find out what an effect it had on the opposite sex. Her father's death had cut her off from the *ton*, but what Mr Brummell had suspected might happen when her confidence grew to match her new-found looks and her intelligence had at last come to pass.

At a signal from m'lord, Mrs Morton led the ladies from the room, leaving the gentlemen to their port and cigars. Emma had hardly taken her seat in the drawing room before Miss Straight made a bee-line for her to begin what was obviously a none too tactful attempt to suggest that she had been forgetting herself over dinner. But she had for once met her match; Emma found a subtle amusement in wrong-footing Lady Clara's crony and self-constituted protectress.

'It must,' Miss Straight announced magisterially, 'be exceedingly difficult for one like yourself, quite unversed in the practices of polite society, to accustom yourself to playing a proper and correct part in it.'

'Not at all,' returned Emma, showing no signs of being nonplussed by such sneering patronage. 'After all, I have the advantage of seeing how you and Lady Clara conduct yourselves, and I could surely find no better examples than you both.'

This came out with such winning sweetness that for once in her life Miss Straight's bullying dominance of all around her, including Lady Clara, was under severe threat.

What to say?

How to answer?

'Miss. . .er. . .Lawrence, is it? I can only commend you for your common sense in choosing us as your guides. One does wonder, however, whether many employers would allow their dependants to sit at table with their guests, thus rendering such self-control necessary. You must not expect others to allow their governesses such a loose rein—we all know what a charming eccentric Lord Chard is, but. . .' And she shrugged her bony shoulders.

'Oh, you have me there,' murmured Emma, putting up her fan and looking at Miss Straight over the top of it. 'You must forgive me if I do not find m'lord at all eccentric. I would have said, rather, that he is emblematic of downright common sense. But then, you and Lady Clara know him so much better than I do. Perhaps you could enlighten me as to his other eccentricities, so that I do not fail in *savoir faire* by unwittingly referring to them when next I speak to him.'

What to say again? Miss Lawrence appeared to be possessed of the ability to deprive the person to whom she was speaking of any reply which did not sound ridiculous or unmannerly. It was, Miss Straight had the grace to acknowledge to herself, really quite wrong of her to have made such a personal remark about Chard to one of his underlings, but she had been provoked to it.

With nothing to say, she retired to talk to Lady

Clara—who had been pointedly ignoring Mrs Morton, who sat placidly embroidering a tapestry cushion. She was compelled to hand the palm to the governess, who sat as demurely as Mrs Morton, before picking up her own canvaswork— a kneeler for the Loudwater chapel with the Hastings arms worked into it.

Boredom reigned. The unlikely quartet was only rescued by the arrival of the men some half-hour later, followed rapidly by the teaboard, brought in by a fleet of footmen. Mrs Morton and her housekeeper ran a tight ship, as Lord Lufton commented—he being neither as malicious nor as rude as his sister to dependant female underlings. Besides, he was trying to keep Chard happy, and had shrewdly noted that his fellow peer did not care overmuch to see his dependants demeaned by his guests. He accordingly vied with John Bassett and Ben Blackburn for the governess's attention, leaving Mr Cross to treat with Mrs Morton in his quiet way.

M'lord thus had Lady Clara and her companion to himself again, and was not sure that he appreciated the honour. Far from it, in fact. He could not prevent himself from looking over to where Miss Lawrence sat, her perfect profile and beautiful shoulders revealed for the first time in her splendid dress. He was surprised to discover how much he resented the attentions the other men were paying to her.

He wanted to go over and push them out of the

way, and have that piquant face and charming voice to himself, but his duty called him, and, as always, he obeyed it with an inward sigh. If Emma noticed his half-turn towards her she gave no sign of it, but continued a calm conversation with Lord Lufton, who was asking her for her opinion of Northumbria. Ben Blackburn, who had drunk more than was good for him, was lounging against the white marble fireplace, his right hand suggestively cupping the breast of the half-naked statue of the goddess Venus holding it up.

M'lord frowned at the sight. He did not care for the way in which Blackburn was eyeing Miss Lawrence, and decided to take a hand in the game himself.

Tactfully, he bowed to Lady Clara and her friend, saying, 'I understand that the party has expressed a desire to visit Hadrian's Wall, which is not at so great a distance from Loudwater as to be too tiring a journey. May I propose the day after tomorrow? That will give me time to send a messenger to The George at Chollerford, where the bridge crosses the North Tyne, arranging for a suitable cold collation to be sent from Loudwater to be served there around midday. Always providing, of course, that the weather is fine.'

'Oh, famous!' exclaimed Miss Straight, before Lady Clara could say anything. Lady Clara was not particularly entranced by the notion of a day spent in the open, but this might be a splendid opportunity for them to have m'lord to themselves.

'I am sure that Clara and myself will be only too delighted by such an expedition. I have never visited the Wall, and have frequently longed to do so. Is not that a famous notion of m'lord's, Clara?'

'Oh, famous, indeed,' returned Lady Clara somewhat grudgingly. 'It will not be too windy, I hope? I declare that of all things I do dislike wind, and I believe that the Wall is in a most exposed position.

'But think of walking where the Romans walked! It *was* the Romans who walked there, was it not, m'lord? I always mix them up with the Danes. Or was it the Anglo-Saxons, perhaps?'

'The Romans it was,' replied m'lord, keeping a straight face with some difficulty. 'Now, forgive me, I must ask the rest of the party if this arrangement is satisfactory to them. I know that it will gratify Miss Lawrence and Tish; they have both expressed great interest in such an expedition.'

He bowed his way over to where he could keep an eye on that bounder Blackburn, and Lufton as well, who had an expression on his face when he looked at Miss Lawrence which m'lord knew from of old boded nothing but ill.

'Oh, bother,' exclaimed Miss Straight inelegantly to Lady Clara as she watched him cross the room. 'I was sure that we had rid ourselves of the governess—and the child as well. Never mind. We can suggest that they remain with the servants.'

'I have no great desire to grub around in the

open,' remarked Lady Clara reproachfully. 'I wonder at you being so set on doing so, Calypso. Not like you at all.'

Really, reflected her companion, there were times when her friend's dull wits were insupportable. To work so hard to achieve a great settlement for her and to gain so little support was the outside of enough. But no matter. It was obvious, even from across the room, that apart from Lady Clara all the party were greatly taken by the prospect of a trip to the Wall. It would make a pleasant change for them from wandering around coalpits and talking to jumped-up colliers like this man Geordie Stephenson whom Lufton was always prosing on about, was Miss Straight's briskly dismissive conclusion.

'So,' finished m'lord, 'we are all agreed. The Wall the day after tomorrow, and Killingworth the following week.'

'Oh, indeed,' replied Lord Lufton. 'Pleasure before business for a change, Chard. You are becoming quite reformed. I never thought to see the day when you placed business second!'

Emma was delighted. Not only would she take great pleasure in seeing more of the starkly beautiful countryside which surrounded Loudwater, but such a trip would give point to the history lessons which Tish was beginning to enjoy under her careful guidance.

She could see Miss Straight's hard and unfriendly eyes on her, as well as Ben Blackburn's lecherous ones, and decided to remove herself as quickly and as tactfully as she could.

Picking up her embroidery, she rose, saying to her employer, 'You will allow me to retire, m'lord. I fear that I am unused to late nights, and I have promised to take Lady Letitia for a long walk after breakfast tomorrow.'

M'lord bowed his permission, and the enthusiasm with which the men bade her goodnight was only matched by the lack of it from Miss Straight and Lady Clara, who nodded their cold farewells from across the room.

Not that that troubled Emma. What did trouble her was the expression on Ben Blackburn's face as he mentally stripped her of her clothing—an expression which she had last seen Henry Gardiner wearing. The sooner she left and assumed once more the drab mantle of the governess, the better—even if she had enjoyed for one brief evening pretending that she was once again the great heiress Emilia Lincoln, who was no longer a small fat girl with a stammer, but someone who attracted interested attention.

Ben Blackburn ceased to fondle Venus as the door closed behind Emma. He yawned, and remarked to the ceiling where yet another Venus was sporting with Mars, 'Time for me to turn in too, Chard. It's been a long day.'

M'lord's speculative eyes followed him through the door. Something odd there. Blackburn never usually turned in before the small hours. He would allow him a small start before breaking up the party, and would then follow him to his room— any pretext for a conversation would serve if the man's intentions were innocent.

He accordingly signified the end of the evening's entertainment, which had the advantage of ridding him of the need to remain with the Lufton ladies any longer.

His duty done, he made his way rapidly up the backstairs to Ben Blackburn's room, to find it, as he had expected, unoccupied.

Emma had almost reached the safety of her room when Ben Blackburn caught up with her. He had seen her walking along the first great landing in the direction of that part of the house where he had earlier discovered that she and her charge were housed, away from both m'lord and his guests. There were no footmen about and she was, he hoped, unaware that she was being followed.

Indeed, it was only when Emma had her hand on the doorknob that she realised that Ben Blackburn was close behind her. He leaned forward, put a hand on hers and, breathing port wine fumes over her, muttered into her ear, 'Well met, m'dear. I like a lively piece, that I do. And now is the time for us to enjoy ourselves somewhat more than we could do downstairs.'

Before she could stop him he had swung her about, pushed her against the wall and thrust his face into hers, his mouth attempting to devour her and his hands rifling her body. He was big, strong and determined, and cared nothing for the woman whom he was assaulting.

Swiftly the dismayed Emma realised that the tactics which had served to overcome the rather more civilised Mr Henry Gardiner would not work here. Worse, she was so hard up against the wall, pinned there by his brute strength, that she could neither push him away nor use her foot or knee to injure him. She gave a little moan and tried to wrestle free of him, only to force from him a low chuckle and the words, 'Come, madam, do not pretend you don't want this from one of us. You may have Chard another day. Tonight you are mine.'

In his mind he was already winning his bet with Lufton, and a rare pleasure it was going to be. He always preferred to enjoy a woman after a bit of a struggle, and madam was duly obliging him.

To resist him simply roused him the more, as Emma was beginning to find. He was holding her with such unkind strength that she could almost feel the bruises starting up on her arms. Her face was raw where his bearded jaw, more than a day away from a close shave, had scraped it, and her hair had already come down.

Fearful from his behaviour that he might do more than simply try to snatch a kiss, there was nothing left for Emma to do but shout for help and damn the consequences in shame and scandal if anyone heard her and came to save her. But even as she tried to do so Ben Blackburn muttered an oath and silenced her by the simple expedient of putting his own mouth over hers and forcing his tongue inside it.

Then, just as Emma began to despair, salvation arrived. Someone was walking briskly along the corridor, and that someone was m'lord. He had seen the pair of them close together and was saying from a little distance, as coolly as he could, 'Oh, there you are, Blackburn. Lost your way, have you? Your rooms are up the other stairs—facing the front lawn.'

M'lord made no great effort to reach them speedily, giving Ben Blackburn the opportunity to wrench himself away from his victim and Emma the chance to repair her dishevelled state. Ben Blackburn took the opportunity m'lord was offering him to pretend that nothing untoward was happening, had happened, or was about to happen, by saying confidently and carelessly, 'Miss Lawrence was just putting me right about my destination.'

Never mind that his face was scarlet, and that he knew only too well that m'lord had known exactly what his intentions were. To say anything else would be dangerous, and might put his social position at risk. Ben Blackburn might be a power in Northumbria, but m'lord was more powerful still, and could ruin a man if he so pleased. He anxiously awaited m'lord's response.

'Oh, indeed. How exceedingly helpful of her,'

intoned m'lord, his expressionless face giving no hint that he was in the grip of a murderous rage which had seized him when he had turned the corner and seen the two struggling figures. 'Well, you had best thank her for her assistance, Blackburn, and bid her goodnight.'

So saying, he stood to one side to allow Ben Blackburn to pass him, which he did, averting his gaze from his host and thankful only that m'lord was choosing to play this particular game with him.

And what was m'lord doing, prowling the corridor where his governess lived? Who was he to keep Ben Blackburn from pleasuring himself with a doxy who was obviously pleasuring her master? No man had a lien on a woman lacking virtue! And he had been so near to winning his bet too. Damn the man! But there was always another day.

Ignoring him, m'lord walked to where Emma was now opening the door to her room. She, too, had her face averted from him, full of shame that she had been discovered in such a compromising position. Suppose he thought that she had been encouraging Ben Blackburn. . .?

M'lord could think no such thing. He could see the bruises on her arms, and on her face, and he knew why she was acting as she did—like a shy fawn which had just escaped a fell hunter.

He had to speak to her, to reassure her that he knew that she had been a victim, not a willing partner in the game of illicit love.

'Miss Lawrence,' he said, his voice as low and gentle as he could make it, 'you must forgive me if I appeared to make light of the shameless way in which Ben Blackburn was behaving towards you, but I did not think that you wished for the scandal which would follow an altercation between us over you. He could survive it, but you could not.

'If you wish me to do more, to forbid him the house, you have only to say so. But I do not think that he will try to force you again, and to send him away might provoke him to blacken your name without you having any form of redress. As it is, we can all pretend that nothing happened.'

Still standing in the doorway, Emma lifted her head proudly and, putting up a hand to tuck away an errant curl, murmured, 'I thank you for saving me, and for doing it in such a fashion as to avert scandal. I am well aware that I am the one who would suffer if what has occurred were to become known.'

She hesitated before plunging on. 'Please believe me—I have done nothing to encourage him, to make him think that he could treat me so improperly. I am sure that he was drunk, and that he hardly knew what he was doing.'

This m'lord knew not to be true. He thought that Ben Blackburn had known exactly what he was doing; he had feared something like this might happen since he'd first had cause to watch Blackburn's conduct towards the governess. That the man was a libertine, he knew. What he could not have known was that he would misuse Loudwater's hospitality to attack a patently innocent young woman.

More, he saw that for all her brave words and manner Emma had begun to tremble, and he could not prevent himself, as her shudders grew worse, from putting out his own hand to touch her cheek where Ben Blackburn had marked it, to stroke it gently and to say, 'No, you must not. . .'

What was it that she must not, and that he must not? Neither of them knew. He lost himself, lost all sense—was no better than Ben Blackburn, even though he used no brute strength, no cold ferocity. He put his arm around her, to hold her shuddering body gently to him, to stroke her silky hair, to press a light kiss on the top of her head, to comfort her, to murmur, 'There, there,' as though she were no older than Tish. To kiss her cheek, the one which Ben Blackburn had violated. . .

To do more than that. To. . .to. . . No! It was necessary for him to spring away, to say almost violently as her great eyes looked up at him, bright with unshed tears, 'No, no. I am no better than he was to take advantage of you when you are still distressed. I am a brute. You must think all men brutes. Forgive me.'

Emma, her mind still reeling from what had passed, and from her body's strong reaction when m'lord had taken her in his arms, looked up at him trustingly and said, 'No, no. You saved me, and you have not behaved towards me at all as he did. No, indeed.'

And then she said, for the thought had just struck her, 'How did you know what his intentions were? How was it that you came so opportunely to save me? Another moment and I should have been lost. She began to shudder again.

'I don't know,' said m'lord slowly. 'Perhaps the manner in which he looked at you in the drawing room.' He must not frighten her further, and, though it was agony not to touch her, he must not do so. He could not trust himself, or the desire which had run through him when he had taken her so lightly into his arms.

He must simply bow and say to her as gently as he could, 'Try to forget what has happened, although I know that will be difficult. Would you like me to send for your maid? Shall I order a soothing drink for you?'

'Thank you, but no,' returned Emma slowly. 'I think that I would prefer to be quite alone. . .and to sleep, if I can.'

'Then you shall be,' he said, and then he was leaving her, walking down the corridor, away from the temptation which she unwittingly presented to him. All the long years since Isabella had died he had felt nothing for any woman. Not even the society beauties who had thrust themselves at him could tempt him from the celibate life which he had adopted. As for marrying for money again— he shuddered at the thought.

And now, this delicate flower—for so he was beginning to think of her—who possessed moral strength as well as grace, was working a magic upon him which he could not resist. And, oddly, it was as though he had always known her, as though she was that part of his life for which he had been waiting all these lonely years.

Had he met her when he was young and brash, he was sure that he might have passed her by, so insensitive had he then been to anything other than the more obvious charms which women possessed. Older, wiser, chastened by life and by the weight of the great responsibilities which he had inherited, he had come to value more than mere obvious surface attraction. The beauty which she possessed was subtle, and enhanced by a good mind— something which the youthful m'lord would have denied a woman possessed, and certainly had not then wanted in his wife.

No, he must stay away from her, not tempt her—even though she tempted him. . .

Behind him, in her lonely room, Emma sank on her bed, clutching her hot cheeks. Much though Ben Blackburn's assault had distressed her, the emotion which had moved her the most was— astonishingly—the knowledge that she loved m'lord.

More, she knew that what she had felt for him nearly ten years ago had been simple hero-worship, a child's love, but that what she felt now was more

complex, more mature. It did not depend upon the
mere trick of him possessing a pretty face and a
charming manner. Instead she had fallen in love
with the strong man he had become.

# CHAPTER SEVEN

'AND did the Romans truly live and work here, Miss Lawrence? How cold they must have found it after Italy!'

Predictably, Tish was the member of the Loudwater party most excited by the trip to Hadrian's Wall. They had started out in the midmorning of a glorious summer's day and had made at once for Chollerford, where there was not only a bridge over the North Tyne but a crossroads where stood an old inn, The George, much used by travellers.

Once the day had promised to be fair, m'lord had sent a coach ahead of them laden with excellent food and drink, as well as Cook and several servants, so that the landlord might have a cold collation ready for them when they arrived. The George was only a short distance from the Wall— too far to walk, but not so far for a party on horseback and in carriages.

M'lord had arranged that they should first visit the remains of the Roman fort called Housesteads, some eight miles from the ford, and then, before leaving for home, they were to rest and refresh themselves at Chesters, where there were the remains of yet another fort. Although now called Chesters, m'lord told them that its Roman name had been Cilurnum. It was situated in the park owned by the Clayton family, who were unfortunately absent in London, but Mr Clayton's agent had given m'lord permission to hold a picnic there.

Fortified by an excellent meal, the whole party sat in the shade of the inn's garden idly admiring the river as it slid slowly by in the pleasantly wooded valley. There was little traffic on the primitive road in front of the inn, even though the small village of Chollerton was only a short distance away.

When they had set out Lady Clara had been annoyed to discover that m'lord could not drive her in his curricle—'Too unsafe, the roads are so poor,' he had told her—so that she was compelled to sit in the open carriage with Miss Straight, Mrs Morton, the upstart governess and Lady Letitia.

Only the fact that m'lord had ridden beside their carriage on his splendid black had kept her happy—that and pointedly ignoring the governess. Her satisfaction in doing this might not have been so great if she had been aware that Miss Lawrence had only been too happy to be ignored, and to talk quietly to Tish about the Wall and the Romans, and the camp which was really a town which they had built at Corbridge and which had never been properly excavated.

Really! thought Lady Clara angrily now. It was too bad that the wretched woman had brought the schoolroom with her, and she was about to say so to m'lord, when he leaned over to remark approvingly to his daughter, 'What a pleasant way to learn your history, Tish—on a fine day, with a well-informed teacher. Pray, where did you gain your classical knowledge, Miss Lawrence?'

He could not resist talking to her though he knew that he should be addressing himself to Lady Clara. Lufton had already pointedly hinted that she would bring a splendid dowry to the lucky man who won her, and that he would be happy for that man to be his friend and neighbour Lord Chard.

Instead, m'lord was trying not to admire his daughter's governess, who had no dowry at all to help him to save Loudwater and develop its lands properly.

'My father had been a good classical scholar, and he was pleased to talk to me of such matters,' offered Emma, well aware of the baleful glances being shot in her direction by Miss Straight and Lady Clara because m'lord was choosing to speak to her at all.

'Then you were fortunate, and Tish has the benefit of it,' returned m'lord, who, becoming aware of Lady Clara's annoyance, now leaned across to speak to her, to ask her if she was enjoying her day, it being so fine, but the heat not oppressive.

'I would be enjoying it the more,' complained Lady Clara ungraciously, 'if the journey were not so long. Hadrian should have built his wall nearer to Loudwater!'

A crass remark which set Emma's lips a-twitch-

ing—especially since Tish, on hearing it, cried
innocently and eagerly, 'Only fancy, Papa! I had
no idea that our house was built in Roman times!'

His daughter's response set m'lord a problem.
To reply to it correctly might make Lady Clara
look a fool, but to say nothing at all would leave
Tish under a serious and rather stupid misunder-
standing about her home. He was saved by
Emma's quick wits. She murmured gently, 'Why,
Tish, when we are back at Loudwater again I must
instruct you on its history. It is most fascinating,
and the site does indeed go back to Roman times.
We must ask Papa for his help.'

She had not meant to look in m'lord's direction,
but some magnetic force compelled her to do so.
His own lips were twitching, she saw. He could not
prevent himself from adding, 'Most apt of you,
Miss Lawrence. I shall be only too happy to assist
in Tish's education. All Northumbria, of course,
goes back to Roman times!'

The look he gave her was the more meaningful
because Lady Clara, at least, had no notion of her
idiocy, but Miss Straight, who was as aware as
Emma and m'lord of her friend's stupidity, tightened her lips and interpreted the look correctly.

Oh, yes, m'lord was interested in the governess,
and if Lady Clara wished to net him she must show
a little more *savoir faire*. But who would have
thought that Lord Chard would be interested in
these erudite matters! Such had not been his
reputation when he had been younger.

Nevertheless Lady Clara, whilst not knowing exactly what she had said which was wrong, was not quite such a fool as to be unaware that something was amiss. Like Miss Straight's, her lips tightened. All this came from dragging along with them a child and a pair of servants—for she was busy ignoring Mrs Morton as well as Emma.

She was ignorant of the fact that Mrs Morton's pedigree was more exalted than her own, and that she was not a servant but was doing m'lord a favour by living with him and providing him with a hostess and Tish with a loving female relative.

The beauty of the day, the sight of the remains of the Wall itself and the knowledge that as they drove along the track—for the road was little more than that—they were almost at Housesteads, one of the more famous sights on the Wall, meant nothing to her.

What exactly she had expected to see she was not sure, and whilst the party dismounted, or were helped down from their carriages by the grooms who had travelled with them, preparatory to walking up to the ridge where the fort had stood, she stared, dissatisfied, at some large stones and broken walls which were the only visible remains of the Roman garrison.

Was *this* what they had driven all these miles to see? Miss Straight, giving Lady Clara a sideways glance, distracted attention from her sullen boredom by exclaiming, as the gentlemen were doing, but in slightly different terms, 'How mysterious!

How romantic. Mrs Radcliffe herself could not have provided us with more of interest.'

Emma could not stop herself. 'Other than offering us a kidnapping, a skeleton behind the ruins and a mysterious stranger wearing monk's robes and about to threaten us—a new *Mysteries of Udolpho*, in fact.'

Miss Straight wished to glare at her, but her good sense and her appreciation of the comic prevented her. She joined the men in their laughter, and even Lady Clara favoured everyone with a thin smile. It was patent that her brother, m'lord and, to a lesser degree, Ben Blackburn were interested in the remains of the Roman occupation, so presumably she ought to show some small enthusiasm for them too. She did not count Mr Cross and John Bassett, who were clambering onto the stones and otherwise amusing themselves—after all, they were only superior servants, like the governess. One wondered why m'lord had dragged them along.

If she married him she would soon cure him of his odd taste for the companionship of underlings.

She sat herself down at some distance from the others, opened her pink parasol and tried not to yawn. M'lord came to stand by her.

'You are not overhot, I trust,' he offered again, trying desperately to think of something—anything—to say to her to which she might reply sensibly. And then, 'The grooms have brought some lemonade along in their packs. If you care to drink any, pray tell me, and you shall be served at once.'

He thought that he had never sounded so inane in his life, and his own *savoir faire* was not helped by the knowledge of the enthusiasm for the expedition which Tish and Miss Lawrence were showing, and which he was unable to share with them because of his commitment as host to his unwanted guests.

Well, he was learning one thing as a result of the day's adventure—that on no account would he offer marriage to Lady Clara Lufton. She would drive him mad in a week—or else have him on the gallows as a wife-murderer! No, not even if she brought the whole wealth of Northumbria to the wedding day. It would be too high a price to pay to save Loudwater.

One such price had already been demanded of him; a second would destroy him.

He was aware that Lady Clara was talking, but he had not the slightest notion of what she had been saying. Nothing worthwhile, he was sure. Ten years ago he would have cheerfully married her for her money, for all her disposition towards the sullens and her woeful lack of enjoyment of anything which interested him. But not now. Never now.

Once again Emma saved him—unwittingly this time. She was walking over to him, her hand in Tish's. 'M'lord, Lady Letitia wishes me to join her in accompanying Lord Lufton and the others for a walk along the Wall, but I felt that we ought to ask your permission first. There might be some small danger: the path is a slight one and stony.'

M'lord thankfully abandoned Lady Clara's wittering. 'You will excuse me a moment, Lady Clara, I'm sure. Yes, Tish may go with you. I am sure that you will be careful.' Then, inspired for he was sure that Lady Clara, her feet clad in pale pink kid pumps had no inclination to explore the Wall, 'If you will wait a moment, I will accompany you. You will allow me to take your arm, madam.'

He held out his own arm to Lady Clara, who glared at it and said crossly, 'By no means, m'lord. Miss Straight and I will sit here to enjoy the afternoon sun. I am sure that she has no more wish to turn an ankle or overheat herself by a long tramp on a hot day whilst looking at a barren view than I have! But go yourself, by all means. Pray do not consider me!'

It was Miss Straight's turn to glare. At Lady Clara. She would have liked nothing more than to join in the proposed walk. Far better than sitting mumchance on a stone beside a companion who possessed no conversation at all. But good manners, and her duty as companion, must prevail.

'Oh!' she exclaimed, a little shrilly. 'I echo you, my dear Lady Clara. Too hot by far for jaunting. Let us sit here and chat about the Romans.'

Emma avoided m'lord's eye again. Which was as well. Good manners demanded that he remain with Lady Clara. But to hell with that, was his inward response. He wished to walk with his daughter where the Roman legions had once marched, did he not? And that was another thundering lie. What he really wished to do was to walk with his daughter's governess.

He bowed at the two women. 'You will forgive me for leaving you,' he said, his hand on his cheating heart. 'But I see little enough of Tish these days, and I would wish to be with her on her first expedition here. She has been waiting for it so long—'

'Oh, yes, Papa,' interrupted Tish. 'Do come. After all, Lady Clara has Miss Straight, has she not? And Mr Cross,' she added helpfully as that gentleman, looking hot in his tight black clothing, decided to sit by Lady Clara, the other members of the party having already begun their walk along the Wall.

Inward giggles consumed Emma as she caught Lady Clara's baleful expression on being gifted with a menial to whom she had no wish to talk whatsoever. Mr Cross might represent salvation to Miss Straight as someone to whom she could usefully converse, unlike Lady Clara, but to Lady Clara he was merely another bore—and a middle-aged one at that.

But Lady Clara couldn't say so. She rewarded m'lord with another thin smile, and through compressed lips muttered, 'Oh, pray, take your daughter for a walk, m'lord, do. I shall be only too happy to remain here.' Then she looked resolutely in the opposite direction from him, wondering, Did I abandon my London season for *this*?

Her inimical stare followed the three of them as they began their walk.

'Thank God,' said m'lord below his breath, loosening his tight cravat as Tish walked happily in front of them, minding where she went as Emma had told her. 'I could not have endured another five minutes of meaningless politeness.'

'Oh, so you do not mean to be polite to me, then, m'lord?' queried Emma naughtily.

'None of that, now. You know exactly what I mean,' he replied, playfully stern, his voice still low, so that although Tish knew that they were talking, she could not hear what they were saying. 'Do not bam me. My temper is a little short. There are some women who would try the patience of a saint, and Lady Clara is one of them. And I am far from claiming *that*!'

'Oh, I quite agree,' riposted Emma, behaving as badly as she could, but unable to resist temptation. 'You have no right to claim sainthood. You are far too human, one must presume—and fortunately so!'

This sally had him staring at her mocking face, at her gently twisted mouth and her shining eyes. 'Oh, dear God,' he murmured, stopping dead and forgetting Tish, who was now well ahead of them. 'Why do you tempt me, here in the open? I want. . . You must know what I want.'

'Yes,' said Emma, 'but not here, on the Wall.

And you must not allow Tish to leave us behind. She may be running into danger. The Wall is not as safe as it was when the Romans built it.'

'Damn Tish, damn the Romans, damn everything,' grumbled m'lord morosely, but turned away from her all the same, to begin walking again. 'And now *you* would try the patience of a saint. Must you always say and do the proper thing?'

'That is a governess's duty, m'lord. Should she fail in it, then instant dismissal awaits.'

It was the turn of m'lord's lips to twist. 'Not from me,' he assured her, his voice light. 'Proper behaviour is more like to earn you that!'

How far they had come! Could the small fat girl of so long ago ever have thought of exchanging mocking innuendos with her godlike hero? Or even the woman who had alighted at his door a few short weeks ago. And Dominic Hastings, now m'lord, was no longer godlike to Emma. He was all too human, and he was rapidly falling victim to the most human failing of all—that of illicit passion between a man and the woman whom he desired.

Did she desire him? The answer must be yes. Revenge for past rejection called, as well as the pull of his powerful masculine attraction. He made all the men around him seem ordinary. And if once he had been a trifle shallow in his understanding of the world, then time and chance had changed that—as it changed everything—as it had changed Emma.

'You are silent, Miss Lawrence?'

He was perhaps being a little formal because Tish had run back to them, saying that they had almost caught the earlier party up. She could see Mr Blackburn, she said.

'You leave me little to say, m'lord,' Emma answered him.

'M'lord! M'lord! Must you always belabour me with my title?'

'As is only proper,' she said.

'Proper,' he replied crossly. 'I am tired of being proper. I have been proper for the last ten years!'

Tish's running back once more, to take her father's hand, prevented Emma from making the kind of reply to that sentiment which she might have wished. Besides, they were rapidly catching the others up, and when they did they must be all decorum.

'Mr Bassett must be tired already,' remarked Tish as they drew near them. 'He is sitting on a stone.'

So he was, and it was soon apparent that there was something wrong. Ben Blackburn was whistling cheerfully, but Lord Lufton was looking grave. John Bassett was holding his wrist and was minus his black silk cravat, which Ben Blackburn had made into an improvised sling.

'Now, what's the matter?' exclaimed m'lord. 'What the devil have you done to yourself, Bassett?'

'Went exploring and fell,' explained Ben

Blackburn, with the cheerfulness of a man who was not injured. Lord Lufton, still standing apart, had assumed an expression between concern and boredom—one suitable for expressing sympathy with an underling.

Ben Blackburn continued his tale of woe. 'He's either sprained or broken his right wrist. My bet is on a sprain. Not much secretarying for you for a time, eh, Bassett?'

'Let me have a look.' M'lord went down on one knee to inspect the damaged member as gently as he could, with John Bassett looking miserably at him the while, his face white.

'I could not help it, m'lord,' he muttered miserably. 'The path off the Wall seemed safe, but. . .'

'It wasn't,' continued Ben Blackburn, still abominably cheerful, and doing his best to ignore Emma—as he had been doing all day.

M'lord continued to be gentleness itself as he undid the sling and examined the swollen wrist, to put it down at last, whilst offering the opinion that, 'Yes, the wrist is sprained, not broken. But it will be painful and not fit for use for some time.'

He rose. 'Never mind, old fellow. We'll soon get you home, and the doctor shall look at you. Try not to jar it. Sensible of you, Blackburn, to tie it up.'

'Damaged my own wrist once,' offered Ben. 'Tying it up seemed to ease the pain a little.'

'Poor Mr Bassett,' said Tish sadly. 'He won't mend as easily as my doll, will he, Papa?'

This delightfully gloomy statement was enough to bring a wan smile to John Bassett's face as m'lord helped him to his feet. He was badly bruised in several places—mostly unmentionable before ladies, so Ben Blackburn didn't mention them. He contented himself with carrying out his self-imposed duties as harbinger of doom, rather, Emma thought later, like a messenger in an old play reporting dire events which had happened off-stage.

Their walk back was distinctly less cheerful than their one forward. John Bassett seemed to have perked up a little towards the end, except that he suddenly stopped dead and announced in tones as doom-laden as Ben Blackburn's had been, 'Oh, m'lord, how badly I have mistimed this! What shall you do now that my wrist is damaged—and you due to go to Killingworth and to Newcastle—without a proper secretary?'

'Do not trouble yourself overmuch on that score,' returned m'lord. 'I shall manage somehow or other, I am sure.' And with that his secretary had to be content.

By the time they had returned to where Lady Clara sat in offended silence she was the only happy member of the party—delighted that John Bassett's misfortune was such that they were immediately to return to the ease and comfort of Loudwater's drawing rooms.

'Such a fortunate turn, that,' she confided taste-lessly to Miss Straight once the ladies were all back in the carriage again. 'I'm sure another five minutes spent in that desert would have had me screaming.'

Emma could not contain herself. 'It was worth the expense of having poor Mr Bassett screaming instead, I suppose,' she said tartly, signalling to Tish to keep quiet.

'And who is Mr Bassett that I should care for him?' was the equally tart reply. 'Still, I suppose that one servant may be allowed to grieve for another. You surprise me, however. I thought that your affections were fixed elsewhere—but perhaps they are distributed indiscriminately. And that being so it is useless to ask Chard to dismiss you for insolence.' She turned her bony shoulder towards Emma and Tish.

'I don't like that lady,' whispered Tish as they descended from the carriage at Loudwater's entrance. 'Cook said that Papa is going to marry her, but I do not want her for a mama—no, indeed! She is not kind.'

Which was as true a way of summing up Lady Clara Lufton as Emma had ever heard.

M'lord sighed. It was going to be damned awkward without a secretary. Damned awkward. He had grown used to John Bassett walking around with him, taking notes, anticipating his thoughts and writing perfect letters which left m'lord time to attend to all the aspects of running a great estate on the verge of bankruptcy.

The doctor who had been summoned on the previous evening had confirmed the universal diagnosis. John had not broken a bone but his sprained wrist must be kept supported. 'And on no account must he try to use it,' he had ended, leaving John looking fearful for his future prospects of employment at Loudwater.

He ventured to say as much this morning to m'lord, who replied robustly, 'Nonsense, man. You have been my right-hand man for some years now, and will be again, I hope, in the future, when your wrist is better again. No, I must either do without anyone, or find a useful deputy. Meantime you must take the opportunity of enjoying a holiday from your duties. You have earned one.'

A deputy. But who? No one immediately sprang to mind. Some clerk from Corbridge would not do. And old Cross would not do either. M'lord imagined him blinking myopically around Killingworth and Newcastle, being infinitely obliging but damned useless.

He had a sudden wicked thought. To be at first dismissed but then to send him haring after John Bassett, who had already reached the bottom of the grand staircase.

'John, a moment.'

John Bassett started a little at m'lord's lack of formality and his strange expression. He was usually 'Bassett' or 'you', even though m'lord was more courteous to his underlings than most.

'M'lord?'

'Is there no one in my household who could fulfil at least part of your duties? I am due at Killingworth in a few days. I have no time to break in someone who knows nothing of Loudwater and its concerns, and who cannot do as good a service for me as you do.'

John Bassett stood irresolute, visibly thinking. He dismissed Mr Cross as his master had done, and then he, too, had an odd thought. No, it would not do. Definitely not. But it must be said.

'I can think of no one,' he began hesitantly, 'except. . . But no. . .'

'Why is it,' asked m'lord rhetorically of the heavens, or rather of the painted ceiling above him showing Jupiter seducing Leda in the form of a swan, 'that these days no one around me can finish their sentences? Vomit up your great thought, man, do!'

John cast caution to the winds. 'Miss Lawrence,' he offered, 'is not only highly intelligent—for a woman, that is—but she writes a good hand and is far better than I am at figuring. You could do worse than employ her—as a stop-gap, that is.'

Done! thought m'lord triumphantly. And I did not even have to propose her myself. He made a pretty show of hesitation.

'Miss Lawrence? A woman? Whatever would Lufton and the rest think? No, no.'

'It would be merely temporary, of course, and they would understand that my accident had left you in a pickle.'

M'lord looked so doubtful that he almost overdid things, and John began a diplomatic retreat.
'Of course, I can see that it will not do. Forgive
me.'

It was essential now, having made a tactful show
of diffidence over the matter, to push things in the
necessary direction. Quickly m'lord responded,
but carefully kept his voice unenthusiastic. 'Well,
it might serve as a stop-gap, after all. If she does
not satisfy—or does not wish to undertake such a
heavy burden—then I must look elsewhere. I will
speak to her. My thanks, Bassett. I might have
known that you would come up trumps.'

So he was Bassett again, thought John wryly as
m'lord left him. Something made him turn to
watch m'lord, usually scrupulous in keeping up
appearances, take the stairs two at a time as though
he were chasing a fox without the benefit of his
horse. Something odd there, but what?

What he could not have guessed was that m'lord
had just played on him as skilfully as a maestro
using his keyboard to conjure up a thrilling
melody, and that he had supplied him with the
excuse he needed to see as much of Miss Lawrence
as a man with a passion for her could desire.

Unaware that John Bassett and m'lord were busy
planning her future for her, Emma was walking
along the terrace which overlooked the west lawn.
She had spent the morning teaching an attentive
Tish about the Romans, and after her mid-morn-

ing cup of coffee and Tish's glass of lemonade she had left her carefully copying a Roman legionary from a large folio which Emma had found in the library with the help of Mr Cross.

She had just reached the turn where there was a small niche with a seat in it, whose occupants could have no sight of her until she passed them, when she heard her own name said in tones of infinite feminine disgust.

Emma sighed. She seemed fated to overhear conversations, and she did not want to eavesdrop on this one. She was about to make some polite noise—a cough, perhaps—when something that was said stopped her dead in her tracks.

'And he's as poor as a church mouse,' Calypso Straight was declaiming derisively. 'Everyone knows that although the third Earl did not quite bankrupt the estates by building the present house, the late and fourth Earl made sure that Loudwater ended up in Queer Street by gambling and losing both on the tables and in ill-advised speculation on the late war. So if Chard marries you, Clara, it will be solely for your money. Since he has eyes only for the governess you cannot pretend that he is smitten with love for you—if he proposes, which I am willing to bet he won't, unless you change your manner to him for the better,' she ended triumphantly.

Emma was frozen, paralysed. She could not go forward after that for it would be plain that she must have heard, and to go back might cause her presence to be detected.

She shrank against the wall to hear Lady Clara pout back, 'I am not a complete ninny, Calypso, although you frequently take me for one. Of course I know he doesn't care for me. What of that? Husbands seldom do care for their wives. And I certainly shan't care for him. It is just that after Lufton has so plainly offered me to him, it is humiliating to be passed over for a governess. Besides, I have a fancy to be Lady Chard.'

'Well, if you *do* want to marry him then you must try harder. Show an interest in *his* interests, flatter him a little instead of frowning at him all the time. After all, he's not going to marry the governess, only bed her. Our kind never marry such creatures—although I am sure that *she* doesn't understand that.'

Oh, yes, she does, was Emma's inward response, so savagely made that she almost missed Lady Clara's grumbling reply to the effect that Chard could do what he pleased with anyone after they were married since it would relieve her from the burden of pleasing him—once she had given him an heir, that was.

Well, whatever m'lord deserved, he hardly deserved Lady Clara. So disgusted was she by what she was hearing that Emma decided to risk walking away, but not before she heard Miss Straight's final bombshell.

'I hope, then, Clara, that you are very sure what

you are taking on: a husband who does not love you, an overburdened estate and a brat who isn't even Chard's own child—everyone knows that, including Chard. One wonders why he troubles with her. There are enough places round here where she could have been farmed out. . .'

Emma was so shocked at this news about Tish that she hardly cared whether her retreat was overheard or not. She almost ran, as lightly as she could, to let herself into the house by the side door, where she was met by a somewhat agitated Mrs Morton.

'Oh, there you are, Miss Lawrence. M'lord has been asking for you. He wishes to see you at once, and he was most insistent on the "at once". Not like him at all!'

# CHAPTER EIGHT

'So my dear Miss Lawrence,' ended m'lord, 'you would be doing me a real service if you could see your way to acceding to my request—and John Bassett would, of course, be on hand to assist you, should you so require.'

'Of course,' murmured Emma, looking beyond him, through the window, at the long avenue of trees which ran parallel with the horizon. Just below them was a small folly in the shape of a Roman temple which she had yet to visit. Mr Cross had once mentioned to her that inside were the most beautiful murals depicting the labours of Hercules.

What mural would depict the labours of Miss Emma Lawrence if she agreed to m'lord's proposal? And why was she standing here, rapt, thinking of such foolish things, instead of giving him an answer?

Because the real question was, Did she really wish to put herself into such a position of intimacy with him? Oh, never mind the slight taint of scandal which would hang over her for agreeing to be such an. . .unwomanly. . .thing as his temporary secretary. That was nothing. What *was* something was that her feelings for him had become hopelessly compromised.

On the one hand she could see the possibility for revenge on him for the past, but on the other hand she had committed the supreme folly of falling in love with him all over again. In the long watches of the previous night she had asked herself whether the naïve child she had once been had nevertheless been capable of seeing below the carelessly charming exterior of him to the possibility of the strong man he had become.

She was also faced by another problem. Deceiving him as to her true identity had been easy at first, when she was not involved with him, but was becoming uncomfortable now that she was. Having fallen in love with him again, she felt that she ought to confess to him who she was. But she was happy at Loudwater, happy with Tish—and most of all happy with him.

But suppose he became angered when he learned that Emma Lawrence was Emilia Lincoln, the fat girl who had jilted him? Worse still, might he not think that now she was poor she had arrived at Loudwater to snare him because she thought he was rich? Such had not been her intent, but, thinking so, he might send her away. . . There was no easy way out of this impasse but to continue as she was and pray that something would happen which might make confession easy.

'Miss Lawrence?' queried m'lord, a trifle puzzled by her long silence and by the almost marble-like calm of her as she looked beyond him. 'Do you have an answer for me? Or do you wish to have time to think before you decide? I am aware that what I am asking of you is unorthodox, to say the least. But it will only be for a short time, I am sure.'

He could not openly say to her, Oh, my dear Miss Lawrence, pray say yes, and make me a happy man who need not skulk about his own home in order to find an opportunity to speak with you and to enjoy your company!

As if she had heard his thoughts, Emma turned back to him and gave him her most dazzling smile.

'Bearing in mind, m'lord, that the measure is only temporary, then I agree. But I dare say that Lady Clara and Miss Straight will see the matter in quite the worst light!'

'No doubt—and damn the pair of them for doing so! Oh, pray forgive me, I had not meant to be quite so blunt, but I fear that I have lived too long among men and have forgotten the delicate fashion in which one speaks in the presence of ladies. Perhaps having you by my side will reform both my speech and my manners. There was a time, although I fear that you will not believe me, when I was quite a *preux chevalier*, who was always able to say the right thing in whatever company I found myself. Pray civilise me again, Miss Lawrence. I have become quite the savage.'

'Suppose I said that I preferred the savage to the smooth, m'lord?'

'Then I might think that you were trying to flatter me—except that I have never experienced any flattery from you. Quite the contrary. I must assume you to be speaking the truth. I can only hope that the savage you admire is the noble one of whom Mrs Aphra Behn wrote so movingly—although I do not live in the jungle.'

'Some might think Northumbria uncommonly wild, though,' responded Emma, her eyes sparkling as she joined in his game. 'It all depends where one stands, I suppose.'

'Indeed. You will forgive me if I do endeavour to become a little smoother, I trust.'

Emma's heart began to beat more and more strongly. Any witness to their conversation would certainly have assumed that they were flirting—especially since m'lord had come from behind his beautiful oak desk to stand near to her. He was in his country clothing again, and she thought that she preferred him in it rather than in the dandy's outfit which he had taken to wearing at dinner. It suited his mature strength, and not what had once been, she shrewdly judged, his youthful weakness.

'Not too much of smoothness,' she said slowly, looking up at him as he towered over her, his own eyes shining, the pupils of them wide, his mouth curling a little as he watched her speak.

'How much?' he asked of her. 'As much or as little as this?' And without touching her, other than with his mouth, he bent to kiss her on her lips, a butterfly's touch, as though he sipped at a virgin flower never before visited by a bee. He thought her untouched, and he was not wrong.

The tender mouth moved under his, so that instead of withdrawing completely, as he had intended once the kiss was over, he lifted his head only a little, before dropping it to kiss her again.

This time it was Emma who moved away when his second kiss ended, her knees weak and her whole body clamouring for her magic moment to continue. If she were to work with him as his secretary this must stop, and now.

'No,' he said a little hoarsely, and came after her, only for her to put out one small hand and push him away, saying, 'No,' in her turn. But whereas his no was there to make her say yes, her no truly meant no, and he knew it.

'You are not to do that,' Emma told him sadly. 'For I cannot be your secretary if you treat me as your whore.'

'Never my whore,' he said passionately, 'but. . .' He paused, for he knew that he lied. He had, as Miss Straight had said, no intention of marrying her.

What, then, did he intend? He did not know. . . and therefore he had no right to kiss her. For if they had an affair, if he made her his mistress, then she would truly become his whore—and as Dr Johnson had once said of another such affair which a friend had tried to prettify, 'The woman's a whore, and there's an end on't!' No soft words could sweeten the brutal truth.

He turned away to stare at the wall, at a portrait of the grandfather who had begun Loudwater's ruin. Oh, if he were to marry once more it must be to wealth—even though he had privately vowed never to sell his soul for money again, seeing what disasters the first sale had brought him!

'But me no buts,' said Emma sadly to his broad back. 'You see why you must try not to make love to me, I am sure. I have a life to live, and all I have is my honour and a few talents. Rob me of one or the other, and I am destitute.'

'There is more than one kind of destitution,' said m'lord, the Earl of Chard to the wall, his voice desolate.

'Oh, indeed,' agreed Emma. 'And some kinds are more deadly than others, as you must surely understand.'

He had never felt so lonely. He had thought loneliness was his friend. That he could forswear friendship and love and live a barren life as happily as a fulfilled one. His one passion had become the saving of Loudwater from ruin, and now this delicate-looking but strong woman had entered his life and cast a magic spell which had left all his resolutions in ruins.

But he must not ruin her. That would be to make him the worst sort of cur. Perhaps he should forget this scheme, which would surely cause gossip. But then, as he turned back to her to meet her great grave eyes, he thought, No, for if I am condemned to wander in the desert which my life has become, God cannot deny me a little water to help me on my way.

'Let us be friends,' he said, as calmly as he could. 'I was mad a few moments ago to do that which would shatter our friendship. I would not hurt you for the world. Believe that if you believe anything.'

Emma bent her head. Tears pricked behind her eyes. 'Yes, I believe you,' she told him simply. 'Now, will you release me? Tish will be wondering what has become of me. You said that you wished me to work for you in the afternoons. That being so, her mornings must be busy, you understand.'

M'lord could not speak for a moment. He nodded, and then said a trifle thickly, 'That seems sensible, Miss Lawrence. I shall expect you here at two of the clock. Mrs Morton will act as chaperon, so that gossiping tongues cannot blast your reputation. She, Tish and Tish's nursemaid will accompany us to the house I have taken in Newcastle when we do our business at Killingworth. You see, I have thought of everything.'

So that was that. He watched her go and, prey to thoughts and emotions which were as new to him as those of first true love were to Emma, strode to the window to glare blindly out, seeing nothing before him but desolation.

Honour and duty were harsh taskmasters, and for the first time in nearly ten years m'lord wished that he was free of them so that he could be as careless and carefree as he had been in his youth, so that he could take Miss Lawrence in his arms and. . .

But in those days you would not have looked at her, a still, small voice told him. For you were not wise enough to tell a real diamond from a false one—so perhaps the hard years have not been wasted after all.

Emma was equally exercised by what she had agreed to. She spent the rest of the morning in a daze. If Tish wondered what had happened to her usually lively governess, who this morning frequently seemed to lose the thread of the lesson, staring abstractedly out of the window at yet another of Loudwater's remarkable views, she did not say so.

Emma ate her nursery lunch in the same detached state, which remained with her when she walked down the broad staircase into the great hall at the bottom on her way to m'lord's study to begin her new duties with him. So much so that, crossing it, she did not see Miss Straight standing there, by Apollo's bust, waiting for her.

'Miss Lawrence. A word with you, if you please.'

The words were polite, but Miss Straight's tone was curt and peremptory to say the least. Emma stopped in some surprise. Miss Straight was smiling a wicked smile.

'So, Miss Lawrence, is it true what Lord Lufton has just told us? That you are to be m'lord's secretary. If so, do I congratulate you—or not? You have played a tricky hand excellently well, but, as you undoubtedly heard me say to Lady

Clara this morning, he will not marry you—however much you please him, in bed or out of it!'

Her eavesdropping had been detected after all. In the strange state in which she had been living since she had accepted m'lord's offer, Emma made nothing of that. Before, she would have been horrified—shamed, even—but now she simply raised her eyebrows and murmured, 'I am astonished, madam, that my humble affairs should have received your attention, or even that m'lord's arrangements to replace his secretary should attract your notice.

'As to playing tricky hands, I bow to your superior knowledge of such matters, and should I require assistance will come to you for your advice. Or would you prefer to sit in as chaperon to m'lord and myself when I act as his secretary and save poor Mrs Morton the trouble? Or, if not you, then perhaps Lady Clara might do the honours?'

Coming out in such coldly bored tones made Emma's insolence sound even worse than it was. But if she refused to be affected by Miss Straight's insults, then Miss Straight was equally determined not to be put down by those of a mere governess.

She clapped her hands together as enthusiastically as though she were applauding Drury Lane theatre's latest and greatest star. 'Oh, my dear Miss Lawrence, pray allow me to congratulate you on your effrontery, if on nothing else. But it will not do, you know, to chase after Chard. And whatever you may think is the reason for my speaking to you so plainly, at least do me the honour of assuming that I have *your* welfare at heart, as well as Lady Clara's.

'When he has ruined you, who will take you in, or confide their children to your care, do you think? The gossip will not be confined to Loudwater. One way or another the *on dits* about such an affair will circulate round the town, I do assure you—and where will you be then?'

So, it was to be blackmail! Leave m'lord alone so that Lady Clara has no rival, or I will tell the whole world of your conduct, was the burden of Miss Straight's song. . .

Emma was silent, not because of fear, but because of the rage which was consuming her. Finally, she said, 'Let me be plain with you, Miss Straight. I care not a fig for Lady Clara or your good self, and I don't accept for a moment that you are moved by pity for my situation *vis-à-vis* m'lord. If you say one more word to me on this matter I shall go *straight* to him—' she leaned heavily on the word straight '—and inform him of the threats with which you have just favoured me. You may be above me in station, and a guest in a house where I am only a servant, but I would not care to bet on what the consequences of my action would be—would you?'

Never, in her whole life, had Emma behaved or spoken as she was doing now. Always she had been outwardly mild and pleasant, and had accepted the blows which fate had dealt her with a becoming resignation. She had learned to swallow the insults put upon her by those who employed her and by their friends. But since she had come to Loudwater the balance of her life had changed, and in the changing she had changed too. Never again would she compromise, and if the consequences for her were to be grave, or even disastrous, then she would face them.

That her defiance had surprised Miss Straight was plain. She gave a little half-laugh, looked her adversary up and down and then, almost unwillingly, came out with, 'I have half a mind to admire such audacity. Very well, play your dangerous game. But remember that you have Calypso Straight on the other side of the table, and I am as great a plunger in the gambling line as you are revealing yourself to be. You may leave me, Miss Lawrence, and go to your lord. Be very sure, though, that what I have said of him is true. Adieu.'

They were quits. If they had been fighting a duel, as men did, with naked swords, then they would have fought to a draw. Each turned their back on the other—Miss Straight to return to her protégé and Emma to go to m'lord. How the game of which Miss Straight had spoken would end was as yet unknown to either of them.

'Oh, Papa, am I really, truly, to go to Newcastle with you?'

M'lord nodded. Tish was seated by Emma in

the Egyptian room enjoying a cup of tea with the grown-ups after dinner. Since Lord Lufton and party had arrived she had been eating her late afternoon meal in the nursery.

'It can scarcely be called dinner,' she had told Emma reproachfully, thinking of the large number of dishes from which she could choose when she ate with Papa, nursery food being of the take it or leave it variety. She had, however, been allowed to join him and his guests at the teaboard afterwards.

'Yes, my love. Since Miss Lawrence is coming with me as my secretary, then you may join us and she can fit in some lessons for you when she is not otherwise occupied. It is not just a holiday for you, you know.'

This news pleased Lady Clara, if no one else. The governess could hardly be instructing Tish and charming m'lord at one and the same time. Emma, for her part, was surprised all over again at the loving way in which m'lord treated the little girl who was not his daughter. Was Miss Straight correct in her supposition that Tish was simply his faithless wife's child? And, if so, what did his obvious care for her tell Emma about his character?

M'lord had other fish to fry than Tish's welfare, though. He was the only person standing, his back to the empty fireplace which was filled with large blue, rose and white jars from China, stuffed with flowers from Loudwater's ample gardens. He pulled a paper from the pocket of his well-cut breeches before addressing the company.

'A letter from Sir Thomas Liddell arrived by special messenger today,' he announced a trifle dramatically—rather like the compère at Astley's amphitheatre, was Emma's irreverent reaction. 'He tells me that next week, on the twenty-fifth of July of 1814, as ever is, Geordie Stephenson will be conducting trials on the new travelling steam engine which he has been building for the last ten months to replace the horses which pull the wagons on the tramway at Killingworth. He recommends that we arrive in time to be present.'

He looked around the beautiful room. 'That being so, may I suggest to you all that we up sticks and set off for Newcastle as soon as possible, instead of leaving it until next week as planned? Will that be possible for you, Lufton? I know that Blackburn is used to setting off at a moment's notice, but you have the ladies to consider.'

'Oh, pray do not consider *us*,' shrilled Lady Clara. 'We are entirely at your disposal where matters of business are concerned.' This remarkable and uncharacteristic statement from her was the result of much coaching by Miss Straight on how best to please m'lord, and was rewarded by him with a grateful smile. Further to demonstrate her willingness to fall in with his lightest wish, she asked him in a dramatic voice, 'And Sir Thomas Liddell—pray what is his interest in this?'

Her brother chose to answer her rather testily.

'Do you never listen to me, Clara? I have told you a hundred times of Sir Thomas's involvement with Geordie Stephenson. He believes that the man has the answer to the problem of moving coal cheaply. Chard and I—and Blackburn, of course—are interested in discovering whether there is anything to it. I must say, Chard, here and now, that I have my doubts. But perhaps the twenty-fifth of July will settle all!'

Lady Clara's pout was monumental, but the men were so absorbed in discussing Lord Lufton's possible heresy that they took no note of it. Emma, as a result of her week spent as m'lord's secretary, already knew that Sir Thomas was the leader of a small band of Northumbrian aristocrats and gentlemen who owned most of the iron foundries and coalpits in Northumberland and Durham. They called themselves the Grand Allies and were financing Stephenson's modifications to the primitive steam engines on tramways or rails with which Mr Blenkinsop of Leeds, and Mr Trevithick were already experimenting.

'I didn't tell Lufton,' said m'lord to Emma, smiling a little when, after their tea, he asked her to write the letter to Sir Thomas which would inform him that the Loudwater party would be delighted to see Stephenson's travelling engine at work on the twenty-fifth, 'but what Sir Thomas actually wrote was that I ought to see that Lufton rattled his hocks a little, if he wanted to test his scepticism about the effectiveness of Stephenson's engine. I thought that it might not be diplomatic to repeat such frank language aloud!'

At first when Emma had worked for him he had been a little stiff with her—put off, no doubt, by the presence of Mrs Morton, who sat in the corner of his study doing her embroidery and acting as chaperon. But as time had passed he had become more and more easy, and though his language to Emma never became as frankly masculine as it was when he discussed matters with John Bassett, he was beginning to forget that he had a lady with him.

'And Bassett was right,' he exclaimed, picking up his accounts, which Emma had brought up to date earlier that day. 'You are not only as accurate as he is, but neater. I have noticed before that the handwriting and numbering of ladies is more legible than that of men. What I had not expected was that you would be as conscientious.'

Emma bristled a little. 'Why, m'lord, given the chance I think that we might do as well as the men—if not better. *I* have noticed that men are more slapdash than women when performing tasks which are required to be both meticulous and precise.'

M'lord raised his handsome head and said softly, 'Ah, Miss Lawrence, as usual you do not hesitate to correct me. I must beg your pardon if I sounded patronising. Bassett himself could not have done better for me than you have done this week.'

Their eyes met. His were warm, and gave a great deal away. Emma's were more guarded, but she could not prevent herself from smiling back at him as he praised her. He put out a hand to give her Sir Thomas's letter, and the reply which he had drafted in rough.

Now it was their hands which met.

Nor did they wish to part.

He did not will it, by no means, but m'lord dropped his head and kissed her small paw which lay so lightly in his.

'Oh, you please me, my little bird,' he whispered.

'No, m'lord,' Emma whispered back, trying to reclaim her hand from his. 'You promised to be good—'

'Not exactly,' he said. 'I only hinted—'

'Mrs Morton will hear you,' warned Emma.

'Hear what? I have said nothing.'

'But looked a great deal.'

'Oh, looks.' M'lord smiled, then added more soberly, as she continued to gaze steadily at him, 'but I must heed what you say.'

'Indeed, you must,' said Emma, and then, a trifle naughtily, as she cast her eyes over the draft he had given her, 'You will allow me to correct your grammar a little, m'lord?'

'Since you venture to correct everything else I do, and by more than a little, then correct my grammar "a little", by all means.'

Mrs Morton's eye, a trifle puzzled, was on them

as they whispered together. Emma shook her head, moved away and sat down at John Bassett's desk. She picked up her quill and began to write as though her life depended on it. M'lord sat down at his desk, propped his chin on both hands, smiled at Mrs Morton, who had returned to her needlework, and then studied Emma as she copied his letter for him.

Emma was aware of his scrutiny. Wryly she sanded the letter and considered the unlikely fate which had been hers since she had arrived at Loudwater. She had become the object of every man's pursuit. She had earned the dislike of Lady Clara and, oddly, the unwilling admiration of Calypso Straight. Ben Blackburn's chasing of her had been muted since m'lord had found him attacking her, but his place had been taken by Lord Lufton, who frequently found occasion to engage her in conversation, and it was he whom she was trying to avoid.

He seemed to think that m'lord's making Emma his secretary had altered her status for the worse— or rather, he chose to think the worst of m'lord's relationship with her, even though, in public, m'lord was now scrupulous in his manner towards her to the point of coolness. Lord Lufton, by contrast, grew warmer towards her each day.

Now, that she did not want, and the thought that it would be more difficult to escape his attentions in m'lord's rented house at Newcastle, since it would be so much smaller than Loudwater, was not a pleasant one. It was all very well to be m'lord's temporary secretary and enjoy his company every day, but there was a price to be paid for it, and that price was not one she necessarily cared to pay.

Even Tish had noticed that Miss Lawrence was not her usual composed self, and Emma had to hope that being translated to Newcastle and then to Killingworth would give the men something else to think about than the seduction of one poor governess. . .

Fortunately for Emma, m'lord decided that he would take John Bassett with him to Newcastle to lighten the burden on her. John's damaged wrist still prevented him from writing, but he could act as an aide in other ways, and would thus direct attention away from Emma's unorthodox position.

But, in solving one problem for Emma, m'lord had unwittingly created another for her. John's intentions towards her were honourable, not predatory, but they were not welcome. Emma began to feel like a large goldfish in a very small bowl round which a clowder of cats circled, their feral eyes on her. What made it worse was that common sense said that she ought to encourage John. Marriage to him would solve all her problems; she would have a comfortable, if not a rich home with him, and it was very much the best which she could expect from life, given her lowly position and lack of fortune.

Common sense had nothing to do with it! She

had fallen in love with the man who had despised her ten years ago.

All the way to Newcastle, and later, on the journey to Killingworth, she asked herself despairingly what kind of a fool she was to hold off a man who admired and respected her—even if she did feel nothing for him but friendship. Common sense might say, It would be wise to marry John Bassett and settle yourself for life, but meeting Dominic Hastings again had driven common sense out of her head.

Which left her with nothing to do but be patient. . .and wait for what the future might bring.

# CHAPTER NINE

IN THE end everyone, including Mrs Morton and Tish, accompanied the two Earls to Killingworth to see Geordie Stephenson's engine at work. Even Lady Clara, who had privately announced that she did not propose to spend the day scrambling around coalpits among smelly machinery, had been firmly spoken to by Calypso Straight. Even so, she still refused to wear her stoutest shoes, preferring her pretty kid ones—although she did go so far as to try to please m'lord by pretending great interest in his business concerns.

It was a cold July day, the twenty-fifth, when Emma climbed into the open carriage with Mrs Morton, Tish, Miss Straight and the bored Lady Clara. The sun was shining, but a strong breeze kept the ladies shivering in their light clothes. The men, in country dress and heavy boots, were luckier—as Lady Clara constantly complained, being safely away from m'lord, who was in the leading carriage.

Once outside Newcastle-upon-Tyne, they travelled north through wild country on the turnpike road to Scotland; it was country which Emma had never seen before. She looked interestedly around her, particularly when they reached the crossroads where they turned west on the North Shields turnpike which led to Killingworth.

Killingworth proved to be one of the small villages lost in the moors beneath a wide sky. The coalpits surrounding them, with their pumping houses, chimneys and spoil heaps, gave the villages purpose and employment. The High Pit at Killingworth, sunk by Sir Thomas Liddell three years earlier, was situated on the West Moor, where the colliers' cottages ran in a row alongside it.

The end one was the home of Mr George Stephenson, High Pit's enginewright and the builder of the travelling machine which they were about to see. And at the far end of the row was a rude hut where the horses which drew the wagons were stabled. A grimy boy was walking one of them up and down, staring blankly at all the excitement.

Immediately behind the cottages, and parallel with them, was a slight incline upon which the engine was to make its first run—if all went well, that was. All work seemed to have stopped for the day, and there was already a large crowd assembled—colliers, local gentry, and now, with the arrival of m'lord's party, the nobility also were present.

As m'lord handed Lady Clara down from his carriage a voice shouted from the milling crowd, impatient to see the engine run, 'Cum to see wor Geordie's *Blutcher*, has'ta?'

Emma, who was already standing by John

Bassett, watching Tish, her nursemaid and Mrs Morton stare at the incline, the railway and the ragged crowd who stared back at them with equal interest, murmured, '*Blutcher*, Mr Bassett?'

John shook his head to acknowledge that he had no idea what the fellow meant, but m'lord, ever on the alert where Emma was concerned, leaned towards her and said, 'I believe that that is the name which Mr Stephenson has given to his engine. He wanted to name it after Sir Thomas, who provided most of the capital to enable him to build it, but Sir Thomas declined the honour!'

'After the great Prussian soldier, Blucher, one presumes,' ventured Emma in reply. Lady Clara yawned her boredom, but took m'lord's offered arm as he told Emma that he would enquire of Mr Stephenson from whence the name originated. He set off towards the end of the tramway, where Sir Thomas Liddell, Stephenson and other assorted gentry awaited them. Lord Lufton followed, squiring Miss Straight.

Ben Blackburn offered Emma his arm, whereupon she looked steadily at him and said, 'Pray excuse me, Mr Blackburn, but it is my duty to look after Lady Letitia, and I may not easily do that if I allow you to monopolise me.'

'Oh, forgive me,' he riposted nastily. 'I thought that it was your duty to look after Chard, not his daughter! But presumably that is reserved for the night-time, not broad daylight. Respectability and Lady Clara claim him then. I would commiserate with you if I were not sure that you were succeeding in all your objectives. I wonder that he allows his doxy to nursemaid his daughter!'

This came out with the utmost snarling good humour as Ben took advantage of the fact that Emma was on her own—John Bassett having been held back by Mr Cross, who was asking him concerned questions as to how Stephenson proposed to prevent his machine from falling off the smooth rails of the tramway.

'Most dangerous,' he announced reprovingly. 'Particularly if, as I am assured, the brains of the man driving the engine will certainly boil, thus destroying his judgement, if the machine travels at a pace faster than that of a good horse!'

Emma turned away from Ben Blackburn to hold out her hand to Tish, who eagerly ran to take it. Once his insults would have disturbed her, but she had grown a second skin off which they harmlessly bounced, as those of Mr Henry Gardiner and his predecessors had done.

She became aware that John Bassett, who was now walking on her right-hand side again, had said something to her, and she had not the slightest idea what it was. She blinked at him and he repeated in his kind manner, 'I trust that you are not cold, Miss Lawrence. Northumbria can so often be cool, even in high summer, and today it is cooler than usual.'

Emma pulled her light shawl around her and thanked him for his concern for her. 'I am far too interested in seeing how Mr Stephenson's engine will perform to trouble about the weather, Mr Bassett. M'lord told me yesterday that he is sure that the travelling engine will replace the horse, if only it can be made to work properly.'

'Oh, I very much doubt that,' exclaimed John eagerly. 'Consider, a horse may go wherever there is room for its passage, but a travelling engine will always require a set of rails—and I cannot see sufficient of those being built around England to replace stage-coaches and wagons. No, no, depend upon it, m'lord is being carried away by his enthusiasm for novelty. Not,' he hastened to add, 'that he has not succeeded in making Loudwater more profitable than it was through the many innovations he has introduced since he inherited.'

Emma thought a moment before saying slowly, 'I understood that as a young man m'lord was somewhat wild. He seems uncommonly steady and businesslike these days.'

'Oh, it was the inheritance which changed him— that and. . .' he hesitated '. . .other things.'

She did not enquire what the 'other things' were, but suspected that one of them was his wife. Something had engraved those lines of pain and suffering on his face. It was not only the parlous condition in which he had inherited Loudwater which had changed him so much, she was sure.

Tish was pulling at her. 'Oh, do hurry, Miss Lawrence. I am sure that the engine will be starting off any minute, and I do so want to be there when

it does. Papa is talking to Mr Stephenson. Kettie
told me that her elder brother worked with Mr
Stephenson when he was a young collier, and he
was well known for his—' she screwed up her face
to indicate that she was greatly puzzled '—feats of
strength. Surely she meant strong feet!'

Exlaining what feats of strength were occupied
Emma until they caught up m'lord again. Seen
near to, Mr George Stephenson was a big man
with a strong face full of the shrewd and independent humour of the Northumbrian working man.
Emma thought that m'lord had been greatly influ-
enced by it in his years in the North, and that it
was partly responsible for the marked change in his
manner.

Introductions were made all round. M'lord
made sure that no one was left out, and Mr
Stephenson confirmed to Emma that *Blutcher* was
indeed named after the Prussian general. 'All my
travelling engines are given names,' he told her, 'as
stage-coaches are. It distinguishes them one from
the other.'

Presently all was ready for the demonstration to
begin. *Blutcher*, belching smoke and smuts, set off
slowly up the tramway, pulling eight loaded
wagons totalling thirty tons in weight behind it. Its
chimney resembled that of the colliery chimneys
which they had passed on the way from Newcastle
to Killingworth, and the engine was, m'lord
explained to a totally uninterested Lady Clara,
simply a boiler placed on its side, to drive the

wheels which were attached to it and so pull along the wagons filled with coal from the pit.

As it chundered along a cheer went up from the ever-growing crowd of colliers and their wives and some of the good burghers of Newcastle who had come along to see the fun, as well as Sir Thomas and his business allies. The only persons not impressed by this revolutionary sight were Lord Lufton, Lady Clara and Mr Cross, who thought that the whole thing was simply an example of the degeneration of the times in which he lived.

'So dirty,' he kept exclaiming dolefully as *Blutcher* roared and clanked past them on its way up the incline. 'So noisy and so smelly. What will this dear land of ours come to if such devil's ingenuity is let loose upon it?'

But he was careful not to be too loud in his criticism, knowing that his employer saw the salvation of Loudwater bound up with the travelling engine which was ascending the slight incline at a steady four miles per hour.

It was this speed which, when it was announced, was causing Lord Lufton to say with sneering condescension, 'Chard, my dear fellow, all this money, time and iron spent to carry wagons at a speed which any horse could easily match. Where is the profit in that? No, no—' he echoed John Bassett '—all this botheration to do what could be done more simply. Throw your money into the Tyne if you must, by investing in it, but I shall have the good sense to save mine to buy a pair of good horses and a carriage.'

'But this is only the beginning,' said m'lord, nothing daunted. 'And Stephenson tells me that as a result of the experiments he has already conducted he is sure that not only will he be able to double and treble the speed of the travelling engine, but he will be able to increase the load far beyond the capacity of any train of horses.'

The crowd was evenly divided between these two contrary opinions, and when *Blutcher* and his eight wagons reached the end of the incline another great cheer went up—principally from the colliers, Sir Thomas Liddell, his Grand Allies and m'lord. To say nothing of Tish, who jumped up and down, clapping her hands and exclaiming excitedly, 'Oh, Miss Lawrence, if only I were a boy, then I might grow up to be the man who drives the travelling engine!' Then she added sadly, 'But I do not think that Papa would approve.'

'Is that all?' exclaimed Lady Clara in a bored voice. 'Have we really come all this way just to see that smelly monster and a pack of dirty peasants?'

Calypso Straight, who was privately of the same opinion as m'lord and Sir Thomas, thought it politic to affect indifference—particularly as Lord Lufton, whom she was hoping to charm, continued to express his reservations about the whole 'ill-starred enterprise', as he termed it.

'I shall stick with the old ways,' he ended

vigorously. 'And you, Blackburn, what is your opinion?'

'The same as yours, Lufton, the same as yours. I wonder at Chard, I really do—halfway up the River Tick and minded to go the whole way with "wor Geordie".' This last was said with a half-sneer and a sideways glance at Emma.

M'lord himself, talking eagerly with Stephenson and Sir Thomas about future developments, was out of earshot, making his way to the top of the incline, so that Ben felt safe in taunting the lowly governess. 'I suppose that *you*—' he trod nastily on the word '—are all enthusiasm for this silly business, seeing that Chard has lost his senses over it! He's busy talking nonsense about tramways over England and monstrosities like *Blutcher* running along them pulling men as well as coal. Can't he see he'll ruin the whole country with such nonsense—inn-keepers, saddlers, coachmakers, all with a living to lose! Has the world run mad?'

Ben was merely echoing the opinion of many of his fellows, who were vowing to keep their money in their pockets rather than throw it away on steam engines running on rails.

Emma was saved from replying to this piece of jealous nastiness by Tish, over whose head all this was flying, saying eagerly, 'Oh, Miss Lawrence, I have been talking to Robert Stephenson. He goes to school, he says, and his uncle Jem is the man who is driving the engine! And only think, when they first ran *Blutcher* and it stopped outside Jem's house he called his wife Jinnie, who was hanging the wash out, to push the engine for him so that it might start again! And it did! Oh, look! Papa is signalling to us. I do believe that he wishes us to join him. Oh, please, Miss Lawrence, do let us, please! I do so wish to see *Blutcher* near to!'

This opportunity to escape from Ben Blackburn's unpleasant attentions was rapidly taken. Emma, Tish and Kettie all set off, leaving Mrs Morton behind. 'Pray do excuse me,' she murmured gently. 'I am too old to find entertainment in such novelties. I am inclined to Lord Lufton's beliefs, but if m'lord wishes to take an interest in Mr Stephenson's work then we must agree with him. But we need not completely share his enthusiasm for it.'

This was as far as Mrs Morton was inclined to go in criticism of her cousin and benefactor. She accordingly sat down on a dry stone wall and opened her parasol, attended by Mr Cross, who was still busy lamenting the death of the past which he was dismally sure *Blutcher* would bring about.

Shoulders shrugging, Ben Blackburn, Lord Lufton and his party also followed them. Lady Clara achieved about four reluctant paces before complaining, 'Oh, this path is hurting my feet! I will join Mrs Morton in remaining behind. You will accompany me, Calypso, of course.'

Nobly refraining from reminding her that she had been recommended to wear stout walking shoes rather than the elegant kid slippers which she had insisted on because they matched her dress, but which did not protect her feet at all, Calypso Straight shook her elegant head. 'Pray forgive me, my dear. Whilst sharing Lord Lufton's reservations about the merits of the engine, I would very much like to inspect it near to.'

Lady Clara's pout was monumental. She removed herself as far as she could from Mrs Morton and Mr Cross, opened her own parasol and stared in the opposite direction from all the excitement, muted now. She was not missed.

'Oh, there you are, Tish,' exclaimed m'lord. 'I thought that you would like to meet Mr Stephenson and see *Blutcher* nearer to. And Miss Lawrence, of course. This is a historic day, I do believe.'

So Tish achieved her heart's desire and had Mr Stephenson himself in his deep voice explain a little of what made the engine run. A twelve year old boy, standing beside him, did not appear to be at all daunted by the great folk around him. He turned out to be Geordie's son, Robert, who had been ordered to look after Lady Letitia by his father whilst their elders discussed the implications of what they had just seen—*Blutcher* gently belching smoke the while.

This *Blutcher* did to such effect that Emma, listening closely, suddenly let out a little shriek, put her hand to her face and exclaimed, 'Oh, I do believe that I have a cinder in my eye!' She scrabbled in the reticule hanging from her belt for her handkerchief to help her to remove it.

All the gentlemen swung round. Lord Lufton thought, on seeing Emma's bent head, that this was simply one more proof of the unsuitability of the whole enterprise. Not only was the noise of escaping steam when the engine ran frightening all the animals in earshot, but the notion of it cascading smuts and cinders over the landscape was insupportable.

It was m'lord, face anxious, who moved forward to lay a gentle right hand on Emma's arm, at the same time pulling his own handkerchief of fine lawn from his breeches pocket. 'Pray allow me, Miss Lawrence. Lift up your head so that I may see what damage has been done.' Emma did as she was bid, showing him a rapidly watering eye, whereat he carefully lifted the lid to discover that a large smut had indeed lodged itself in the corner.

'I think I see the problem,' he announced gravely. 'Now, if you will hand me your handkerchief—the linen is finer than that of mine—I will try to remove the obstruction for you.'

To have him so near—and for such a respectable reason, even though the whole party was gazing at them in fascination—was both heaven and hell for Emma. She knew once again that revenge or no, she loved him.

'Try not to blink,' he murmured. There was a moment's pain for her and then the smut was out, and, although Emma's eye watered even more heavily at the moment of its passing, the relief from discomfort was immediate. M'lord was having the greatest difficulty in not succumbing to an intense desire to kiss her damask cheek, so invitingly close to his lips.

'Oh, thank you, thank you,' she breathed, looking up at him so earnestly that his desire grew with what it was feeding on.

'Not at all,' he returned, still entranced at having been so near to those beautiful eyes and at having given relief to one of them. 'By no means—a most trifling service.' Which was a lie; there was nothing trifling about it in view of the delightful agony into which touching her so intimately had thrown him.

He was in danger of forgetting that they had an audience, whose responses ranged from the merely interested one of Geordie Stephenson and the mocking one of Calypso Straight to the intensely jealous one of Ben Blackburn. Worse, although neither of them knew it, they had, in that brief moment, given themselves away—both by the immediate reaction of m'lord to Emma's distress and her tender response to him.

No one now could have any doubt of what m'lord and his governess so inconveniently felt for one another.

# CHAPTER TEN

UNAWARE that she and m'lord had betrayed themselves, Emma was inclined to think that the visit to Killingworth had been an interesting experience in more ways than one. The manner in which each member of m'lord's party had reacted to the visit to see Geordie Stephenson's travelling engine had been such a revelation of their true character that the expedition might well have served as a moral example in a book written to illustrate the seven deadly sins!

Emma did not exempt herself from her criticism of her fellow men and women. She was only too aware that where m'lord was concerned she was not merely in two minds, but possibly in three or four. She had arrived at Loudwater determined to forget the past and to behave as impersonally and correctly as any young woman hired to look after the daughter of the house ought to do—she would simply regard m'lord as her employer, not as someone she had once known who had hurt her cruelly.

Alas, this noble resolution had soon been forgotten in her discovery that the man he had become was a man whom she could respect, and consequently the childish love which she had once felt for him had been born all over again. Only this time her own maturity had transformed that love into something more deep and enduring. Where once it had been enough for the young Emilia Lincoln just to be with him, to admire his charm, the older Emma Lawrence wanted much more than that from him. . .

If she were truthful, she wanted to be held and loved by him. She had discovered that his lightest touch set her whole body vibrating. What, then, would happen if he were to do so much more than that? If he were to. . . At this point in her thoughts Emma would blush and tremble all over. She must not think such shameless things. And if once she had believed that she might lure m'lord on, only to drop him when she had secured some sort of declaration from him, then that desire for revenge had long since left her.

As he had begun to show that he was attracted to her, so her feelings for him had burgeoned and grown. And, of course, it was hopeless. She was simply his paid servant, his daughter's governess, a nobody. He might make her his mistress—although so far she knew that he was resisting the desire to. . .to bed her, which was the least shameless way in which Emma could think of what becoming m'lord's doxy would really mean.

She did not need Calypso Straight to tell her that m'lord was most unlikely to marry her.

Their return to Loudwater served only to remind her the more of the vast social distance between herself, m'lord, Lord Lufton and even

Ben Blackburn. It was a distance rendered greater by the fact that they disagreed with m'lord over the value of Stephenson's invention. M'lord was well aware that they were no longer his allies. Both would stand against any further development of travelling engines, both in parliament and out, but they still needed m'lord's co-operation in the county on other matters. Not that m'lord stood to lose by their desertion.

'You see,' he said to Emma when they were back in his study again, 'Sir Thomas has agreed that I may become part of his Grand Alliance, principally because I am prepared to risk a substantial part of my loose capital in promoting Stephenson's work. Not that I think that there is any real risk to be run. I am convinced that we shall be successful.'

He spun round to look out of the window at the smiling landscape. 'Tell me, Miss Lawrence. Do you think that I am mad? I know that Lufton does. But you were at Killingworth and saw the trial, and you are a woman of sense and I respect your opinion. I know, too, that you will be honest with me, and not tell me just what you think that I wish to hear.'

Now, that was a hard thing, for she was not being honest with him, was she? Even the name she was passing under was not her own. What would he say if he were to learn who she truly was? Emma gulped a little. Well, at least she could answer his present questions honestly.

'No,' she said quietly. 'I agree with you. I was

most impressed, not only by belching *Blutcher* but by Mr Stephenson. I have seldom met a man of such integrity and intellect combined. And I understand that he began life as an unlettered collier, which makes his present grasp of matters the more admirable. Yes, if I were a man, or I had money, I would support him in every way I could. No, I don't think you mad. I merely think Lord Lufton and Mr Blackburn shortsighted.'

'Oh, you gratify me strangely, Miss Lawrence,' exclaimed m'lord. 'I had begun to think that *I* was odd, seeing that Lufton and Blackburn changed their minds once they had seen *Blutcher* perform.'

'I think that they were expecting too much,' returned Emma, who had put her pen down. 'They thought that they were going to see something much more remarkable. But these matters must proceed slowly if they are to succeed, one supposes. Or so my father always told me, when discussing new projects of this nature.'

In her enthusiasm and her desire to support the man whom she loved, Emma had forgotten that she was lowly Miss Lawrence, and had become once again Emilia Lincoln, the daughter of a man who had discussed important business matters with her. Fortunately m'lord was too happy to have her support to notice that she had suddenly acquired a father able to have firm opinions on investment and development.

'That, too,' agreed m'lord. 'Between ourselves, I think Lord Lufton a little stick-in-the-mud, whereas Ben Blackburn is a man in a hurry and *Blutcher* was not sufficiently miraculous for him.'

Emma's agreement was patent.

Mrs Morton's mouth dropped open as m'lord and his new secretary discussed such arcane and unladylike topics so enthusiastically. It was time that John Bassett was sufficiently recovered, she thought, so that Miss Lawrence could be relieved of such heavy masculine responsibilities.

She sighed heavily, and sighed again when John came in, his right arm still in a sling. He had a ledger under the left. He had been checking the state of m'lord's finances, and had come to report on how much m'lord might safely invest. It was plain that Miss Lawrence's secretaryship still had some little time to run.

The rest of the afternoon was hard work. With John's help Emma wrote several letters and laid out a balance-sheet for Loudwater. It was plain that although m'lord was not out of the financial wood, Loudwater's affairs were in a much healthier state than when he had inherited.

M'lord wrote to Sir Thomas Liddell in his own hand, notifying him of his intention to join in supporting Stephenson financially. He had, although he was unaware of this, impressed Sir Thomas with his common sense, and relieved him more than a little. He had been told that Chard had been a bit of a wild man when he was young, but it had become plain to him, and to all Northumbria, that the latest Earl was a man of

sterner and more sensible stuff than his predecessors.

It was almost time for dinner before the trio had
finished their work. M'lord's agent came in shortly
after John, and was told of the latest developments.
He made it plain that his approval depended on
them not interfering with m'lord's projected
improvements to the farms on the estate. When
informed that they would not, he announced that
he would support them.

'And if, in the long run—for there will be little
return in the short run—we gain as much as I
hope, then *all* my many plans for the improvement
of the estates can go ahead,' ended m'lord, just as
he pulled out his watch to note, with some surprise, that they must finish talking for dinner
awaited them.

'No time to change,' he announced briskly. 'I do
believe, Miss Lawrence, that since you took a hand
in our affairs they have moved with more
expedition. No offence to you, Bassett, but you
really had too much on your plate, and your
sharing the work with Miss Lawrence has been a
boon I could not have expected when you chose to
throw yourself off the Wall!'

'Oh dear, m'lord,' twittered Mrs Morton a little
anxiously. 'I do hope that does not mean that you
intend to make Miss Lawrence's position a permanency! I must remind you that it would be most
unfitting for a young female. A stop-gap, yes. But
a permanency—no, indeed.'

'If, Mrs Morton,' said m'lord, smiling tenderly at Emma, 'I agree with you, it is with a little sadness. I could not have hoped for a more willing and careful secretary. If I had any reservations that a lady might find the task beyond her, then I have lost them for good. You do your sex credit, Miss Lawrence.'

Mrs Morton stared at him and at his tender look. He must not, he really must not encourage Miss Lawrence to think wrong things. He had never misbehaved himself with or exploited any of the young women who had worked at Loudwater before her, but there was always a first time.

'Besides,' she said loudly, 'Tish needs her governess.'

'Oh, Mr Bassett's wrist will soon mend,' riposted Emma briskly, 'and then Tish will have all of me, and not just the mornings.'

'And I will hire a clerk to help you, Bassett,' added m'lord. 'Loudwater's affairs have become so much more complicated over the last few years that I can plainly see that you need assistance. So your damaged wrist was a boon for you, after all!'

In this jovial mood they all repaired to the drawing room to discover the idle members of the house-party waiting for them to arrive so that they might have dinner.

But m'lord's guests had decided to stay for more than dinner. After many years of refusing to leave his own home, Lord Lufton had become entranced by the notion of visiting the homes of others. A somewhat near man where money was concerned, this visit to Loudwater had convinced him of the financial advantages to be gained by living at someone else's expense.

And, since Ben Blackburn was little inclined to retire to his own lonely and run-down mansion, he also had decided that to spend the rest of the summer at Loudwater was by no means a bad idea—besides, it was time to renew his pursuit of the governess. Her behaviour with Chard had convinced him that she was as much of a lightskirt as most women were, however hoity-toity they pretended to be.

Wherever Emma went, she found that Ben Blackburn was sure not to be far away. Even Tish noticed.

'I do not like that man who follows you about. He does not mean what he says,' she announced firmly one afternoon after Emma had returned from her duties with m'lord. They were on the lawn, having an impromptu lesson out of doors, and Ben Blackburn had followed them out to make coy advances to Tish, but, having little notion of what interested a child, was making a singularly bad fist of it.

'You like the fine weather, hey, Lady Letty?' he asked as he approached them, falsity in every syllable of his speech. 'And your governess too, I'll be bound.' He was making a point of being almost servilely pleasant and civil to Emma. 'I wish that

I'd had lessons in the open when I was a lad. But then I didn't have a charming young lady to be my tutor—only a bear of an Oxford classicist.'

If he had been hoping to placate Emma, to make her forget his attack on her, he was singularly failing. 'You will forgive us, I am sure, if we leave you,' she said, rising, 'but we are to botanise this afternoon. Lady Letitia and I are on the way to the brook which runs through the park by the folly, and I would wish her to concentrate on her studies.'

It was difficult for him to pursue them after that, and he watched them walk away, his face ugly. It grew uglier still as he espied m'lord approach them by the path which led from the stables and saw Tish run to him, unchecked by that damned doxy. M'lord lifted Tish up and shook her playfully before setting her down, and the three of them then made their way to the brook, Tish skipping along, her hand in her father's.

Ben stared after them, swearing to himself, until they disappeared from his view. His determination to teach Chard a lesson—as well as the governess— had been reinforced by the sight of the little group's obvious happiness.

He would have been more angered still if he could have heard the light banter which m'lord was using to Emma.

'I had thought,' he said, 'that after a hard afternoon's work you would have given Tish a holiday so that you might enjoy one yourself.'

'Not at all,' riposted Emma with a smile. 'She has already lost so many lessons with me that I cannot allow either of us to malinger further.'

Tish, who had now skipped ahead of them, turned her head to say, 'Oh, Miss Lawrence, pray what does malinger mean?'

'To pretend to be ill in order to be idle,' replied m'lord before Emma could answer. 'Something of which Miss Lawrence cannot possibly be accused.'

As Tish ran even further ahead, to chase a butterfly, he added in a low voice, 'Was that fellow troubling you again, Miss Lawrence? If he has been, then I shall suggest that he leaves immediately. I do not think that he has learned his lesson, and only my good manners are preventing me from punishing his bad ones. He has invited himself to stay even longer, and as I do not wish a confrontation with him which would cause trouble in the county I have to endure his company—but not if he insults you. I will try to do it without causing scandal which might damage you.'

'Oh, no.' Emma was swift. Like m'lord she wanted no scandal. 'He said nothing wrong.' Which was true, so far as it went. It was his tone which had been wrong.

'You are sure?' asked m'lord anxiously. He was experiencing an odd feeling, one which he had never felt before—that of a knight wishing to defend his lady.

'Quite sure. Tish's presence rendered him a little toothless, I think.'

M'lord was entranced all over again. The notion of a toothless Ben Blackburn was particularly delightful.

'You have a way with words, my dear,' he could not help saying. After all, Tish, now on her knees watching fish in the brook, was out of earshot.

'And so I should.' Emma was looking up at him, her face all mischief whilst m'lord's stern one was softening more than ever as she continued. 'Being a governess, whose trade is words.'

'Your predecessor's wasn't.' M'lord's smile was wider than ever. 'Miss Sandeman was mistress of few words, and few of them apposite.' It was ungallant of him, he knew, to criticise an absent woman, but it was the truth. Emma Lawrence was like no other woman he had ever met. Simply to be with her was making him feel happier than he had been for years.

There was a bench among the trees, and he motioned to Emma to sit there with him so that they might watch Tish enjoy herself in comfort.

Seated out of the hot sun in the green shade, his long legs stretched out before him, m'lord was having another revelation. He wished that the three of them were truly a little family, and that they would be returning to a house empty of all but themselves and where, once they had eaten *en famille*, he would take the quiet woman beside him up to his room and they would. . .

In the balmy warmth of the afternoon, at peace with himself as he had not been for years, m'lord fell into a light sleep. All his cares, which had hung around his neck like so many millstones, had fallen away.

Tish looked up to call to him, and saw Miss Lawrence's finger on her lips demanding quiet. Papa was alseep! In the day! What she could not see was that before he had fallen into his doze Papa had taken Miss Lawrence's hand in his and was holding it gently to his breast.

Her Papa was dreaming, and in his dream he was strolling in Loudwater's grounds. Before him Tish was walking, not running, because somehow she had grown into a pretty young woman. She was holding by the hand a little trotting boy—and he, what was he doing? Why, he had a woman's delicate hand in his. Who could the woman be? And the boy child, who was he? He turned to look at the woman, who. . .was. . . Who. . .was. . . Something startled him, and he was suddenly wide awake. Grown-up Tish, the little boy and the unknown woman had disappeared into the dark.

Emma was on her feet again, and had taken Tish by the hand to join her in watching for fish in the water. The peace of the afternoon still wrapped him around. . .until he heard approaching footsteps and voices. The sound was coming towards them, along the brook's path, and it was that which had caused Emma to leave him and join Tish, in order to restore a ladylike decorum to her and m'lord's idyll.

It was Ben Blackburn who had come after them.

Maddened by m'lord's non-appearance after he had disappeared into the trees, he had hailed Miss Straight when she had walked onto the lawn, offered her his arm and suggested that they stroll to the folly by way of the brook. He had not the slightest desire to see the folly or the brook, or to walk with Miss Straight, for that matter! What he wanted to do was to catch m'lord in a compromising position with his governess—and with La Straight as a witness. She would be invaluable. He didn't ask himself whether m'lord was scoundrel enough to make love to the governess with his daughter standing by! He judged other men by himself.

But, alas! All that he caught out was Tish! Excited by having Papa and Miss Lawrence with her, she threw off Emma's hand, ran along the muddy bank to follow a small shoal of fish, skidded—and fell headlong into the brook with an almighty splash.

Only to stand up, nothing daunted and dripping water, just as Ben and Calypso Straight arrived, a wriggling fish clutched triumphantly in her right hand.

At the same moment, m'lord, now chastely far away from his governess, also sprang to his feet and rushed forward to rescue his child. He jumped into the brook after her, caught her up in his arms and, to the amusement of Calypso Straight, at least, emerged nearly as wet as Tish. A scene which Ben Blackburn had hoped might be a Saturnalia had turned into a nursery game. There were no nymphs, shepherds or satyrs—just a father and his daughter enjoying themselves.

The face which m'lord turned on them all was one none of them had ever seen at Loudwater, so happy was it. Only Emma felt a pang, for here again was the carefree Dominic Hastings she had known of old, full of the joys of life. And then the moment was gone. A grinning Ben Blackburn and a concerned pair of females watched m'lord stride off towards the house, a dripping Tish in his arms, commanding as he went by Emma at the double, 'Miss Lawrence, pray follow me. I have caught a large fish in the brook and I fear that the pair of us will need a bath and clean linen.'

Nothing loath, a now amused Emma followed him—at a slightly slower pace. Ben Blackburn's grin turned savage at this further evidence of m'lord's involvement with the governess. Calypso Straight, highly amused, was a curious spectator of his anger as m'lord and Emma disappeared in the direction of the house.

Sat the wind in that quarter, then? Was there to be no end to the governess's triumphs? And how deeply was m'lord engaged with her? And what were his intentions? There was no doubt that a clever woman might turn such a situation to her advantage, and Miss Straight had long thought that the governess was clever. Was she clever enough to catch either of the two Earls like Lady Letitia had caught her fish?

Ah, but was she, Calypso Straight, cleverer than the governess?'

'A word with you before you retire, Miss Lawrence.'

It was m'lord speaking to Emma as the ladies left the gentlemen to their after-dinner port. He had had his bath and had chosen to be a dandy again. His guests hardly ever knew which version of him they were going to see. The rough countryman or the London tulip of fasion. Tonight he was a veritable dandy, with his cravat tied in a Napoleon and his blond curls brushed out, not sleeked down. His jacket, black silk breeches and delicate black leather shoes with silver rosettes all proclaimed the man of fashion he had once been.

His command to Emma was an order to ensure that she did not retire to her quarters once the ladies reached the drawing room. Tish was not with them; both Kettie and Mrs Morton, on hearing of her descent into the brook, had ordered that she must go straight to bed to avoid the cold which would surely follow such a drenching.

Tish's protests had been in vain. She had already bemoaned the fact that Papa had thrown the fish which she had caught back into the water and had not allowed it to be carried to the house to be cooked for her dinner.

'And to go to bed early as well,' she had complained. 'It is not to be borne. Dear Miss Lawrence, pray tell them that falling into the brook was no worse than having a bath which I had not expected.'

Emma quite agreed with her, but could not outface the combined might of the two women. Nor would it, she realised, have been tactful to try to claim some sort of extra authority over Tish. Both Kettie and Mrs Morton were a trifle worried about m'lord's preference for the governess. It would not do to make them even more resentful of her than was necessary.

She ruefully conceded that she was now left without a friend either upstairs or downstairs. Each party had its own reasons for disliking or mistrusting her, and it was not a pleasant sensation to be so isolated. Always before, by her careful and discreet behaviour, she had kept the respect if not the friendship of those both above her and below her. But now, apart from m'lord and John Bassett, she had no friends. She was regarded either as prey by her superiors, or as on the game by her inferiors.

This dismal thought sat on her shoulders as she stitched her canvaswork as though her life depended upon it. Lady Clara, Calypso Straight and Mrs Morton talked together and ignored her. The arrival of the men, slightly happy through drink, did not mend matters at all, as it soon became apparent that their real target was Emma; they only tolerated the other women.

Not that any of them behaved ill. But in such a close-knit society it was impossible not to read their body language, which was somewhat at odds with what they were saying.

John Bassett strode immediately to where Emma sat on her own, neglected by Lady Clara and Miss Straight—a fortunate circumstance for him.

'My dear Miss Lawrence,' he began enthusiastically. 'I have been reading the précis which you prepared for m'lord detailing the nature of the trials at Killingworth and the consequences which might flow from them. A masterly piece of work! I could not have equalled it! M'lord says that he will be writing to Sir Thomas again, and he will take your account as the basis of his letter since it cannot be improved.

'Upon my word, were you a young gentleman instead of a young lady I should fear for my place! As it is, I regret that m'lord will not have the benefit of your skill much longer. My wrist is mending rapidly and I shall shortly regain its full use, which will mean that I shall soon be able to resume my duties. That will lift a grave burden from your shoulders. M'lord says that you have most nobly continued to instruct Lady Letty as well as carry out all my duties. He and I agree that we fear for your health if we continue to allow you to work so hard.'

'Oh, but the work is so interesting,' returned Emma earnestly. 'I have quite enjoyed myself, and I much prefer being busy than not.'

'So m'lord and I have noticed.' John's enthusiasm could not be contained, and his eyes on her were admiring. 'My dear Miss Lawrence, pray allow me to speak to you tomorrow, at a time of your choosing, on a matter which is most dear to my heart. You will allow?'

If ever eyes could be called speaking, his were. Emma knew immediately what the matter was which he wished to raise. And, oh, it was hopeless, quite hopeless. She could only accept him as a friend, never as a lover. And now she would spend a sleepless night trying to think of a form of words which would allow her to let him down gently. Except that she, of all people, knew that such a thing was not possible. Say what she might, she must leave him desperately unhappy.

But she could not answer or deter him now. He continued to talk on and she replied mechanically, telling him that he might speak to her at ten of the clock and trying to hide her true feelings as she did so.

Except that she could not, for presently, when he left her, Calypso Straight came over to sit in the chair which he had vacated, to say, 'Another devoted admirer for you, Miss Lawrence? And one who I am sure will make you an honest offer. Though he is perhaps not the admirer from whom you most wish it!

'I very much fear that all your superiors in station will admire you enormously, but any offer which they may make you is bound to be unsatisfactory. The satisfactory ones will be from those of your own station or your inferiors, and *they* will be unsatisfactory for quite another reason. That of having not enough to offer you in the worldly sense. I do hope that you will ponder on what I have just said most carefully, and act as sensibly as befits a nobody of no station.'

This was said so pleasantly that any spectator might have thought that the two women were the best of friends. Emma, indeed, smiled sweetly at her would-be tormentor. She decided to be as blunt with Miss Straight as she had been before when the other woman had tried to intimidate her.

'I note your advice, Miss Straight, and, as with all advice, from whomsoever it comes, I will adopt that part of it which seems to me to be sensible and useful and ignore that which is not. Will that do? And would you like me to offer *you* some advice? I believe that you may need it as much as I, since I imagine that your situation is not perhaps so dissimilar from mine as you might like me to think.'

This frontal attack was not at all what Calypso Straight had expected, and, what was worse, the governess was even cleverer than she had thought if she had detected the hidden flaw in Miss Straight's social armour—that her birth might be impeccable, but that her supposed wealth was non-existent!

She was so surprised that she almost gave herself away. 'How—?' she began, and then, softly, 'Oh, no. That would have been a trick worth playing, would it not. . .?'

'For you to confirm by implication,' Emma said sweetly, 'that what I have just suggested of you is true.'

This time the victory had gone to Emma, but she had not time to savour it. Miss Straight, seeing m'lord walking over to them, decided to obey the old maxim that he who fights and runs away will live to fight another day, and rose rapidly to her feet.

'I will leave you to your lordly admirer,' she announced a trifle defiantly, 'and I will not wish you good luck, for you do not seem to need it!'

Emma's reply to that was a smile which m'lord took as meant for him, and he rewarded her with his own smile, rarely seen at Loudwater until the governess had arrived. But his native shrewdness had not departed him, for he said as he sank into the chair which Miss Straight had vacated, 'I trust that she has not been troubling you. She has the reputation of possessing a forked tongue.'

'Oh, no, not at all,' Emma reassured him. 'On the contrary, I find her conversation most entertaining—and enlightening.'

Up rose m'lord's perfect eyebrows, giving him a haughty look reminiscent of the spoiled and conceited Dominic Hastings.

'Now, Miss Lawrence,' he said softly, 'having been the target of your two-edged remarks, you must forgive me if I take that one with a pinch of salt. Attic salt, as the Greeks used to say, hidden beneath the honey.'

Emma pretended not to understand him, which had him laughing fondly at her. 'Oh, no, that will never do. I know you too well. Cruel Miss Lawrence who stabs everyone to the heart with the needle of her intellect.' Then he leaned forward to say more softly still, 'Look how mine is bleeding. Did Miss Straight's bleed?'

'No, but Lady Clara's will if you speak to me so urgently in public.'

'That is because you will not allow me to speak urgently to you in private,' he told her naughtily.

'Oh, I asked for that, did I not? Recollect again, m'lord, on who we are—and our relative positions.'

'And was that what Miss Straight was saying to you? She looked urgent enough to repel a dozen rivals.'

'Oh, I doubt that you are her target, m'lord.'

'Dominic, Miss Lawrence. My name is Dominic.'

'And mine is Emma—but you do not have my permission to use it—*m'lord*.'

'There, you have stabbed me again, and the target Miss Straight attributes to you is Lord Lufton—failing me, of course.'

His smile as he said that was wicked, and, his face being towards Emma and away from the rest of the room, it was for her alone.

'I have no interest in Lord Lufton.' She said nothing of her interest in him.

'Oh, I believe you. But *he* is interested in you. And poor Bassett—does he have an interest in you?' This was carelessly said, but there was anxiety in m'lord's tone. Was he fearful that his secretary pleased her more than he did?

'Tell me,' said Emma, picking up her canvas-work and staring unseeingly at a dragon which ramped across it, belching fire. 'Am I cast as Circe, Messalina or the pious saint who chose martyrdom before the loss of her innocence? I forget her name. Tell me, m'lord, why do we always forget the innocent and remember the guilty?'

Now, this was near the bone, and m'lord winced. 'Touché,' he said, and was staid m'lord again, nothing of Dominic Hastings left. 'You remind me of my honour. Can you be surprised that my heart bleeds—especially since I must leave you and talk to Lufton.'

He was about to rise, but Emma said, 'You asked me not to retire early for you had somewhat to say to me. Was that the truth? Or was it merely a convenience to keep me waiting until you returned to the drawing room?'

M'lord sat down again. 'Why, I think that John Bassett was before me there. I was going to tell you that he has almost recovered and will shortly be resuming his duties with me. And that, Miss Lawrence, does not please me—for reasons I leave you to puzzle out. Not that I do not value John—

but there, my heart is bleeding again, and yours does not. You call me m'lord always, which proves that yours is made of stone.'

Emma's reply was simplicity itself—and it silenced him. 'Why, that is how I always think of you.' Then, almost forgetting herself, because truth and simplicity go together, and truth betrays the speaker, she said, 'I never think of you as Dominic Hastings.'

No sooner had she said it than she quaked a little. He saw nothing untoward at the time, although later, undressing before going to his lonely bed, he puzzled a little—not at her words, but at the tone, which struck again to produce an echo of something once known but long forgotten.

And Emma in her lonely bed thought of m'lord in his, as he thought of her. And I am no longer truly innocent, she thought, for I have eaten of the Tree of Knowledge, and, knowing at last what love means, I cannot go back to what I was before I came to Loudwater—and met him again.

# CHAPTER ELEVEN

THE clock in the schoolroom chimed ten. A little earlier Kettie had removed Tish to take her for a short walk so that Emma might fulfil her promise to see John Bassett. She had put on her oldest gown—a dull grey—had dressed her hair as plainly as possible and wore the most unbecoming lace cap which she possessed in the hope of deterring him from what she was sure would be a proposal.

Vain hope! The moment he came through the door his eyes lit up at the sight of her, drab though she had made herself. Cupid, the little god of love, who flew with happy abandon in almost every painting at Loudwater, had pierced John Bassett's heart with his most potent arrow. Do what she might, whenever he looked at Emma he saw the most desirable woman in the world—charming, attractive and with the happy knack of speaking to him with such a mixture of playfulness and common sense that she made very other woman he had met seem a pale shadow beside her.

Like Emma, he had dressed himself with care. Unlike Emma, he had sought to make himself as attractive as possible. He looked every inch the gentleman's son he was. Emma's tragedy was that she liked him but she could never love him. She would have wished to save him from the disappointment which he was going to feel when she refused him.

He resisted the impulse to throw himself immediately on his knees before her. That would be importunate, and no gentleman must be that! So he manfully spoke of the weather, which was good, of the view from her window, which was better than good, and of his luck in serving a thoughtful master who had been patient enough to continue employing him when he had injured his wrist and transformed himself into a man of leisure.

Emma would have preferred him to get to the point.

He was in one fever.

She was in another.

In the middle of a rambling sentence in which he was congratulating her on the vast improvement which she had wrought in Lady Letitia's manners, he suddenly threw himself on his knees before her and began in a hoarse and broken voice, 'My dear, dear Miss Lawrence. . . But, oh, pray, allow me to call you Emma.' So saying, he took her hand in his and continued as he had begun—ecstatically.

'My dear Emma, I cannot tell you how happy you have made my life at Loudwater since you first arrived here! Your charm and beauty have transformed not only Lady Letitia but all around you— myself most of all.'

He pressed her hand to his black and white striped waistcoat—there was no way in which she could withdraw it—and looked up into her eyes, his own shining with love and admiration. 'My very dear Emma, I beg of you that you will allow me to keep your hand in mine as a token that I wish to care for you for ever, and that the only happy future which I can see for myself is one in which we are husband and wife. Believe that I would ever be your most loving husband and servant, my dearest Emma.' He removed her hand from his breast and began to shower it with kisses.

Of all things, she had never expected this! He had always been so reserved, so proper, that his ardour quite overwhelmed her. But not in the fashion after which he had hoped. Oh, no, it merely served to increase her distress.

'Mr Bassett,' she said as gently as she could, 'pray release my hand, if you would be so good, for I wish to give you my answer as plainly and calmly as possible, so that you do not misunderstand me.'

He was no fool. He knew what she was about to say. All the bright eagerness fled from his face as a meadow loses colour when a cloud passes over the sun. But he was a gentleman, and a good man as well. He gave Emma her hand back and she fought for words to answer him which would wound him as little as possible, though wounded he would undoubtedly be.

'You do me great honour, both by your offer and the sincerity with which you have made it, but, alas, I have to tell you that all I have to offer you in return is my friendship for you—which I hope will sustain us both now that I am compelled to refuse you. I wish, oh, I most dearly wish that I could give you another answer, but I cannot marry where I do not feel love, for such a marriage would bring distress to both of us, and you deserve more from your future wife than I can offer you.'

She fell silent and for a moment they remained as they were, he on his knees, looking up into her eyes, and she looking down at him, an expression of the deepest sadness on her face.

Of Emma's sincerity there was no doubt, as she had no doubt of his. He rose slowly to his feet, most admirably retaining his dignity; once again he was standing before her, and he said, with no passion in his voice, but only a quiet determination, 'I would marry you on such terms if you could bring yourself to accept me.'

'Kind though your offer is, and most handsomely made, I could not cheat you by accepting you,' returned Emma. She, too, had risen, and she put out a hand to him. 'Say that we may remain friends, I beg of you. I have not so many that I can afford to lose one.'

This brought a faint smile to his lips—which did not meet his eyes.

'You are an honest woman such as I have never expected to meet,' was all he said. 'Yes, if I may only have your friendship—then that I will treasure. Your love,' he said slowly, greatly daring, 'may be given elsewhere, and it would be unmanly of me to repine. I hope that you may achieve the happiness which I am denied.' He bowed low to her, as though he were a courtier before his queen, and left the room which had seen the death of his hopes.

Emma watched the door shut behind him and felt as though she had struck a helpless child. But she must be true to herself in order to be true to him, and she could only ask God not to subject her to any more such trials.

Her wish was not to be granted.

For the moment she awaited Tish's return, when she might try to forget what had passed by teaching her about such neutral matters as the early kings of Saxon England, and particularly the much to be admired Alfred, who had burned the cakes. Fortunately she was not required by m'lord that afternoon, and would be able to take her bruised self away from the house which had suddenly become a prison and try to forget the misery which she had been compelled to inflict on a good man.

Another vain hope! As the sun rode over the back lawns of the house she carried the embroidered bag containing her canvaswork and a copy of Mr Lewis's *The Monk*—that delightfully gruesome tale which she had never yet had the good fortune to read—in the direction of the folly, a favourite spot of hers on days when the summer sun became a little oppressive.

Before she arrived there she walked along the bank of the stream in which Tish had fallen and mused on the strange direction which her life had taken since she had agreed to come to Loudwater. So rapt was she that she failed to hear the sound of someone approaching until he was almost upon her.

It was Lord Lufton. He had hurried so much that his face was even more scarlet than usual, and he was mopping his forehead with a large handkerchief which he stuffed into his breeches pocket when she turned to see him.

'Miss Lawrence. How fortunate to meet you here! I collect that you always take a stroll in the open on the days when Chard does not require your. . .er. . .services.'

If there was something of a double meaning in this last sentence, Emma chose to ignore it.

'Indeed, m'lord,' she replied coolly. 'The folly is not too far from the house, and it is pleasant to sit in the shade and read and do my canvaswork.' She made to pass him, for he had placed himself directly in her path. He made no move that might allow her to do so, and continued as though she had said nothing—a habit of his with people, that Emma had already noted.

'Perhaps you would allow me to stroll with you, Miss Lawrence.' He put out his arm for her to take, and made a gesture as though to carry her bag.

What to do?

Emma had not the slightest wish to walk with him. What she had seen of him she heartily disliked, as she disliked the way in which his eyes roved about her body whenever they were together. But good manners dictated that she accept his offer, so she reluctantly handed him her bag and took his arm. He began to walk her along the bank which was hidden from the house, chattering to her loudly and inconsequentially about nothing at all until they reached a small clearing where he came to a dead stop.

He removed his arm, so that she could no longer hold it, and said to her, leering as he did so, 'You are a deuced pretty filly, Miss Lawrence, as I am sure you know. And if Chard is being backward with you, and Ben Blackburn too, then perhaps you might favour an older, more experienced fellow. And damme if I am not the man for you!'

Without more ado he dropped her bag and, before she could stop him, pulled her to him so strongly that she could smell the smoke of the cigar he had indulged in before he left the house and— even this early in the day—the scent of port wine on his foetid breath.

Emma put her hands on his breast and tried to push him away as firmly as she could.

'For shame, m'lord. I have done nothing to deserve this.'

He was not as crass as Ben Blackburn; he did not try to force her immediately. Instead he smiled cunningly at her and said in what he doubtless assumed was a winning manner, 'My dear, do not try to play the innocent with me. I have seen the way in which you look at Chard, and Miss Calypso Straight informs me that you seem to know full well what you are doing. Now, I have more to offer you than Chard. My estate is not encumbered as his is, and I would settle a little income on you. Has he offered you as much?' He moved closer to her again.

Emma retreated. But with the stream being behind her and he in her way there was nowhere for her to escape from him.

'Forgive me, m'lord, if I do not answer a question which demeans my honour. I have no wish to become any man's doxy, least of all yours. I trust that now I have given you an honest answer you will allow me to pass.'

No such thing! He still stood there considering her. He had thought that it would be easy enough to buy her; his opinion of women was so low that he simply assumed that he had not offered her enough to tempt her to him. She was a clever whore, was she not? He would try again.

'A larger income,' he offered with a grin. 'Would you like me to set a figure for you? I have never bargained with a woman before—but shall we bargain now?'

Emma closed her eyes with a sigh. This was not as bad as being Ben Blackburn's prey, but it was bad enough.

'No, indeed. I want nothing of you other than that you will allow me to pass. It would do you honour, as well as me, if you would stand aside.'

As though he had given her his consent, she made to walk past him.

He considered her for a second longer. 'Like all women, your yea and your nay are difficult to untangle, madam. Well, I will desist for now. But do not think that you have heard my last offer. We Luftons never give up easily. "We will have our way" is our motto.'

All the same he stood back and allowed her to walk by him, although as she did so Emma shuddered a little at the possibility that he might leap on her at the last moment. She was lucky, she thought, that he wanted an easy conquest—a woman he might buy, not one whom he would have to use force to obtain. He was not as brute a beast as Blackburn, but he held all women in as low esteem. She shuddered for Calypso Straight as well, if she succeeded in tying herself to such a creature.

She was alone at last. Lord Lufton had, for the time being perhaps, surrendered the field—or rather, Emma thought somewhat sardonically, more appropriately the park. The afternoon seemed sweeter with his going.

But not for long. She had hardly settled herself on a seat in the folly from where she could admire the murals showing the labours of Hercules—the day was too hot for her to do her canvaswork comfortably outside—when a shadow fell across the open doorway and a man came in to join her. For a moment—seeing that he was against the light and she could distinguish only his outline—she hoped that if it were anyone it would be m'lord. Alas, it was not. Instead it was her *bête noire*, Ben Blackburn.

Emma had no wish to be alone with him. She pushed her embroidery into her bag, rose and walked towards the door. But he stood there, immovable, grinning at her.

'Not so fast,' he told her, his eyes cruel. 'I saw that you held off Lufton. Were you waiting for Chard to join you here? If so, you will be disappointed. I left him in the house.'

'I was awaiting no one,' was all she said, as coolly as she could, for her heart was thumping cruelly so fell was the expression on his face. 'And it is time that I left to go to attend Lady Letitia.'

'Oh?' He leered at her. 'Now, that does surprise me, madam. Seeing that you must have arrived here only a few moments ago, after you gave Lufton his *congé*. Never tell me that you are running from me?'

He moved nearer to her, pushing her towards the opening which led to the interior room of the folly, from which they would be invisible to anyone strolling in the park.

Perforce Emma was thrust backwards, but though inwardly trembling she tried to show no fear. She put on a brave face and said, 'I had forgot the time. You will allow?' And she tried to pass him again.

He would have none of it. Instead he leaned

forward, put his large hand on her breast—for now they were almost touching, he having pushed her to the back wall of the inner room—and said suggestively, 'I have a mind for entertainment, madam. You are Chard's doxy, and therefore you are anyone's doxy. Ply your trade with me willingly, and I shall pay you for it.'

So saying, he put his left hand into his pocket, keeping his right cupped on her left breast, and threw two guineas on the floor. 'My money is as good as his, and I have more of it.'

This was Lord Lufton all over again, only worse. Emma said, as levelly as she could, 'M'lord told you not to trouble me, Mr Blackburn, and I think that you would be wise to heed what he told you.'

'Oh, damn that,' he shot back. '*Then* I wanted to retain his interest, but now I have no intention of financing Geordie Stephenson's ugly toy—so any hold he had on me is gone. I have a mind to enjoy myself before I leave Loudwater. I would ask you to go with me if you please me. You would have a better life with me than you have running after Chard's by-blow.'

'I do not wish to have anything to do with you, Mr Blackburn. Regardless of what you appear to think, I am an honest woman and intend to remain one.'

She tried to be as calm as possible in the hope that if she were calm she would not inflame him, but it was a useless hope. He pulled her towards him, saying, 'Not for long, madam. Not for long.

Besides, I do not believe that you are honest. I know what Chard's reputation was, and a man does not change for ever—not even Chard, monk though he may have been lately.'

It was hopeless. Struggle as she might, she had no chance of escaping from him. Nor could she hope for help. He had said that m'lord was back at the house. Perhaps it had been foolish of her to come here alone, but she had not thought that Ben Blackburn would try to force her again.

None the less, she shouted for help as loudly as she could whilst trying to fight him off, but it was useless. He was not a tall man but he was broad and heavy, and she was a small woman whom he was able to control without using his full strength. He began to tear at her dress, hurting her with his heavy hands and grinding his face into hers as he pushed her towards the sofa which stood in the corner of the room.

Impossible to hope that by some miracle she would be saved from him again. . . Stars danced before her eyes and her senses began to fail her under the relentless nature of his assault. He had reached the sofa, and there he pushed her onto her back, his heavy body on top of her. Still she tried to fight him, determined not to succumb without a struggle, but whatever she did was to no avail; his mouth and hands were all over her.

But just when all seemed lost, when, swearing and laughing, he was on the very verge of success, his weight on hers, and when she was lost in the blackness into which she was descending because she could scarcely breathe, his weight was suddenly gone. Voices were shouting—one was m'lord's. Emma sat up slowly, her ebbing consciousness restored now that she could breathe properly again.

Slowly and systematically m'lord, after pulling him off her, was giving Ben Blackburn the kind of drubbing which only a strong man trained in the skills of a pugilist could give another who was not. One last blow had him on the floor at Emma's feet.

M'lord, still cursing him, bent down, seized him by the hair of his head and lifted his bruised and marked face towards Emma. 'Damn you, Blackburn, apologise to Miss Lawrence before I have my footmen whip you out of the grounds,' he ground out. He was quite transformed from his usual quiet and pleasant self.

Emma recoiled from the bruised and tortured face turned towards her. 'No, no, I don't want his apologies. Nothing, no, nothing can wipe away what he has twice tried to do to me.' She turned her own bruised face away from that of her tormentor and stared desolately at the mural of Hercules strangling a snake in his cradle.

All the fight had gone out of her assailant and m'lord dragged him to his feet. His breath recovered, Ben snarled, 'I'll not apologise to your damned doxy, Chard, nor to you,' only to be struck again by m'lord, enraged by his continuing impudence.

This blow was so strong that Ben Blackburn was thrown to the ground beneath Hercules slaying the Nemean Lion, where he lay unmoving and half-conscious. Which did not stop m'lord from hauling him to his feet and beginning to strike him again.

He was stopped by Emma clutching his arm so strongly that he perforce let go of Blackburn, who fell to the floor to land this time in front of Hercules killing the Hydra. M'lord, as roused by anger as the god Hercules himself, cried out hoarsely to Emma, his eyes wild from the grip of the berserker rage which had seized him and in which he did not know his own strength.

'My darling, you must not stop me from punishing him for his wickedness to you. I should have done this when he attacked you before, instead of foolishly letting him go to attack you again.'

'No, no,' panted Emma. 'You saved me, and that must be enough. Think of the scandal if you should kill him, as you are like to do. You have already marked him for life. Let that be enough.'

They were interrupted by a groan from Ben, who had begun to crawl towards the door. He had never in his wildest imagination thought that Chard was other than the pleasant, highly civilised man whom he had always privately despised for his softness towards his friends and his servants.

M'lord's face changed. Sanity returned to it. He acknowledged ruefully to himself that on seeing Emma attacked so vilely his one instinct had been to kill the man who was trying to violate her. He stood back and said to Ben Blackburn as he hauled himself painfully to his feet, 'You will say nothing of this to anyone, nor will you mention Miss Lawrence's name publicly again—or I will call you out and make your punishment final.'

'Damn you, Chard,' Blackburn began, but feebly, with little trace of his former arrogance.

'And damn you too, Blackburn. If you won't give me your word that here is an end of it, that you will never go near Miss Lawrence again or seek to blacken her character, I shall finish what I have begun—despite her generous pleas for mercy for you.'

Head hanging low, the words, 'I promise,' were wrenched from Ben.

'Louder, man, louder,' said m'lord, all arrogance now, truly the Lord of All as he never usually was.

'I promise,' howled Ben, his look for them both one of thwarted malignance.

'Then go,' m'lord ordered sternly. 'But leave Loudwater immediately, making what excuse you like for doing so. You hear me, man?'

Ben nodded sullenly and stumbled out of the door, his hand to his ruined face.

Her legs failing her, Emma sank onto the wide sofa. Warm though the day was, she had begun to shiver and shake. She had rearranged her torn clothing and had pulled her light shawl from her bag to throw it about her shoulders—but still the hateful cold gripped her. M'lord, his face a mask of concern, came over to sit by her. He was careful not to touch her, for he was not sure how she would react to being so near to a man after Ben Blackburn's treatment of her.

Her shivering had now grown so strong that m'lord stripped off his countryman's jacket and hung it around her shoulders. She did not try to avoid his touch, but looked at him with great eyes, whispering, 'Why do I feel so cold? The day is hot.'

'They say that after being wounded in battle, men grow cold and shiver and tremble,' m'lord returned gently. 'And after some fashion you have been wounded in battle too.'

For a time they sat there in silence. Presently Emma found that the dreadful shuddering had stopped, although she still felt very strange— almost as though she were outside herself and had been watching something which had nothing to do with her. She said so to m'lord, and so saying felt the shivering begin again.

As he sat beside her the rage leached out of m'lord to be replaced by the most protective love. He put an arm around her to draw her to him so that she might share the warmth of his body, and Emma did not resist him.

She thought with a kind of tired wonder that whilst Ben Blackburn had repelled her even when he was not assaulting her, and she might have thought that she would feel the same for all men, m'lord's gentle touch soothed her, and as his warmth was transferred to her it became something inward instead of outward. He was her knight who had defended her, who had almost destroyed the man who had tried to rape her, and knights deserved their reward. She could not continue to hold him off, he who had saved her.

So presently, despite himself, m'lord's other arm crept around her and he dropped a kiss on the dark silk of her hair. For a moment Emma stiffened—it reminded her of Ben Blackburn—and then she thought drowsily, for the shivering had stopped and sleep seemed near—the sleep of recovery— Why should I fear him? For do I not love him, and has he not saved me?

There seemed only one answer to this, so that the next time m'lord kissed her—on the lips—she kissed him back, entranced, almost absentmindedly.

M'lord was in agony. He had just half killed a man for daring to force himself on her, and now here he was, growing the more roused by the minute as he held his darling in his arms. How could he, in decency, force *himself* on her, even though he might do so gently? But he did not need to use force. Emma, in the grip of relief, reaction, admiration and gratitude towards her saviour, who was also the man whom she loved, was kissing him gently on the cheek and on the back of the bruised hands which had defended her so nobly.

All the good resolutions of both of them had flown away. Emma's that she would defend her honour to the end against any man—even m'lord whom she had come to love; m'lord's that he would not take advantage of someone who served him and who should be able to trust him to behave correctly towards her. The struggle between love and duty for both of them had never been greater.

M'lord could not offer her marriage, because if he married again duty said that it should be to someone who could bring him the fortune which Loudwater needed, and his love was more penniless than he was! So it was his duty as well as his honour which bade him not to despoil her—as it was Emma's duty to refuse him, to keep her honour intact.

But time and chance had conspired to undo them and nullify all that had kept them apart. The caresses which had been offered in tenderness by m'lord in an effort to calm and reassure his love, and which had been returned in simple gratitude by Emma, gradually changed into an open expression of the unspoken passion which lay between them.

The tender exchanges grew stronger. M'lord's hands grew urgent, though not cruelly so, like Ben Blackburn's had been, for his great strength was subdued by his desire not to hurt his love. But he wished to do more than kiss her, and as Emma showed how willing she was to return his caresses tenderness became passion, freely given and freely taken. The afternoon sun streaming through the doorway gilded their love.

At what point they passed into the realm where the two of them desired to become one, neither knew. They only knew that to be lost in the other—who was also themself—was the one thing which they both wanted. Duty, honour, the proprieties and all the other things which had kept them apart were forgotten. They lay naked in one another's arms, beneath Hercules and his dear wife Deianira, and like them they celebrated their love after the fashion of all the men and women who have ever lived and loved on earth.

Breast to breast, heart to heart, all else was forgotten—even the pangs of lost virginity restrained neither of them. It was only that m'lord muttered thickly at the end, 'I am a brute beast to force myself on you. . .'

But Emma put her hand on his lips and said, 'Hush, m'lord, for I wanted this as much as you did.'

It might be all that she ever had of him, but it would have to be enough, and for the moment she wanted to savour what they had shared, not be ashamed of it, and she would not have him ashamed either.

Presently they slept for a time—the little sleep which follows great passion. They awoke to find they were still in each other's arms, the busy, curious world oppressing them again. It was imperative that others did not realise that both of them had disappeared at the same time—particularly if Ben Blackburn had not been cowed enough to prevent him from suggesting what she and m'lord might be getting up to if they were left alone with one another all afternoon. Neither of them could be sure of that—but still they dallied.

Emma was lying in the crook of m'lord's arm, and his first words were as tender as he could make them. 'I would not have your name and fame traduced, even though I am the one who has laid you open to the insults of the wagging tongues of the world. . . Say you forgive me.'

'Nothing to forgive, my dear lord,' replied Emma steadily. 'For I was your most willing accomplice.'

Afterwards she was to think with some amazement that the one thing which ought to have occupied both of them had never entered their heads: the possibility that she might be with child from their passionate encounter. It was as though they were living in Arcadia, where there were no consequences from passion fulfilled.

'I think, my heart, that you might call me something other than m'lord, seeing what we have just shared,' he said in a loving voice, putting both arms around her, still wanting her to be part of him even though they were now separate.

Emma shook her head. 'No, you will always be m'lord to me. I cannot think of you as other than that.' She did not wish to call him Dominic. That would be to acknowledge the past of which she had not yet told him and now feared to. The time when she might conveniently have confessed her true identity to him had long gone.

His next words served only to confirm that belief. 'The thing I value most in you,' he offered, turning his blazing blue eyes on her, 'is your honesty. Of all the women I have ever known you are the only one I can trust to tell me the truth. And if that truth means that I am m'lord to you, then so be it.'

No, she could not tell him now. Not after that. For Emma knew only too well that her honesty had its limits, and what would he think if he knew that everything about her, including her name, was a lie?

So she said nothing, and m'lord, still holding her tenderly to him, his eyes closed, mused on. 'I have to confess that like Lord Byron not only did I, as a young man, pursue, but I was also pursued—by those women who only wanted my name and the possible title I might inherit. I was not so conceited, then or now, as to think that I was such a catch for myself alone—though God knows, I was a conceited boy.'

He moved restlessly, as though his memories pained him. 'I remember one who pursued me relentlessly after her fashion. A small fat girl with a stammer, almost a child, and I—God forgive me—would have married her for the fortune she would have brought me. But for some reason—and why, I shall never know—she turned me down. Much to my chagrin, for I had thought that she cared for me—embarrassingly so. And whether that was a good thing or a bad thing I shall never know, for I sold myself after that to a beauty for her money. You see, I am trying to match your honesty, and if you despise me for what I was, then so be it. The time for lies has gone. Our marriage was a disaster.'

Silence followed until he spoke again. 'Whilst you—' he kissed her cheek reverently '—you are the other half of me. How strange. . . When I was scarce fledged—a mere boy—an old gypsy woman told me that I was one of the lucky ones, that I would find my own true love one day, yet when I first met her I would not know her. But, later, when I met her again, I would recognise her immediately as my other self. How wrong she was! I knew that you were meant for me when I first saw you standing in the hall. You are my better angel, come to save me. I do not believe that you are pursuing me because I am Earl. I know you too well for that.'

'M'lord. . .' Emma began, but could not finish. How could she tell him the truth now? Where would his belief in her honesty and her integrity be then? And what would he think of her when he discovered that she was the small fat girl whom he had despised? That she, whom he thought of as the soul of honour, had deceived him again and again. Had concealed her true identity from him. If he had known from the beginning that Emma Lawrence was Emilia Lincoln, who had jilted him

so cruelly, he would never have employed her. . . .
Her tormented thoughts went round and round.

'My love?' His voice was tender but drowsy. He
wanted to tell her that he was sorry for the poor fat
girl, who had probably been as lost as he had been,
and who, shortly afterwards, had disappeared from
society because of her father's ruin. But that could
wait. He also wanted to tell her that come what
may he loved her dearly and would marry her—
even though in worldly terms she would bring him
nothing. She would bring him love, and that was
more than enough. But he did not want to spoil
the tender spell which had brought them together
by dwelling on such sordid considerations. There
would be world enough and time to tell her of all
that she meant to him.

She had brought him peace and would continue
to do so, he was sure of that, and so he fell asleep,
content.

Emma could not sleep and was not content. She
was that lost child again—whom he had met and
had not known. He had changed, had he not? And
so had she. And, much though she loved him, she
would never be his mistress, would not creep
stealthily to his bed. She loved him too much for
that. His honour—and hers—must remain intact.
She had shared with him a precious moment
outside time and that must be enough. He had
never mentioned marriage to her, and she would
neither mention it nor demand it.

She slipped out of his arms and began to dress

herself. She must leave him before they were found. Pretend that what had happened had not happened, and make the pretence come true.

Tidy at last, she gave him one final look. To discover that in sleep the years had fallen away from him and he had the look of the handsome boy whom she had once known. Emma shuddered a little. She wished to kiss him goodbye, but she dared not wake him. And, thinking so, she picked up her bag and walked out of the folly into the late afternoon sun, praying that no one was about or had seen m'lord on his way to rescue her.

Luck was with her. She walked on, down by the stream, making a great circle to come to the house from a direction far away from the folly—one more deceit to add to the list of all those which she had practised. But nothing mattered now other than her determination to leave Loudwater and her love as soon as she could, hard though that might be. He deserved more from life than an illicit affair which would bring shame and scandal on them both.

All the way to her room she hugged to herself the thought that she was loved and had loved, and that was more than most women ever experienced, even though all she would have would be the memories of her one encounter with him.

# CHAPTER TWELVE

'HAVE to go,' muttered Ben Blackburn thickly, trying, ineffectually, to hide his damaged face in his handkerchief as he passed Lord Lufton in the hall on his way to his waiting carriage. 'Message from home—wanted urgently.'

There was no one else about, so Lord Lufton caught him by the arm, smiled nastily and said, 'Chard's handiwork?'

'Eh? What's that? Oh, my face. No, took a fall on Rufus this afternoon. Good thing I got off so lightly.'

'Oh?' Lord Lufton was derisive. 'Not Chard, then? Had another go at the governess, did you? Followed her to the folly? Never saw you on Rufus.'

Ben snarled viciously at him. 'Spying on me, were you, Lufton?'

'Have a mind to win my bet, Blackburn. Caught you at it, did he? Was she with him when you left? I saw him on his way to the folly too, after I left her. No sign that either of them is back yet.'

'Damn you, Lufton. I told you what happened. Now let me go. Matters at home urgent.'

'Not before you pay me what you owe me now you've lost your bet. My turn to try to thwart Chard now.'

The much battered Blackburn had had enough. He dropped the handkerchief which had been muffling his face and his voice, and snarled, 'And much good it may do you. He's broken my nose for nothing. God knows what he'd do to you if you put a foot wrong. And if it'll keep you quiet here's an advance on the fifty guineas you claim I owe you for losing the bet—not that I did, mind.' He threw some guineas on the floor at Lord Lufton's feet, as he had thrown them at Emma. 'I'm admitting nothing about the governess—but anything for a quiet life.'

'Properly cowed you, didn't he?' grinned Lufton. 'Threw you out and told you to keep quiet, didn't he? I'll fetch a footman to pick up your guineas, and you can forward me the rest. You may be sure I shan't put a foot wrong where the governess is concerned. I value my nose too much for that.'

'And damn you too,' muttered Ben as Lufton strode away, whistling gently, amused at a rival's downfall. 'And if I don't pay Chard back for what he's done, my name's not Ben Blackburn.'

All the way home he had but one thought, and that a black one. One way or another he would break more than Chard's nose for him.

There were two missing at dinner that day: Ben Blackburn and the governess. M'lord had woken up to find that his love had fled. He took it for granted that she had chosen the way of prudence, but he wished that she had not. He had wanted to hold her in his arms again and tell her that she should be his Countess and they would try to save Loudwater together. He could hardly wait to see her again.

Even so Mrs Morton's informing him that Miss Lawrence had a severe headache and consequently would not be down for dinner did not serve to depress him overmuch. He thought even more tenderly of her for not wishing to face the stares of others after their passionate encounter. Ben Blackburn's absence would have been passed over in silence had not Lord Lufton, more than ever sure now how m'lord and the governess had passed their time in the folly, said meaningfully, 'Hear that Blackburn had to leave suddenly, Chard. Affairs at home claimed him, he said.'

He managed to make the two last words sound sinister, a feat in itself, but m'lord was not to be drawn.

'So I understand,' he almost drawled, and attacked his dinner with gusto at the thought of Blackburn being driven home nursing his nose. He looked a little sideways at Lufton, thinking for the first time that he might have to protect Emma from him. On the other hand he thought that Lufton might be a little more subtle in his approach to her. In any case, once the world knew that she was to be Lady Chard she should be safe from those who might choose to prey on mere governesses.

He considered for a moment going to her rooms

to speak to her, but dismissed the notion. He must not expose his dear love to idle and unpleasant comment before he had the right to protect her as his betrothed.

Calypso Straight, who knew nothing of what had passed in the folly that afternoon, had already asked where Miss Lawrence was, and, on being told by Mrs Morton that she was feeling a little unwell, had chosen to sigh, 'Oh, indeed? One is not surprised. She does so much, does she not?' An ambiguous comment which she could not resist making and which set Lady Clara tittering—at what, she was not quite sure.

At the same time Miss Straight was relieved to learn that she would have Lord Lufton's sole attention over dinner instead of having to share it with the governess. She would have been even more relieved to learn that Miss Lawrence was not stretched out on a bed of pain but was packing to leave, and was also working out how best she could get safely away without m'lord or anyone else stopping her.

The only thing which sustained her was the memory of lying in m'lord's arms—a memory which was all that she would take with her from Loudwater. Honour demanded her flight, but her eyes filled with unshed tears not only at the thought of leaving m'lord but of deserting Tish, whom she had come to love. She could hardly write the letters which she was leaving behind her, so blinded was she by her tearless emotion.

No matter. All through the long night watches she sat at her bedroom window, for she knew that she would not be able to sleep. She would leave at first light. She would go to the stables and ask one of the grooms whom she knew would already be on duty to drive her to Alnwick where she would board the stage for London. She would tell him that her news from London was so urgent that she had no time to waste before she left. If he thought her behaviour was strange, then so be it. If he would not do as she wished she would walk to the nearest village and hire a carriage to take her to the stage.

She dozed a little before morning came, and then she picked up the two small bags containing her few possessions and set off for the stables, hoping that she would meet no one on the way. It was a wish which was almost granted—until at the last turn of the stairs whom should she encounter but. . . Calypso Straight!

She was wearing a light bedgown over her night rail. Her hair was down and the look of shock on her face when they met mirrored that on Emma's. Emma knew at once where she had spent the night. Where else but in Lord Lufton's bed?

Miss Straight spoke first. Her eyes took in Emma, her neat travelling coat and bonnet, and the two bags she was carrying. 'So, you are leaving us, I see. I suppose that he bedded you, and, that being so, you are sensibly leaving him. I commend your common sense in doing so, seeing that he will never marry you.'

Emma shivered a little, but could not resist saying quietly, 'But you, I believe, *are* lacking in common sense. Lord Lufton will not marry you, I think.'

'Oh, but there you are wrong,' returned Miss Straight triumphantly. 'You may congratulate me, for he has asked me to marry him and has written to the *Morning Post* informing them of our betrothal. I would not have indulged him else.'

The look she gained in return was a steady one. Emma felt a great sadness sweep over her for the other woman, whose plight was so similar to her own. It was that, not spite, which caused her to say, as gently as she could, 'There is an old proverb of which you might take note: There's many a slip 'twixt cup and lip.'

'Oh, I leave *you* to consider that.' Miss Straight's tone was contemptuous. 'Well, well, I will not keep you. The London coach does not wait long at Alnwick, and you will want to be on your way. Goodbye, Miss Lawrence. I wish you better luck in your next adventure.'

Emma inclined her head and continued on her way down the stairs. Miss Straight was at least correct in one of her suppositions: time was short and she had a coach to catch. It would not do to miss it, to have m'lord come after her once he realised that she had gone. . .

* * *

It was some time before m'lord knew that his love had deserted him. The need not to offer Lord Lufton's party any ammunition with which to attack her prevented him from rushing, once breakfast was over, to the schoolroom to be with her. No need; the whole day lay before them.

He was seated at his desk in the mid-morning, trying to concentrate on the accounts which his agent had brought him, when all he could think of was what he would say to her when next they met. For years he had never felt so light-hearted, so carefree.

Thus the sudden and agitated arrival of Mrs Morton, her kind old face agitated, came as a most unwelcome surprise.

'Oh, m'lord, I have the strangest news for you. Miss Lawrence has gone. It seems that she left Loudwater at dawn. Sim drove her to Alnwick to catch the London stage. She left letters for you, myself and Tish on my work table. I took the liberty of reading mine at once, and Kettie has given Tish hers, and she is inconsolable, and I have brought you yours.'

She held it out to him. M'lord, who had grown white to the lips at her news, was so stunned that although he rose he did not take it from her.

'No.' He almost stammered. 'No, that cannot be. She cannot have gone. You must be mistaken. I am sure that you are.'

'No mistake, m'lord. Read your letter, I beg of you.' She waved it at him.

He could not believe what he was hearing. Gone? After their afternoon of passion? He took the letter from Mrs Morton, and said numbly, 'I must ask you to leave me while I read it.'

'Of course, m'lord.' And then, because he looked so ill, she asked, 'Are you quite well? May I bring you a cordial?'

He, who was usually so well-mannered, did not answer her, but feverishly ripped open the carefully sealed letter to learn that, yes, his love had left him. He was alone again, and this time for life. There would never be another woman for him now.

My dear lord,
    If I leave you it is not because I do not love you dearly, but because I do. I found our loving so sweet that if I stay I shall be unable to resist the temptation to taste that sweetness again and again.
    And if I did I should become your mistress, and that would be not only to commit a sin but would surely end in unhappiness for us both. In honour I cannot stay, and in honour, things being as they are, you would not wish me to. I write this with a breaking heart, but break it I must.
    Remember me, Emma Lawrence.

Remember her! How could he not remember her? She had brought hope and joy into his life again. He crushed the letter slowly in his hands. She could not leave him! He would not let her! He would follow her—to hell or to heaven; it mattered not which. He would find her and tell her that even if, at first, he had wished to make her only his mistress, his love had grown so great that he wished her to be his wife.

And why had he not told her so immediately? What had possessed him to believe that she would know of his intentions? Why had he not had the wit to see that living as she did in their world she could only believe that a great gentleman who bedded his daughter's governess would never marry her? He had said and done nothing to make her believe otherwise. Every look, every comment made on her situation by others whilst she had been at Loudwater would only have served to remind her of her place—that of someone who was neither a servant nor a lady, and therefore not to be considered.

And why was he standing here? He must go after her, find her and bring her back.

And then he remembered that his sister had engaged her, and that he had never known where she had lived before she came to Loudwater—and why was he dallying, lost in grief? He must be on his way to Alnwick—the coach might have been delayed; anything might have happened.

He had been fearful that his errand might be fruitless, and so it turned out to be. He returned to Loudwater alone again, having tasted Paradise. He had loved an honourable woman, and because he had not spoken his mind to her she had behaved honourably and left him. Even his sister, when he wrote to her, could not tell him of Miss Lawrence's home address, because she had hired her for him on the recommendation of Mrs Gardiner, who was now in Paris.

In his desperation, he even applied to her for help, but she knew of no other address for Emma than that of the last position which she had held before she hired her. . . Unconsidered, humble Miss Emma Lawrence was unknown to society, and his chances of ever finding her again were small.

'Papa is so sad these days,' Tish confided miserably to Mrs Morton. 'And I am sure that it is because Miss Lawrence has left us. Oh, why did she have to go? I liked her, and so did Papa. Surely she could have stayed. I thought that she was happy here.'

Mrs Morton, more wise in the ways of the world, said gently, 'I think that she left us because she felt that she ought to, my dear. It was probably a hard decision for her.'

Unaware of m'lord's wish to marry Emma, she privately approved of Miss Lawrence's decision to sever herself from him. Nothing good could have come from such a liaison—even if m'lord's distress at her going was so patently obvious. He had been like a madman on the day of her disappearance, all his usual calm control quite gone.

And now that she had departed for good he had

become again the withdrawn man he had been before Miss Lawrence had arrived to be his daughter's governess. It might have been better, after all, if she had consented to be his mistress! One had to hope that without a reference from m'lord she would be able to find another post. . .

'My dear!' exclaimed Mrs Gore when Emma suddenly and surprisingly arrived at her little house near Clapham Common. 'I did not expect to see you again so soon, without warning. I have so much to tell you. Your arrival is most providential—it has saved a great deal of time and trouble. I have had your late father's lawyers here. They have been trying to trace you for some months. They were unaware that you had changed your name, and they had almost given up their search for you when someone remembered that you and I were friendly. Two of them came to see me this morning, to discover whether I knew where you might be found.'

She paused for breath as Emma, stunned by this news and tired from her long journey, collapsed into an armchair.

'Why?' she asked fearfully. 'Why would they want to speak to me after all this time? I hope that you did not inform them that I was at Loudwater!'

'No, indeed, for you had begged me never to give anyone a hint of your whereabouts. I said that I knew where you were living and that I would write to tell you that they wished to speak to you.'

She waved an excited hand at the table where an inkstand, a quill pen and paper were all laid out and a letter was half-written.

'And did they give you any hint of why, after all this time, they were so desirous of finding me?'

'None at all. Only that the matter was of the utmost urgency. Wait! They gave me their address and said that if you were in London you were to visit them immediately. To do so would be greatly to your advantage! What could they mean by that? I asked, but they would not tell me. It was you to whom they wished to speak.'

And then she looked at Emma's weary face. 'Oh, my dear, I am so excited that I have forgotten what a hard journey you must have had. Let me brew you some tea. You will want something to eat and a comfortable bed, no doubt, and then you must be off to the lawyers in the morning!'

Emma could not share Mrs Gore's excitement. She was too weary, too stricken at the thought of the number of miles which separated her from m'lord. All the same she felt a faint wonder at what her father's lawyers could wish to tell her that was so important that they had succeeded in exciting the usually placid Mrs Gore by their urgency.

She would think about it in the morning, after a good night's sleep.

By morning, indeed, her indifference had been succeeded by a vague sense of excitement, which grew even stronger when she was shown into the office of Mr John Manson, the senior partner of

Manson and Wade. She remembered them as superior beings who had had business with her father.

Mr Manson, a tall, thin man with a clever face, greeted her with unusual warmth. 'My dear Miss Lincoln, I am so relieved that we have at last found you. We have great news for you! You remember my partner, Mr Charles Wade?'

Yes, Miss Lincoln remembered Mr Wade, who now looked at her with open admiration. Obviously being made love to by m'lord had subtly increased her ability to attract other men. She said nothing, however, but a cool, 'I remember you both. I am sorry to learn that you had so much difficulty in finding me. I changed my name to Lawrence when it became plain that no one wished to hire the daughter of the disgraced suicide Mr Henry Lincoln.'

Mr Manson looked a little uncomfortable at this reminder of his late patron's fate, but he soon brightened up, saying jovially, 'But that is one of the matters of which I wish to speak to you. It appears that your late father almost certainly did not commit suicide, that he was, in fact, murdered by the person who swindled him and stole his fortune, leaving you to live in penury.'

The room swung around Emma. She was aware of young Mr Wade saying agitatedly, 'Drink this, Miss Lincoln,' and holding out a glass of water which he had poured whilst Mr Manson had been supporting her lest she fall from her chair.

'Foolish of me,' chattered Mr Manson, 'to break it to you so abruptly.'

'No,' retorted Emma, her colour returning as she drank the water. 'Foolish of me to be so weak. But it is a great shock, as I am sure you understand—particularly about poor Papa. He was so vilely traduced in the newspapers at the time for being a swindler himself. When did you discover this, Mr Manson? And why do you wish to speak to me?' She put the empty glass down and folded her hands together, awaiting his reply.

Both men were full of admiration for her common sense and for her swift recovery of her self-control. Mr Manson said, 'You knew, of course, that your father had a junior partner—a Mr George Swain. Your father trusted him, but it was he who embezzled your father's funds and brought him to bankruptcy and ruin. It was thought that he was ruined too, but after a time he started a business with what he said was a small legacy left him by an aunt, and he was successful. What no one knew was that his fortune was infinitely greater than that his business made for him, and that he lived in luxury and comfort on what he had stolen from your father.

'Earlier this year he visited Swanage for a holiday with his family. He had a wife, a handsome and clever son and a daughter. One day he took them sailing. There was an accident. He was rescued, but his wife and children were drowned. He was naturally distraught and took it as God's judgement on him for what he had done to your father.

'He shot himself, but not before he had sent me a letter in which he told me in detail how he had ruined your father and made off with his fortune. He then killed him after such a fashion that it appeared that he had committed suicide. He was fearful that your father, being a clever man, might discover what he had done.

'Enclosed in the letter was his new will in which he left everything he possessed to you, as some expiation for what he had done. You are a rich woman again, Miss Lincoln, and may resume your rightful place in society.'

'I am sorry for the deaths of his wife and family,' said Emma slowly, 'but I cannot forgive him for what he did to my father. This news is of no benefit to him, other than to restore his good name. As to my rightful place in society. . .' She shrugged. 'I have no notion what that now is! I have been a governess for almost the last nine years.'

Both men looked profoundly shocked. Mr Manson said, 'I know that your father had no living relatives, but what of your mother's family, Miss Lincoln? Did they do nothing for you? I own that I was surprised when I applied to them as to your whereabouts and they said that they had had nothing to do with you since your father's disgrace.'

'Nothing,' replied Emma steadily, neither judgement nor reproach in her voice. 'They did nothing for me. Had it not been for the kindness of my dear friend Mrs Gore, my father's house-keeper, I should have starved. As it was, she gave me a home until I found my first post as a governess.'

She did not say that immediately after her father's death she had gone to her aunt's home for help and refuge and that her uncle had told his servants to turn her from the door, seeing that her father had impoverished him. He had had a great deal of his fortune invested in her father's ventures, and it had all been swallowed up in the bank-ruptcy. For that he could not forgive either his brother-in-law or his daughter.

Mr Manson tut-tutted over such heartlessness for a few moments, conveniently forgetting that though he was an old friend of Henry Lincoln, he too had done nothing for his daughter. 'I see no difficulty with probate, Miss Lincoln. Under English law, Mr Swain's ill-gotten fortune will revert to you in any case—seeing that he has confessed both to the embezzlement and your father's murder—and so your father's will, made in your favour before he died, will stand.

'A criminal cannot profit from his crime. He has simply made your inheritance easier. I shall be happy to advance you monies so that you may be able to live a life commensurate with your fortune until all the legal formalities of inheritance are complied with.'

'There will, I suppose,' said Emma, rising, 'be a large number of documents for me to sign.'

'Oh, indeed. But later, later. I shall inform you as soon as possible when you are required. You will leave me your address, and inform me of any change in it? Mr Wade will be only too happy to assist you should there be anything that you require between now and then.'

She had become exceedingly rich again, so Mr Manson was only too happy to fawn on her. What he and Mr Wade would have made of poor Miss Emma Lawrence was quite another thing!

So overcome was she by the bittersweet nature of the news which she had so suddenly and surprisingly received that it was only when she was on the way home to Mrs Gore's in the cab which Mr Wade had summoned for her that Emma thought again of m'lord.

What was he doing, back in Northumbria? Was he thinking of the poor governess who had left him as she was constantly thinking of him? At least she knew that when he had made love to her he had not done so because she was rich Miss Lincoln.

And that was a thought to hug to herself in the long days and long nights which followed her restoration to the world of wealth and society.

# CHAPTER THIRTEEN

MISS EMILIA LINCOLN'S reappearance in the *ton* was one of the most remarkable events of the year. It was equalled only by the news of Napoleon's flight from Elba and that Lord Lufton was to marry a simple nobody—even if she was of good, if not distinguished birth. Before the next season it would all be forgotten, but meantime the *on dits* flew around society. Letters from those still in town were written to those exiled in the country, and excited letters flew back again. The scandal sheets were full of hints, blanks, exclamation marks and suggestive cartoons.

The reverberations of Emma's changed fortune—she could not think of herself as Emilia; she had been Emma too long—were many and varied. . .

A notice from the columns of the *Morning Post*, September 1814:

We have received advice that the death some years ago of Mr Henry Lincoln was attributable not to suicide, as was supposed, but to murder committed by his junior partner Mr George Swain, who by prolonged embezzlement caused the collapse of the House of Lincoln. Mr Swain, overcome by remorse, has himself committed suicide after confessing his crimes and restoring the Lincoln fortune to Miss Emilia Lincoln, the late Mr Lincoln's only child. Thus is obeyed the old maxim, *Magna est veritas et praevalet*—Great is truth and it prevails.

An extract from Miss Emilia Lincoln's private journal, September 1814:

I cannot but regret that today I have discovered that I shall not be having m'lord's child. However inconvenient it might have been to produce an illegitimate offspring, it would have been some memory of our love, and therefore would have been most welcome to me. . . Shall I ever see him again? And, if we were to meet, how would he behave when he learned that I had deceived him as to my identity? 'O what a tangled web we weave, When first we practise to deceive. . .'

Sir Thomas Liddell to the Earl of Chard. November 1814:

I have some good news for you. The withdrawal from our little syndicate of Lufton and Blackburn has been more than made up for by my receipt of a draft from Coutts Bank. It is on behalf of Miss Emilia Lincoln, who has indicated that she wishes to join us in investing money in Mr Stephenson's engine! She has instructed me that she desires to be kept in touch with Mr Stephenson's progress. I am more than happy to oblige her. . .

Anne, Lady Fontaine, to her niece, Miss Emilia Lincoln, November 1814:

My dear niece,

I write this letter with some natural diffidence since I am asking you to forget what happened between us some nine years ago so that I may be able to call upon you when next we visit London.

My husband, whose cruel edict I was most sorrowfully compelled to obey when he forbade you to enter our house after your father's death, is overcome by remorse since he received the banker's draft from Coutts which restored his lost investments to him in full. It was drawn up on your advice, but arrived with no word from you.

I am aware that in asking you to forgive us for refusing you help and succour when you so greatly needed it I am asking of you that which you may not be prepared to grant, but you are my sister's child, and I acknowledge that you have been most grievously wronged. . .

Mr Ben Blackburn to Jacob Stroud, City of London Moneylender, December 1814:

How dare you send me such a curst peremptory letter demanding that I settle at once the bills I have taken out with you? I'll have you know that as a gentleman I am not prepared to accept such insolence from those of a lower station than mine. You shall have your money when I am ready to pay you, and not before. In the meantime, cease to dun me.

Miss Emilia Lincoln to Lady Fontaine, December 1814:

In replying to your letter I was at first tempted to adapt the famous words of Dr Samuel Johnson to Lord Chesterfield, when he was in a similar case to mine. 'The notice which you have been pleased to take of my labours, had it been early, had been kind; but it has been delayed till I am indifferent. . .till I am known, and do not want it.'

But I cannot forget that you were my dear mother's sister, that like most women you have no control over your husband's actions and that I am alone in the world and will remain so if I leave unrecognised the claims of those relatives I do possess—even if in my greatest need they deserted me.

Of course you may call on me, and we shall endeavour to forget the years which have passed since our last meeting, and think and speak only of the future.

Anne, Lady Fontaine, to her niece, Miss Emilia Lincoln. January 1815:

You are too generous. . .

A notice from the columns of the *Morning Post*, February 1815:

> The marriage which had been arranged between Augustus, third Earl of Lufton, and Miss Calypso Straight will not now take place.

Miss Calypso Straight to Lord Lufton, February 1815:

> How could you be so cruel as to humiliate me before all the world by informing the *Morning Post* that you had called off our marriage before informing me? I had spent the morning with the lawyers, arranging the details of my marriage to you, and the afternoon buying my bridal wear. In the evening I attended Lady Cowper's Ball to find myself the subject of the jeers and smirks of all those who had read the announcement in the public prints—as I had not done.
>
> I cannot believe that you mean this. Say that it is a hoax or a dreadful mistake, for if it be the truth I am ruined. . . .

Lord Lufton to Miss Calypso Straight, February 1815:

> I can only suppose that the damned letter telling you of my decision to call off the marriage went astray on the way to London. You must admit that I proposed to you in a moment of madness—it wouldn't have done at all. Particu-

larly when you were so free with your favours to me without the benefit of marriage.

In consequence, when the madness had passed, I was a little troubled by the notion that once married, you were like to be as free with others as you were with me. I enclose a banker's draft to cover the cost of your bridal wear.

You will not, of course, return here to be my sister's companion. It would not be proper.

From the columns of *The Times*, March 10th, 1815:

It is reliably reported that the usurper, Bonaparte, having escaped from the Isle of Elba to which he had been confined, is on his way to Paris. . .

Mr Ben Blackburn to Mr Jacob Stroud, City of London Moneylender, March 1815:

Damn you for sending the bailiffs in. This is no way to treat a gentleman. I was obliged to retreat to the nearest inn to find a bed and they had the impudence to demand their money in advance, since your men had been running around the district gossiping about my debts. . .

Miss Emilia Lincoln to Sir Thomas Liddell, April 1815:

I write to tender you my most sincere thanks for the information which you have sent me on the progress of Mr George Stephenson's travel-

ling engine—or locomotive, as it is now known.
Should you require further capital to support his
venture, do not hesitate to inform me at once. . .

The Lady Letitia Hastings to her father, the Earl
of Chard, April 1815:

When are you coming home from Newcastle,
Papa? I am very unhappy now that you as well as
Miss Lawrence have left Loudwater. You said
that you would not be away for long, but you
have been gone a month. Mrs Morton is kind,
but she does not know very much about the
Romans. I miss Miss Lawrence very much. Why
did she have to go?

The Earl of Chard to his daughter, Lady Letitia
Hastings, April 1815:

I am sorry that I have been compelled to be
away from home for much longer than I had
expected. I may, indeed, have to travel to
London soon. Mrs Morton informs me that you
have been a good girl and have shown great
diligence in your studies with her. I have not yet
been able to find a governess whom I consider
suitable to instruct you. As Mrs Morton
observes, Miss Lawrence will be hard to replace,
and I am aware that you feel her loss keenly. . .

M'lord put down his pen and passed his hand
over his eyes wearily. Tish was not the only one to
miss her governess. She could not regret her loss

more than her papa did. All efforts to trace her had come to nothing. The ill-fated house-party had broken up the day after her flight, and he had severed all his connections with both Lufton and Blackburn.

Blackburn he would never willingly speak to again after his treatment of Emma. The wretch ought to count himself lucky that he had not been brought before a court of law! He also suspected that Lufton had pestered Emma, but he had no proof of that. M'lord's breach with him came as a consequence of two events which had occurred after Emma's departure.

Before he'd left Loudwater, Lufton had offered him the hand of his sister, Lady Clara.

'You see, old fellow,' he had drawled at m'lord, 'I would value an alliance with you. Of course, if you do accept her I would carry on supporting Stephenson. Otherwise. . . Need I say more?'

'No, indeed.' M'lord was curt in dealing with this crude attempt at blackmail. 'But much though I value both you and your sister, I must inform you that I have no mind for marriage. You must do as you see fit over the business of investing in Stephenson.'

'Oh, I quite understand.' Lufton's tone was as nasty as he could make it. 'About marriage, I mean. Much better to bed the little governess, was it, rather than commit one's self to a new countess? After all, she might cuckold you as the last one did. I'm surprised that you give houseroom to another

man's leavings, though. Noble of you to acknowledge the child.'

Lufton's anger was caused by m'lord's failure to
take his sister off his hands. She would be around
his neck for ever; that was plain. As plain as
Calypso Straight—who was foolish enough to
think that she had caught him. She would soon
learn differently, but that piece of spite could wait
until he was away from Loudwater. As for investing in Stephenson, Chard must be mad to think
that there was any future in locomotives running
on tramways!

M'lord was too dispirited by his loss to take
offence at what Lufton had said. For a moment the
rage which had overtaken him when Ben
Blackburn had tried to force Emma rose again, but
if he let it overcome him he would be in danger of
handing Lufton a bigger beating than the one he
had handed Blackburn. But to what avail? It would
not bring Emma back to him.

No. The simplest way to deal with Lufton was
to ignore the insult to Emma and make sure that
their paths never crossed again. So he said nothing
and let the man and his unlovely sister leave
Loudwater, never to return.

I shall become a hermit, he thought savagely.
Only to discover when he went to Newcastle to
meet Sir Thomas Liddell and Stephenson again in
April that there was no danger of that.

'You must go to London,' Liddell told him
eagerly. 'To try to convince them down there that

we, here in the North, hold the future in our hands. I want you to lay the groundwork with your fellow peers so that when we put forward a Parliamentary Bill allowing us to build a railway across country we shall have made enough converts to support us.'

M'lord demurred a little. 'I have little influence in the political world. . .' he began.

'Nonsense,' returned Sir Thomas vigorously. 'You are related to nearly all the great men who rule us. I know that you have been an exile in the North for many years, but it will not take you long to be accepted once again, and then you may put forward our plans and say how well and speedily they are progressing.'

M'lord opened his mouth to argue with him, and then closed it again. Why not go to London? It was years since he had left—nearly nine to be exact. And if he did might there not be a slim chance that he would find news of Emma?

Sir Thomas was speaking again. 'And while you are there,' he continued, full of enthusiasm, 'you must try to meet Miss Emilia Lincoln. She has written to me again thanking me for my kindness in sending her information on Geordie's progress. It would be of all things the best if one of us was to thank her personally. You are such a steady fellow, Chard, that I have the utmost trust in your judgement.'

To meet Emilia Lincoln again and thank her! Thank the woman who had jilted him! The small fat stammering girl—who must now be a small fat stammering woman, still unmarried—who had unexpectedly recovered her fortune. It was the last thing which he wished to do, but he could hardly tell Sir Thomas so.

'Very well,' he said grudgingly. 'It would be pleasant to see London again, I suppose, and renew my acquaintance with William Lamb and the rest of the cousinry. Like me they will have grown older—and, I suppose, steadier.'

So Liddell considered him to be a steady fellow! He thought ruefully that Sir Thomas would be most surprised to learn what a conceited, selfish and unsteady fellow the young Dominic Hastings had been. He supposed that his old friends might be equally surprised at the change in him when they met him after so many years.

'I shall go to Loudwater first,' he said, 'after you have briefed me, and then travel to London as soon as I can arrange it. I shall have to open the house off Piccadilly again. I suppose that so early in the season town will be half-empty.'

'Not necessarily,' Sir Thomas returned, happy that he was not having to travel to the Great Sewer—his name for London. 'If it is half-empty—why, so much the better. The dinners are smaller and better—and that goes for the balls and receptions too. I quite envy you.'

M'lord did not envy himself, but there was nothing for it. He owed Liddell a debt of gratitude, and the only consolation was that he might be able to trace his lost love, who was continually in his thoughts and dreams.

'No, Miss Emma,' said Mrs Gore briskly, 'I cannot be your companion now that you are back in society again. I shall be happy to be your housekeeper and your friend, but you need a lady to accompany you in your new circumstances.'

However much Emma argued with her, saying that she had no intention of going into society again and would be leading a quiet life, she would not give way. 'That is what you say now, my dear, but the time will come when you will change your mind—mark my words.'

The consequence was that after she had written to her old duenna, Miss Dacre, that lady consented to return—as her companion this time. Emma had bought a little house in Chelsea and had filled it with small treasures—china, books, music—and old pieces of furniture which resembled those which had once filled her own home. That was long gone—sold to pay Henry Lincoln's supposed debts—and Emma's childhood had gone with it. She had lost everything—even the dolls and the various trinkets which her father had lavished on her. They had all been sold to help to pay his many supposed debts. . .

'My dear,' her aunt said, embracing her on her first visit. 'How handsome you have grown! Far from diminishing you, the years have brought about a great improvement.'

'Come, come, Aunt.' Emma smiled. 'I am past my last prayers, as you well know. I shall become a busy spinster lady.'

'Oh, no—' her aunt was shrewd '—not with the Lincoln fortune, my dear. Suitors will be beating a path to your door, and your mantelpiece will be full of invitation cards from every London hostess worth the name. I shall be only too happy to sponsor you.'

Emma thought wryly of the lost years, when no one had sponsored her, but she said nothing of that, only, 'Fortune-hunters all, my dear aunt. I had my fill of them when I was a young girl.'

'But now you are mature enough to sort out the good from the bad, my dear.' She hesitated. 'There was one thing which puzzled me, my love. Why did you refuse Dominic Hastings when he offered for you? He was perhaps not a great catch then, but your father and I thought that you liked him. He is now, in case you are unaware of it, the Earl of Chard. He made, they say, a most unfortunate marriage. His wife died some years ago—I believe there was a child, a girl. I thought you most suited, and to have married him would have meant your escaping the ruin which followed your father's unhappy death.'

She coloured a little, remembering how little support Emma had received from any of her mother's relatives, and said faintly, 'You will allow me to introduce you into society again, I trust. I see that you have got Dacre back. I am in trouble over my own companion, Miss Harley. She is to marry, despite her advanced years, a most respectable clergyman. I am pleased for her, but I shall miss her. We have sorted so well together for so long. I shall find her difficult to replace.'

Emma nodded and her aunt swept on. Emma had forgotten what a gossip she was. 'I shall be compelled to tell you of all the *on dits* and scandals so that when you do accompany me you will be sure not to say the wrong thing.' She launched into a series of stories and recitatives about persons of whom Emma had never heard, until her attention was caught by Miss Calypso Straight's name.

'Such a scandal, my pet.' Aunt Fontaine could not find enough loving names to shower on Emma. 'Imagine, Lufton jilted her even as she was buying her bride clothes. The whisper is that he did so because she had been a. . .little. . .forward with him, and consequently he drew back. I am sure you know whereof I speak!

'Of course she will not be received—except by those cousins of hers, the Straights of Shropshire. One fears for her future. She had been part of Lufton's household as his sister's companion, I hear, but that will never do now—and she as poor as a church mouse too.'

The Straights of Shropshire! Emma remembered Miss Straight's catechism of her and of her supposed family, and knew that they were two sides of the same coin. Both had lost their place in society, both had been poverty stricken, living on the mercy of others in return for the services they could do for them as governess and taken-for-granted companion.

Then Emma had been down and Calypso Straight had been up, hoping to be Lufton's Countess. Now she was down and Emma was up. Would the coin be tossed in the air again, and if so, how would it fall? Emma thought not. It had been tossed for good and all.

Pity swept over her—a real pity, not the easy variety her aunt was offering, with poor Calypso being given idle lip-service before she passed on to retail the next bit of delicious scandal to her newly found niece.

Emma could not but wonder how her aunt had spoken of *her* after her ruin. Not once did she ask her about her years of exile, and Emma made a point of never speaking of them. They were gone, as m'lord had gone. She was unlikely ever to meet him again, for she knew that he never came to London and Emma had resolved never to visit Northumbria. The only contact there would be her letters to Sir Thomas.

Mr Manson had been patronisingly amused about her interest in Mr George Stephenson. 'A dreamer,' he had said. 'I am sure that nothing will come of this engine you speak of, but no reason why you should not invest a little in him. Speak to Mr Coutts of it first, though.'

Mr Coutts had been more encouraging when she had visted him at his bank—partly to arrange

the draft for Sir Thomas, and partly to discuss the
enormous fortune which his bank had held for her
since Mr Swain's suicide. 'An excellent project,'
he had said. 'I have heard good reports of Mr
Stephenson. I am told that he is your true hard-
headed Northerner, as I understand Sir Thomas
is. I will see to it for you.'

He did not mention the name of the Earl of
Chard, and nor did Emma. She might think of him
continually, and wake up in the night with the
tears running down her face, but she never spoke
of him to those around her. Mrs Gore had no idea
that he had once been the Dominic Hastings
whom Emma had refused. She had assumed that
Emma's connection with her employer, Lord
Chard, had been that between a great gentleman
and a humble servant, and Emma had not disa-
bused her of that belief.

A new life. That was what she must make for
herself, and eventually, as Mrs Gore had said that
she would, she gave way to Anne Fontaine and
agreed to enter society again. After all, apart from
m'lord and the Gardiners, her previous employers
had been relatively humble people and were
unlikely to frequent the drawing rooms of the *ton*.
She wished Emma Lawrence to be dead and
buried.

'Such a charming young person, Miss Lincoln!'
was the verdict of society on her. 'Who would have
thought that she would turn into someone with so

much presence? He will be a lucky man who wins her.'

Society was unaware that Emma did not wish to be won by any man, lucky or unlucky. Only she knew that her heart was irrevocably given to m'lord. If she could not marry him, she would marry nobody, and as she had said to her aunt, 'I intend to become a domineering spinster, much given to looking after pug dogs and deploring the manners of the young.'

'Never say so, my dear,' her aunt had implored, and then, seeing the mocking amusement on Emma's face at her light words being taken so seriously, 'Oh, I see that you are funning. Of course you will marry. You must choose the best amongst those who daily besiege you.'

Besieged by suitors Emma might have been, but she distributed her favours equally among them. She could never forget that all these grand men and women who fawned upon her because of her great wealth had ignored her in her time of trouble.

Not that she allowed this cynicism to be detected. She used the charm which loving m'lord had increased to keep people at bay and her air of pleasant reserve was much commended. So much so that the great Lady Cowper, William Lamb's married sister and one of society's most sought after hostesses, took her up, constantly invited her to ride in her carriage in Hyde Park, introduced her to everyone who mattered and talked politics with her, discussing everything from Napoleon's attempt to reconquer Europe to what that conquest might do to Lord Liverpool's government.

In after years Emma remembered that London season as a mixture of glittering occasions rendered the more poignant because of the unspoken fear of what Napoleon's escape from Elba might entail for the future of them all. Many of the great families whose houses she entered had sons, fathers and brothers with the Army which was going to march against him.

'And, my dear Miss Lincoln,' said Lady Cowper one afternoon when they were being driven out of Hyde Park, having spent the afternoon bowing and being bowed at, 'with so many having gone to the Continent, I shall rely on you and Lady Fontaine to add your presence to all those events in the season which might be less brilliant without you. I shall expect you both to attend the ball which I am giving tomorrow night.'

Useless for Emma to plead that she was growing weary of balls, dinner, supper parties, little jaunts to Vauxhall and Ranelagh and boating parties on the Thames; she knew that all her objections would be charmingly dismissed. Besides, Emma also knew full well that even if Lady Cowper was being kind to her, she was being so because Emma was the season's latest novelty, and it was her pleasure to monopolise her to show that her social power was still intact.

'Depend upon it, we shall both come,' exclaimed Aunt Fontaine, before Emma could answer. 'We should not wish to miss such a splendid event.'

'Then that's settled,' smiled the Lady.

'Oh, Aunt,' said Emma, after the Cowpers' coach had delivered them to Chelsea. 'I was so looking forward to a quiet evening at home. I have had so few lately.'

'Nonsense.' Her aunt was firm. 'You have had so many quiet evenings at home over the last few years that you now deserve as many lively ones as you can contrive. Besides, who knows? Tomorrow night you might meet the one man who will be able to dismiss from your mind this ridiculous nonsense of being a spinster for life.'

'Oh, I doubt that,' returned Emma drily. 'I doubt that he exists, and if he does he is hardly likely to be present at Lady Cowper's ball.'

It was a saying she was to remember the following evening. For shortly after she had mounted the stairs at the Cowpers' London mansion, walking between her uncle and aunt Fontaine, and had entered the brilliantly lit reception rooms, the footman they had passed at the bottom of the stairs bellowed the name of Lady Cowper's latest guest. 'M'lord, the Earl of Chard.'

# CHAPTER FOURTEEN

M'LORD had gone to Lady Cowper's ball much against his will. He had already spent a month in London, and, although he had been busy carrying out Sir Thomas Liddell's first wish that he publicise and promote Stephenson's revolutionary invention among his fellow peers, he had not yet carried out his second.

He had been told that Miss Emilia Lincoln now lived in Chelsea, but he had not been able to bring himself to visit her and to pass on Sir Thomas's good wishes.

Memories of Emma only served to increase his distaste at the notion of meeting the unprepossessing young woman who had jilted him. He had been told more than once the strange story of how she had regained her fortune. Petersham, whose judgement he had always thought faulty, had described her as strangely attractive.

Strangely attractive! Could that really be believed of the stammering fat child he had known? He had expressed his doubts as to her looks and Petersham had laughed and muttered, 'Really, Chard, do have a little faith in my ability to know a beauty when I meet one—even if Miss Lincoln's is not of the more obvious kind.'

'I knew her once,' he had said stiffly, 'and she was certainly not beautiful then.'

'Oh, yes,' Petersham had drawled. 'Offered for her, didn't you, before her Papa lost her money? Refused you, didn't she? Refusal probably affected your judgement. None of us like to hear the word "No" from an heiress. Why don't you have another go? Might be more successful next time.'

'God forbid,' he had said, and changed the subject. He really did not wish to discuss Emilia Lincoln, or meet her again, but he was duty bound to carry out Liddell's wishes. Perhaps he could wriggle out of the obligation by writing her a letter. Duty and honour said no. He had given his word, dammit.

Even Lady Cowper could not let this occasion pass without dragging Miss Lincoln's name in again. She was the toast of the season, of all unlikely things.

'My dear Chard,' she said on meeting him—and he thought that she had kept her looks when many had lost them. 'What luck that you are back with us. Even better luck that you have chosen to honour my little *affaire*. I hear that you are in London as Sir Thomas Liddell's envoy. I compliment you on your friend—a sounder and more sensible fellow never existed.'

She ran out of breath, tapped him with her fan and gave him an arch smile. 'And Miss Lincoln is here too. You will have a chance to make your peace with her. She is here tonight—and greatly in looks.'

M'lord could only suppose that Lady Cowper, like Petersham, had run mad. Miss Lincoln in looks! He bowed a little stiffly and offered her an aloof smile, before saying, 'I shall seek an occasion to speak to her, madam. I have been charged by Sir Thomas Liddell with the duty of remembering him to her. She has joined the syndicate financing tramways since her recent accession to fortune.'

'Goodness.' Emily Cowper smiled, tapping him with her fan, thinking that he had greatly changed but was more attractive now as a somewhat harsh man than he had ever been as a mere pretty boy. 'She is most enterprising these days—as you are, Chard. I must reintroduce you to her. You would have much in common. I cannot remember, though, that you were interested in such matters when we were boy and girl together.'

M'lord bowed. 'Nor was I then, madam, but times change and we with them.'

'Well, you have changed, Chard, and for the better, I think,' she told him, frank impudence being her middle names. 'I insist that you go and find the lady. If you fail to do so in this great mob, I shall make it my business to bring you together again. She is charming these days.'

Every woman of great wealth is bound to be charming, thought m'lord cynically, making his temporary adieux and walking into the great reception room to find those he might know, determined to dodge Miss Lincoln as long as possible.

It was as he was hailing a few old acquaintances from his younger and wilder days that he saw his lost love. No, it could not be Emma, not here. . . He stopped dead in mid-sentence whilst talking to young Worcester, and said hastily, 'Excuse me a moment, pray. . .'

Without further ado he strode across the ballroom to where he had glimpsed her. But in the moment or two which had elapsed she had disappeared through the double doors into the ballroom, crammed with people, and was lost to sight.

Nothing to it but to return to young Worcester. He must be dreaming—so besotted, so lost to everything since her disappearance that he imagined her everywhere! Impossible for her to be Lady Cowper's guest, the poor young governess that she was.

So impossible that he was not surprised that she did not reappear. And then, when he was leaning against the wall, watching the dancers, bored beyond belief, wondering how he could once have spent his nights engaged in this sort of nonsense, he saw her again.

And it was his Emma.

There was no doubt of it this time. But she was strangely changed.

Instead of the drab but decent gowns she had always worn, except for that one evening when she had captured the attention of both Ben Blackburn and Lord Lufton, to say nothing of poor young Bassett, she was most sumptuously attired. She was wearing a cream silk dress, high-waisted, low-necked with an amethyst-coloured sash and a small train of amethyst gauze which floated behind her. There were amethysts around her neck, her wrists and on her dark curls in the shape of a small tiara. She had never looked so enchanting, his Emma.

Jealous rage overcame m'lord, blinding him, filling him with the most dreadful grief. She had left him to find a new lover, that was it! All women were the same, it seemed—faithless creatures who flitted from one lover to the next. Oh, yes, she had found a lover who showered presents on her and had introduced her to society. Well, he would kill him before her, and damn the consequences—even if he swung for it!

His expression was so grim that Lady Cowper, who had been searching for him, took a step backwards.

'Why, Chard, I vow that you look as though you are present at an execution, not a ball! Come, my friend, I will introduce you to Miss Lincoln when the dance is over. I see that she is on the floor.'

Damn Miss Lincoln! He had not seen her on the floor and did not wish to. She was nothing to him. Emma was the only woman he wanted, and what he wanted most of all was to. . .to. . .

Somehow he pulled himself together and spoke calmly to Lady Cowper—although he had no idea of what he had said. It must have been something suitably banal, for she gave a tinkling laugh and struck him on the arm again with her fan.

The dance was ending, the dancers were leaving the floor, and Emma was walking away from him on the arm of the damned dandy with whom she had been cavorting—was *he* her lover? No, he would not endure this! But he must. For Lady Cowper was exclaiming, 'A moment, Chard. Pray stay where you are—I shall return presently,' and walking away from him.

Nothing for it but to obey her, since curious eyes had been on them both. He stood there, stiff and stern, to see Lady Cowper returning with Emma of all people on her arm, talking earnestly to her. What games were they playing with him?

'You see,' Lady Cowper had said to Emma as she had caught her up on the verge of being taken to the supper room by young Lord Simon Winchester, who professed the utmost admiration of her, 'I promised to introduce you to all the most interesting people in society, and I always keep my word. You will allow me to entertain your partner for a moment, Lord Simon. I promise to return her as soon as possible.'

What could he say to that, other than what the Lady expected? And, talking all the time, all pretty and conscious vivacity, Lady Cowper engaged Emma's interest until they reached the spot where m'lord stood, his face white, his whole posture that of a man ready for battle, waiting for them.

At the last moment Emma looked up—to see m'lord, standing before her, his face first grim and then bewildered as Lady Cowper said prettily, 'Miss Lincoln, may I introduce you to the Earl of Chard, whom I believe you once knew as Dominic Hastings. I know that you will have much to say to one another, so I will leave you for the present.' And she tripped away, conscious of duty well done.

So much to say to one another! Face to face, stranded on the edge of the ballroom floor, with all society staring at them, remembering that Emilia Lincoln had once jilted Dominic Hastings after all the *on dits* had said that they were sure to marry, neither of them could speak.

It was as though they were alone. The noise of the ballroom faded into nothing, the curious watching eyes disappeared. And still neither of them spoke. Which of them was the more shocked at meeting the other had to be a matter of some doubt.

M'lord spoke first. His voice was as grim as his expression. 'Well, madam, am I to say well met after all these years? What possessed you to deceive me so cruelly? What game were you playing at Loudwater, that you pretended to be who you were not, calling yourself by a name which was not yours? Did some kind of revenge inspire you to seduce me? And for what?'

All the weary months since her disappearance he

had imagined what he might say to her when he found her again. Always he had heard himself pouring over her passionate words and broken phrases which would convince her of his love. Never in his strangest imaginings had he conceived that once he found her he would begin by hurling words of reproach.

Emma lifted her head proudly. Like m'lord, she had sometimes imagined what they would say to one another if ever they met again, and, like him, she could scarce credit what she was about to say.

'Pray do not reproach me, m'lord. I was a poor governess when I was at Loudwater. No word of a lie. My change of circumstances came after I had left you. As to deceit, I rechristened myself as Emma Lawrence since no one would hire Emilia Lincoln, the disgraced suicide's daughter, to be a governess and teach their children. If I had applied to you in the name of Emilia Lawrence, would you then have employed me?'

He waved a lordly hand, as much as to say, Explain it how you will. You still deceived me— and I thought you honest. . .

She would not plead with him, by no means. She would not tell him how desperate she had been these last ten years. He could have no notion of what it meant to face starvation—and even, if all else failed her, whoredom in order to stay alive. He could not know that when the position at Loudwater was offered her she had not dared tell him the truth lest he refuse her, sight unseen. And why should she explain herself? Why tell him that she had, as he surmised, dreamed vague dreams of revenge on one who had demeaned her, but had forgotten them once she had fallen in love with the man he had become? And that once having done so she had found it impossible to tell him the truth about herself.

Instead she simply said, 'I owe you no further explanations, m'lord.' Then, seeing avid eyes on them, she tried to compose herself. 'I fear that we are becoming a raree-show.' It was plain to the watchers that some great emotion was passing between the pair of them, even after so many years apart, and there was more than one who wondered what was afoot.

'True,' he said, still stern, and unbending. 'And that being so let us adjourn where we may be private. I believe the double doors behind us lead to a corridor at the end of which is an ante-room where we may speak without the whole world trying to conjecture what we are at.'

This was the last thing Emma wanted. To be alone with him would be torture. She wanted to throw herself at him, to say, What happened to all the love which passed between us at Loudwater? Why are you so cold? But she knew why. It was she who had abandoned him for the second time—and now that he had found her deception out, his love had turned to hate. He thought that she was all deception, like the woman whom he had married and who had betrayed him.

'No,' she said. 'I see no need for us to engage in further conversation.' But her heart was breaking at the sight of his stern face, of his resolute unfriendly stance.

He would have none of it.

'No?' he announced. 'No? Indeed not. Your answer must be yes. You owe me that and you *will* come with me.' He put out his arm for her to take after such a fashion that for her to refuse to accept it would draw upon them even more attention than they would attract by disappearing together.

Nothing for it, then, but to take the offered arm and process out of the room into an ante-room very like the one in which she had overheard him making mock of her so long ago.

It was small with a beautiful fireplace, the mantelshelf upheld by two water nymphs delicately carved. Exquisite porcelain figurines were displayed in the alcoves on each side of the hearth and deep armchairs stood before a low bookcase filled with the latest novels. Lady Cowper's embroidery was on a pole stand.

It might as well have been a labourer's hovel so far as the two of them were concerned. M'lord released her and waved her to a seat. Emma refused and said, 'I will stand, m'lord.'

'Stand, sit—it is all one to me,' returned m'lord unkindly. Then, in a more human tone, he went on, 'It may be weak-minded of me to revert to it, but what in the world happened to your stammer? You could barely manage a sentence without it overcoming you, but now you possess a flow of speech which a Parliamentary orator might envy!'

Emma could not prevent herself. She broke into helpless laughter and had the pleasure of seeing his grim face soften. And if there was more than a touch of hysteria in her mirth, then what mattered that? For the Polar ice-cap which lay between them had been narrowed.

Her eyes watering as she hiccuped into silence, Emma found m'lord offering her his handkerchief.

'Come,' he said, more kindly, 'you must admit that you have undergone the strangest transformation—'

'From the fat lady at the fair to woodland sylph,' interrupted Emma, wiping her eyes. 'But mine is no more of a transformation than yours.'

'Mine?' queried m'lord. 'Now, why ever should you say that? I own that I am a little more serious than I was—'

She interrupted him again. 'I acknowledge that you possessed nothing so unfortunate as my stammer, which miraculously disappeared on the night of Lady Corbridge's ball, but do admit that you were the most mindlessly inconsequential dandy who ever graced a London ballroom—and look at you now. So serious that an Oxford Fellow might envy you, wrapped up in the management of mines, estates and the promotion of tramways and travelling engines, usually dressed more like one of your gamekeepers than a beau of the *ton*. Why, I hardly recognised you when I met you again.'

'And I did not recognise you at all,' returned m'lord hardily. 'Although there were many times when some imagined resemblance in you struck me, though I never knew to what. . . And that last catalogue of remarks merely serves to reinforce my admiration of your control of language—so different from your silences when I first knew you.'

'Why are we doing this?' muttered Emma helplessly as she handed him back his handkerchief— which he refused with a wave of his lordly hand.

'Doing what?' M'lord was a trifle puzzled.

'Reproaching one another for having changed.'

'Oh, I am not reproaching you,' riposted m'lord, a trifle nastily. 'On the contrary, I am full of admiration for the double-dealing, over-articulate temptress which you have become.' Then, with pathos in his voice, he asked, 'Why did you run away, Emma? Why did you refuse me ten years ago and then compound that refusal by deserting me again?'

'You did not want me ten years ago,' Emma answered him truthfully. 'You wanted my money.'

M'lord bowed his head. He could not deny what she had said. He remembered what the old gypsy woman had told him—that when he first met his love he would not know her. . .and he had not.

'That was then. You were not the woman who was Tish's governess. Tish was broken-hearted when you disappeared. And I did not. . .take. . . you in the folly at Loudwater because I wanted your money. I thought you penniless. I ask you again. Why did you refuse me twice?'

He would not use the word 'love'. The burned child fears the fire. She had uttered no word of love to him, and the fear of yet another refusal held him back from uttering it to her. A little while ago, when he had first seen her, he had been beside himself, thinking that she had left him for another lover or had found another lover after she had left him. He was sure now that that was not true, but the shock of finding her, changed again, had made him uncertain, fearful of yet another rejection.

All the selfish certainty which he had once possessed, the notion that whatever Dominic Hastings wanted would always be granted to him, had been burned away in the harsh years of toil and exile whilst he tried to save Loudwater.

He had wanted to marry riches. He had done so and the riches had turned to dust and ashes. He had wished to love and to marry beauty, and his wishes had been granted. But his beauty had never loved him. Instead she had betrayed him over and over again. He had hoped that one day he might attain the dizzy heights of being the leisured Earl of Chard who owned the beautiful palace called Loudwater. He had become the Earl of Chard, and the title, and Loudwater, had been millstones around his neck. Instead of leisure he had been condemned to the backbreaking work of saving his inheritance.

Emma was right. He had changed profoundly. If

he were young Dominic Hastings once more, conceited and selfish, would he make the same mistakes again? He tried to believe that he would not, but he knew only too well that the years of suffering and hard work which had followed his disappointments had made him more careful of others and more forgetful of self.

Except that he did not wish to be hurt again—or to hurt another.

She was speaking, and he must listen to what she was saying.

To watch him struggle with himself, as he was so plainly doing, was beginning to move Emma so much that she knew that she must tell him the truth—about what had happened ten years ago and in the more immediate past at Loudwater.

'I will tell you first why I fled Loudwater,' she began, 'and it was for the reasons I gave you in my letter. You spoke no words of love to me, nor did you mention marriage. And, judging by your early approaches to me, you did not begin your campaign against me with any intention of marrying me if it succeeded. You thought of me only as a likely mistress, which was why I held you off for so long. In the end I fled rather than become your mistress.'

He bowed his head. He could not say her nay, for that was the truth—at least it had been in the beginning. Love had come later, when he had begun to understand the strength of her, the steel which complemented his.

She continued. 'I will also tell you why I refused you when you proposed to me ten years ago, even though it will cause us both great pain. Me in the telling, and you in the hearing. You may or may not remember that we met in Hyde Park the day before you proposed to me. You asked me if I intended to go to Lady Corbridge's ball that night and I told you that I did not, for my father was expecting guests for dinner and I must be present.

'But when I informed him that you were coming to see me and then him on the morrow, he told me to go to Lady Corbridge's so that we might be together. I went there with such high hopes. . . I know now how unattractive I must have seemed to you, but I thought at the time that you cared for me a little, whilst I. . .' She paused, for although she had thought that she had exorcised that long ago pain, Emma found that it was suddenly as fresh again as it had been on that evening ten years ago.

'Whilst I—and I must say it—I worshipped you. You were so handsome and charming, and you were so kind to me that I foolishly thought that I meant more to you than my money.

'I could not find you in the ballroom, and someone told me that they had seen you leave by the west door. I followed you and found you. . .

'You were in a side room with some other young men, all half-drunk, as you were, and you. . . I can hardly say it. . .you were being hatefully cruel about the necessity of having to marry such a plain fright as I was, and they were agreeing with you! I overheard every dreadful word, and without revealing myself I crept away.

'All I wanted was for you to suffer as I had done. So I refused you, pretended that you had meant nothing to me, that you were misled. And every word I uttered was a lie. I loved you then—which is why my grief was so great—and I love you now, but with a deeper, truer love.'

Emma was silent.

M'lord was silent.

She had said that she loved him. In the past. . . and in the present.

As she had reached the end of her painful confession he had turned his face away from her. He could not bear to look at her, for every word she uttered was a dagger in his heart.

She spoke again.

'They say that listeners never hear any good of themselves. And so it proved for me. But some strange good did occur. I never stammered again after I had overheard what you—and those with you—had to say of me. I also determined that I would no longer be a fat girl, and that I would not enter society again until I had changed myself for the better. The only person to know how much I had altered was poor George Brummell, who came to see me nearly a year later. But before the season began my father was ruined, and so no one ever knew how much Emilia Lincoln had changed.

'I came to Loudwater because I was desperate—

I had just lost a good post because of my employer's husband's would-be lechery, and I hoped that you would not recognise me and send me away. I had not been at Loudwater long before I saw how much *you* had changed, and that I had not been wrong to love you all those years ago because I had somehow known that what you then showed the world was not your true self. That self belonged to a man I could love and respect.

'But even so, in honour, however much I loved you, I could not become your mistress. And so I left Loudwater.'

And now she was silent. M'lord had walked to the fireplace and his head was bowed over it, in his hands. He was remembering the little girl he had mocked so cruelly and so often. He thought that he had rightly been punished by fate for his unthinking cruelty to her.

After a moment he lifted his head and turned to her.

'Useless for me to try to apologise. What words of mine, what expressions of bitter regret can wipe out what you heard? I remember that night—just. I cannot remember exactly what I said, but I know that I was given to such boastings and braggings to my hangers-on when I was in my cups. It explains only too well why you refused me as you did. That hurt the conceited fool I was, because I had believed that you had admired me; I had counted my fortune yours. I was well served when I at last married beauty as well as money and the owner of them was faithless, and betrayed me again and again.

'The only extenuation I can offer for my conduct when you overheard me is that very young men often say such things in order to assert their masculinity when alone with their friends. More, I must have known that I had lost something worth having, for over the years the memory of that small girl stayed with me, and it explains why I found you so familiar when I met you again—although I was sure that I had never seen you before.

'But what can I say to you now? What will wash the stain of those cruel words away? And how to apologise for my original wish to seduce you, make you my mistress when you came to Loudwater?'

He turned away from her again, and said, in a sudden violent and remorseful burst, 'After all that I have said and done how could you bear to touch me, then or now? You refused me once, when you were rich and I was poor. Believe me when I tell you that on the afternoon we made love in the folly I had made up my mind to marry you, and was prepared to propose to you when next I saw you—only to awake and to discover that you had gone. Not only gone then, but gone the next day, without speaking to me first—simply leaving me a letter which broke my heart.

'Truly the gods are making me their sport—to have me love you and wish to marry you when you were poor, and not be given the opportunity to tell you so, so that if I offer for you now, you and the world must believe that it is solely because you are rich again! The cruel jest is that I would have married you when you were penniless, and would have brought me nothing!'

Emma said numbly, 'No, m'lord, I did not know that—that you wished to marry me when I was a poor governess at Loudwater.'

'Yes,' he said fiercely. 'But knowing what I had said and done before, it was not unnatural of you to think me such a cur that having robbed you of your virginity I would then make you my mistress, to suffer the insults that would inevitably follow. Why should you believe that I would treat you any differently from the way in which Lufton has treated poor Miss Straight? You must have thought that I was as bad as Ben Blackburn, who wished to force you! At least I did not force an unwanted child on you.'

'Oh no, m'lord,' she said softly, his distress becoming hers. 'I never thought you like them. Not even on that night when I overheard what I should not have done. Honesty compels me to admit that you were saying nothing but the truth— about both of us. Oh, no, m'lord,' she repeated, and then, under her breath so that he could not hear her, 'The child would not have been unwanted.'

'M'lord,' he said slowly. 'Oh, I know now why you call me that. To say my true name would be too painful a reminder of the past.'

She was quick to shake her head. 'Oh, that is

because when I saw you again you were truly m'lord. The man I thought that I had fallen in love with when I was a girl had come to life, and I could forget the boy you had once been.'

It was his turn to shake his head, to say sadly, 'Oh, you are a sophist, are you not? You chop logic as skilfully as a lawyer. Nothing you say can change that which lies between us. In honour I cannot offer for you, ask you to accept me, poor as I am, damaged as I am. No, you deserve a better man than I, tied as I am to Loudwater and ruin. You need a man who has not demeaned and hurt you— hurt you not once, but twice. I must renounce you so that you may accept someone good and kind, who will treat you as an honourable man should and make you happy.' He turned to go.

'No!' she cried. 'No, I do not want that man. And where shall I find him among the fortune-hunters who surround me?'

He swung round. 'There are many who will court you who have their own fortune, as I have not, and who will want you for what you are and not for your money. Think: unknown and penniless you drew the hearts of all around you at Loudwater. There will be many others to come, I assure you.'

That might be true, but she did not want them. She wanted him and only him. But she could not have him. He made as if to take her hand, to kiss her goodbye, but started back, exclaiming, 'No! Even to touch you, however lightly, will undo me.

Adieu. I wish you all and more than you would wish for yourself. Someone with clean hands and a clean heart.'

And so he left her.

It was the hardest thing he had ever done, and it broke his heart to do it.

Emma wanted to run after him, but she was frozen, turned to stone. As he strode out of Lady Cowper's house she knew without being told that he would return at once to Loudwater, leaving behind the place where he had found her—and lost her for the second time.

Honour! What did men mean by honour?

What had she, a woman, meant by honour when she had left him rather than become his mistress?

But she knew—she knew.

The boy he had been would have laughed at the word. The man he had become lived by it, and in doing so had rejected the chance of happiness which had been offered him because honour said that he was not worthy of it.

But what of my chance of happiness? she thought. What of that? No! He may renounce me, but I shall not renounce him! After all, if we lived untrammelled by the straitjacket of convention, the highest compliment he could have paid me would have been to make me his mistress—the woman he wanted in his bed above all others. We have both paid our debts to honour, and now we are free to start again.

And then another thought struck her. A question which she must ask herself before she made any plans: Should she give up her wealth to gain him? Always it had come between them. When she had been a girl he had wanted to marry her for it, and for nothing else—she had been merely the handle to grasp to win it.

When she had been his governess and had been poor he had courted her because he loved her, and would have married her even though she had nothing. And now. . .now she was rich again, and he would not offer her marriage because of the same wealth for which he had so greedily tried to marry her ten years ago. Such were the ironic reversals of fortune!

Should she, then, go to him with nothing? Emotion might say, yes. Reason said no. That would be to betray her dead father, and the repentant criminal who had returned her fortune to her in expiation of his sins.

No, she thought. If I can persuade him to marry me and accept my wealth, wisely used it will save Loudwater for the next generation. And whatever the Bible or anyone else says in this world, as I have discovered, rich is better than poor.

So, awakening from her stupor, in the grip of a pain even more terrible than the one she had felt ten years ago when she had refused him, Emma was full of a strange hope. Yes, we are quits now, she thought triumphantly. For first I refused him and now he has refused me, and we may start again on level terms!

One way or another I shall get him back. M'lord shall make me his lady, and I shall bear his children. . .

# CHAPTER FIFTEEN

WHAT a damn'd fool he had been, prating about honour, thought m'lord when he reached Loudwater again. Loudwater, where every room, every corner of the gardens brought back memories of her—laughing up at him, teasing him, holding off her insistent and unwanted suitors or would-be ravishers. He loved her, dammit, and if she had not been honest with him, what of that? He had not been honest with her ten years ago either.

The place seemed more of a millstone and lonelier than ever, even though he had learned that some of his London investments were doing well and that the farm accounts were showing a profit, despite the apparently never-ending war. Not only that, but his mines were flourishing, and a letter was awaiting him from Sir Thomas telling him that Stephenson was growing near to being able to demonstrate an improved version of *Blutcher*.

'But not the final one,' he had written. 'Not the engine which will cross country, carrying passengers. More time is needed for that.'

Once he would have been elated by all this good news being decanted into his lap at once, but his folly in refusing Emma haunted him night and day.

His staff knew what was wrong. 'Missing her, ain't he?' said his valet wisely. 'Saw her in London, didn't he? She's a rich grand lady now, and what does he do but refuse her!'

'What?' exclaimed the cook. 'And him willing to make her m'lady when she had nothing! There's a turn-up.'

'Aye,' nodded Louis. 'Light in the attic, as they say. Mark my words, though, it ain't over. Determined madam, our late governess! Anyone want to bet on it? I say she'll get him in the end. And here's my guinea as an earnest on't.'

He grinned as he offered this, knowing he had won the last bet when Tom, the under-gardener, had reported that m'lord and the governess had got up to tricks in the folly after Lord Lufton and Ben Blackburn had failed with her.

'Want to bet against me?' he asked the butler, still grinning.

'Not I,' retorted the butler sturdily. 'You only bet on sure things. Let's have a sweep on how long it will take her.'

Done!' cried Louis. 'Knowing the lady, I'll give her until the autumn.'

And so it was arranged. As usual, the servants knew most of the game, as onlookers always do.

Back in London, Emma was carefully making plans to lay siege to m'lord even as the summer wore on towards the final battle between the usurper Bonaparte and the forces of legitimacy led by the Duke of Wellington, Field Marshall Blucher and the inconsequential Prince of Orange. Emma's forces were neither so large nor so grand, but she was equally determined.

In a letter to Sir Thomas Liddell thanking him for the message of goodwill he had sent by m'lord, the Earl of Chard—m'lord's last act before leaving London having been to send her an impersonal missive on the matter—Miss Emilia Lincoln suggested that she was willing to invest more money in the Stephenson venture and would not be averse to visiting Northumbria. It drew an enthusiastic answer from him.

Whilst Sir Thomas was not able to entertain Miss Lawrence himself, his place being under heavy repair and his wife a semi-invalid, he was able to invite her to spend part of the summer with his good old friend and cousin, Miss Whately, who had a mansion not far from Mr Stephenson's home at Killingworth, where he would be delighted to meet her. She would be pleased to accomodate Miss Lincoln, and he would be more than pleased to show the pair of them around whichever part of the North they might care to visit. And he would make sure that Mr Stephenson was introduced to his new backer as well.

'Never say that you are leaving before the season ends!' exclaimed her aunt. 'Such a success as you have been.'

'Oh, I have unfinished business in the North,' replied Emma truthfully—that business being her campaign to overrun m'lord's position and secure his hand.

'I had hoped that you might wait to come north with me,' mourned her aunt, who lived in Yorkshire. 'Being as yet without a companion, I was looking forward to spending a cosy month or two with you.'

But Emma was adamant—although the problem of her aunt's companion was to be solved in an unforseen manner.

Shortly before Emma left for Northumbria a visitor was announced. 'A Miss Calypso Straight craves the pleasure of an audience with you,' announced the butler, looking severe. All society knew of Miss Straight's downfall.

Calypso Straight wished to see her? Now, why should that be? Emma puzzled on this whilst the butler was sent to fetch her. Did Miss Straight know that Emilia Lincoln was also Miss Emma Lawrence, the unconsidered and apparently poverty stricken governess? As yet no others did, for she and her aunt had said nothing on the matter.

Miss Straight did—and apparently had not talked, since no rumours were flying about that Miss Lincoln had spent the last nine years or so as Miss Lawrence, the poor governess. She was very subdued in manner, plainly dressed, and at once thanked Emma for seeing her. 'You were pointed out to me in Hyde Park by one of my few remaining friends as Miss Emilia Lincoln who had reappeared in society now that her fortune was recovered. You may judge of my surprise, but it is not that of which I wish to speak.'

'No?' returned Emma warily.

'No. I suppose you are aware of the cruel manner in which Lord Lufton treated me?'

'Yes.' Emma was still short. 'You must understand that I could not avoid hearing the gossip.'

'Exactly—and the irony of it is that I was triumphant when you left Loudwater so suddenly, for it seemed that I had succeeded and that you had failed. Strange, was it not, that we each warned the other of the likelihood of receiving such treatment from those we trusted, and that it was I who paid the price for my folly and not you?'

She fell silent. Emma did not speak; she saw that her visitor was struggling with herself. The struggle ended and Miss Straight spoke again, in the decided, slightly superior tones which she had always used at Loudwater.

'I am shortly to retire into a straitened—you appreciate the pun, I am sure—private life. I thought that to make a little amends for the manner in which I treated you at Loudwater I should pass on to you something which you might not know. I had always doubted that Chard was truly attached to you, and merely saw you as prey from the servant class—as Lufton saw me. But on the day you left, I knew better.

'Chard was like a madman in his grief at losing you. He drove to Alnwick after you, and returned empty-handed before we left, in a state bordering on mental collapse. He was as unlike his usual calm self as a man could be. Rumour has it that you turned him down for a second time at Lady Cowper's Ball, but, having seen the strength of your attachment to him, it occurred to me that you were unaware of the strength of his to you.

'Once you were as rejected and poor as I am now. You warned me of what my fate with Lufton was like to be, and I dismissed that warning when I should have heeded you. In return I thought I ought to tell you that if the reason for your refusal of Chard was because you believed that he was solely after your fortune again, then you are mistaken. His attachment to you is a genuine one. That is all. I leave you now, wishing you the good fortune which has been denied me.'

Emma stood there numb. Miss Straight—and society—misunderstood the matter. M'lord had refused her this time, not she him, and she had no doubt that m'lord loved her. Miss Straight's words, however, were a powerful confirmation that in refusing her m'lord was punishing himself for what he saw as his unworthiness. More, this sudden reversal of Miss Straight's behaviour towards her came as a complete surprise.

Once she and Calypso Straight had been alike in being penniless, come-down-in-the-world spinsters, striving not to slip into the gutter which awaited all those single women who had lost everything. That she was mistaken in supposing that Emma had refused m'lord was not to the point, and did not devalue the kindness which lay behind her unexpected visit—unexpected because she might have thought that Miss Straight resented her own good fortune.

My sister, she thought. For all the differences between us, she is my sister. As Miss Straight put her hand on the door to leave Emma spoke one word. 'Wait!'

Calypso Straight's bowed head rose.

'Miss Lincoln?'

'You have nowhere to go? No future?'

'None. But what is that to you?'

'You came to offer me a truth of which you thought I might not be aware. I thank you for your kindness in doing so. My aunt, Lady Fontaine, has need of a companion of good family. If I were to recommend you to her as one who has been greatly sinned against, and suggest to her that she would be making an act of Christian charity if she offered you the post, then I think that she might accept my recommendation.'

So speaking, Emma retired to her little desk, pulled out a piece of paper and quickly and impulsively began to pen a letter to her aunt.

'But my reputation is irrevocably damaged. . .' began Miss Straight dubiously.

'No matter,' said Emma cheerfully. 'My aunt owes me a profound debt for having thrown me off when I was as lost as you are, and I shall tell her that she will reconcile herself to her Maker for having done so by helping you. She is also of an

independent turn of mind herself, and will recognise that you are the same. You will have many a
splendid *cose* together, I am sure. Here.' And,
having signed, sanded and sealed her letter, she
handed it to her bedazzled visitor.

'I did not come for this,' uttered Miss Straight,
'but I thank you. And all the more if Lady
Fontaine disregards the *on dits* about me and
agrees to appoint me. I do not deserve this from
you.'

'Perhaps not.' Emma's response was still cheerful. 'But having been blessed with good fortune
myself, I must be willing to pass a little on to
others.'

Before she left, clutching her letter, Miss
Straight said, shyly for her, 'And may I wish you
more luck with your lord than I had with mine!'

Words which Emma carried with her on her
second journey to the North made in a state quite
different from that of her first. Deference greeted
her everywhere, and, bowling along the drive to
the small jewel of a house of which Miss Whately
was mistress, she had only one thought in her
mind. How soon would it be before she saw m'lord
again—and what would he say when he realised
that she had come after him?

'You did well with Miss Lincoln, Chard,' Sir
Thomas Liddell told m'lord when next they met—
he was unaware that m'lord had once proposed to
her in her younger days. 'So much so that she is

coming north to see Geordie at work. I have arranged for her to stay with my old cousin, Miss Whately at The Dovecote. You must be sure to meet her again. She seems to be a person of sound good sense. I had assumed that she was a lady of advanced years, but Miss Whately seems to think not. I told her that I would ask you which of us is correct. Her preparations for an elderly guest would be somewhat different from those for a young one, I suppose.'

M'lord, whose brain was in a whirl at this news that Emma was following him north, stammered a little in replying. 'An old lady! Oh, no, a young one—not yet thirty. She was little more than a child when her father was swindled of his fortune.'

'Oh, aye,' nodded Sir Thomas. 'A strange tale, that.' And surely Chard's response to it was a little strange too, he thought. He had changed colour, and patently did not want to pursue the matter, so Sir Thomas let the subject drop.

He spoke of it that night to Miss Whately, with whom he was staying. 'Not surprising,' said that lady brusquely. 'Not the sort of thing you are aware of, Sir Thomas, but years ago Miss Lincoln jilted Chard when he was Dominic Hastings and as poor as a church mouse. Everyone assumed that they were to marry.'

'He ain't much richer now,' said Sir Thomas, cheerfully down to earth as usual. 'We must make sure they meet again. To let him have another go at her,' he explained to Miss Whately's raised eyebrows. 'Chard could do with an injection of capital, and no mistake. He has done wonders at Loudwater, but a little help would do even more for him. Ought to marry, you know. He'll need an heir for Loudwater. Invite him to The Dovecote when she's settled in!'

A proposal of which Miss Whately thoroughly approved. Her reception of Emma was a warm one, and the contrast with her first arrival in Northumbria struck Emma all over again. She was given a suite which included the best bedroom in the house and told to rest for the next few days. 'And then,' promised her hostess, 'I shall hold a little dinner party for a few local notables—including Sir Thomas, of course, who will be staying with me. He is most desirous of meeting you.'

She was not aware that Sir Thomas had already met Emma, though briefly, in the guise of Lady Letty's governess, and Emma wondered wryly if Sir Thomas would recognise her in her new splendour. Miss Whately, warned by Sir Thomas to be tactful, had not informed m'lord that Miss Lincoln would be present at the dinner party to which he had been invited, nor had she mentioned to Emma that m'lord would be a fellow guest.

'They might both cry off,' he had declaimed, matchmaking with all his might, 'if they knew that the other was to be present. And that would never do. If Miss Lincoln is nearly thirty she needs a husband as much as Chard needs a wife, and we cannot have them declining to meet. No, indeed.'

His determination to see m'lord settled would have amused Emma, who was quite unaware that, so far as her campaign against m'lord was concerned, Sir Thomas was playing Field Marshal Blucher to her Wellington—the details of the Duke's victory over Napoleon having reached Northumbria shortly after she did.

M'lord had grumbled a little at John Bassett when the invitation from The Dovecote arrived. Miss Whately suggested that he spend a few days with her: 'Sir Thomas will be present and hopes to meet you,' she had written. She said nothing of Sir Thomas's other plans for him.

So it was that when he entered Miss Whately's pretty drawing room it was not Sir Thomas Liddell on whom his eyes first alighted, but none other than Miss Emilia Lincoln. Sir Thomas was there beside her, having immediately identified her as Chard's late governess, and, for some reason which Miss Whately could not quite understand, he was highly amused at the discovery.

She looked absolutely radiant, damn her, thought m'lord disgustedly. She had no business looking radiant. She ought to be wan and overset by his loss. M'lord was human enough to want her to be a little sorry that honour demanded that they should not marry.

There were times when he was beginning to damn honour too. And this was one of them. He was in an absolute turmoil as Sir Thomas, in his role as the senior male in Miss Whately's family, joined her in the necessary introductions, roaring jovially, 'I believe that you and Miss Lincoln have already met, Chard. Years ago and more recently, when chance brought her to Loudwater as little Letty's governess, I understand. Matters better with her now, though.'

'Indeed,' responded m'lord, bowing over Emma's small hand, the merest touch of which sent him into a very stew of desire—and in a maiden lady's drawing room of all places. If he had ever doubted the power which Emma had over him, he was being given a stark reminder of how wrong he was to question it.

And she was so damnably calm. Her great dark eyes were smiling at him as demurely as though she had not tracked him down, chased him all the way to his eyrie with his conquest in mind. Oh, he knew what she was doing! Beneath her charming exterior there dwelt a will of steel. He should have known that all those years ago, when she had thrown him over with such exquisitely insolent despatch, pretending that she cared nothing for him. When all the time. . .'

He might have been a little happier if he had known that Emma was nothing like so calm as she appeared. All the churning emotions which she had repressed since the fateful evening of Lady Cowper's ball were back with her, inducing in her a sensation of strong nausea.

Poor dear! He had never looked so stern and

forbidding—nor so dauntingly handsome. His
strong mouth was turned down a little at the
corners, as though to say to her, No, I will not have
it. You are deflecting me from my duty! And the
more he showed his strength of will, the stronger
hers grew.

What folly for them to be apart when they were
so well matched! Between them they could restore
Loudwater, build tramways across the North and
bring up children to succeed them. Impossible to
believe that the plain stammering little girl and the
spoilt boy whom they had once been had turned
into so strong a man and woman. Emma had no
illusions about either of them. Had they married
ten years ago, what a botch they would have made
of it.

But now!

No such thing. Life had chastened them, and in
the doing they had both matured. It would be a
hard task to ensure his surrender, but surrender he
must if both their lives were not to be ruined.

And all the time she smiled and gossiped about
nothings—and about somethings. The main something was her reintroduction to Geordie
Stephenson—this time as his benefactress.

'And Sir Thomas tells me that Mr Stephenson
will be doing another run to test the improvements
which he has made to *Blutcher* and has created a
new travelling engine which he has named
*Wellington*. He has kindly invited me to accompany

him to it. I should be greatly pleased, m'lord, if you would join our party.'

Now, how could he reject her offer outright with everyone listening, Sir Thomas smiling benevolently and Miss Whately with an expression which echoed his? He could not. So, a little stiffly, he came out with, 'If I can find the time. Certainly.' And what did the little minx have to say to that?

'Why, m'lord, when I was last in the North your enthusiasm for Mr Stephenson's invention was such that I was sure that nothing would have stood in the way of your attending one of his trials. Have you changed your mind about your support for him?'

Of course he had not, and she knew it, so his answer was a feeble one. 'Oh, no, but I am very busy, you understand.'

'Nonsense,' bellowed Sir Thomas. 'Stephenson is your business, Chard, and well you know it. Are you not one of the Grand Allies now? How can you resist such a charming invitation? Neither Miss Lincoln nor I will ever forgive you if you don't turn up. Nor Geordie, neither.'

Concerned, m'lord said, with as much grace as he could muster, 'Well, Liddell, if you are so insistent. . .'

He was clapped on his back for his surrender, and with sublime tactlessness—although *he* considered it tactful—Sir Thomas took Miss Whately by the arm and drew her away, saying loudly, 'Let us leave the young things to themselves, Amy. They must have much to talk about.'

Emma looked up into m'lord's face, no longer grim, for he was smiling ruefully at the way in which every one of his aces had been trumped by Emma and her new-found patron, and said tenderly, 'Have we, m'lord? Much to talk about?'

He was helpless before her. If he had thought her enchanting in her dowdy toilettes when she was being meekly submissive—or pretending to be so—now, in her beautiful new gown, when she was being anything but submissive, she was a very witch, taunting and mocking him—but with such rampant charm.

He put out his arm. 'Allow me to escort you onto the terrace, Miss Lincoln.' Miss Whateley's drawing room opened onto a long walk which looked out towards where the North Tyne ran through green parkland in the distance.

Now it was Emma's turn to submit to his demand. Which did not displease her at all. Far from it, for they would be alone once they walked through the glass doors. Neither of them said anything until they stood before the balustrade at the end of the terrace, when m'lord dropped his arm, saying stiffly, 'I thought that at Lady Cowper's ball I had made my position *vis-à-vis* yourself, Miss Lincoln, quite plain.'

'Oh, yes, m'lord,' retorted Emma cheerfully. 'Quite plain. What is not plain is my position *vis-à-vis* yourself—to adopt the language of business in which you have chosen to speak to me. Allow me to enlighten you: you have renounced me, but I must assure you that I have not renounced you—by any means.'

M'lord could not prevent himself. Forgetting what he had just said, and that they might be overlooked from the drawing room, he gave a little groan, bent his head, swept Emma into his arms and began to kiss her with all the intensity of passion long denied.

With equal enthusiasm Emma kissed him back. Was her campaign going to succeed as easily as this? Would the enemy surrender as the very first shots were exchanged?

Apparently not. For, with another little groan, m'lord stood back. His face was flushed, his hair dishevelled and his cravat awary; his whole aspect was that of a thoroughly aroused man.

'I did not mean to do that,' he announced self-righteously. 'You tempted me.'

'I, m'lord? *I* tempted you? I did nothing.'

'You exist, which is everything,' said m'lord thickly, 'and you challenge me with every fibre of your being, and you have followed me here in order to challenge me. Deny that if you can.'

'Deny what, m'lord? I have come to Northumbria to visit Sir Thomas to offer him, and the Grand Allies, my financial support for a venture to which, I may remind you, you introduced me. You would surely not wish me to withhold my support simply in order to avoid meeting you again? That would be unfair, both to Geordie Stephenson and myself.'

'Why?' M'lord turned his eyes to the heavens. 'Why do I ever argue with you, I ask myself, seeing that I never win? You are the most obstreperous siren it has been my fortune to meet.' He realised at once what an error he had made. He should have said *mis*fortune, but somehow the sentence had come out all wrong, and she would pounce on him—and so she did.

'Your fortune, m'lord? Not your misfortune? Good fortune, I trust. And if you never win, pray explain to me why we—at your wish—are at odds who by every right should be so much at evens that we should be man and wife?'

He closed his eyes. 'I have no further time to argue with you, madam. And if we do not return indoors Miss Whately's guests will be drawing conclusions about us which have no basis in fact.'

'And that will certainly sadden Sir Thomas, as well as myself,' returned Emma saucily. 'He has a great wish to see me married.'

'What, have you won him over too? Does every man who meets you have no other wish than to marry you?'

'No, m'lord. for if that were true then you would wish to marry me—but you aver most solemnly that you do not.'

M'lord paused, thought for a moment, then said simply, 'Here is one argument you will not win.

For what you have just said is not true. I have the greatest wish to marry you, but honour forbids.'

'Ah, yes, honour.' Emma's voice was solemn. 'The virtue which all men summon up when they find it convenient—in conversation and in life.'

M'lord wished that they were both savages, alone on a wide Northumbrian moor, freed from all civilised restraints, where he might do as he pleased with this witch who was taunting him: bear her to the ground and have his way with her. His Viking blood was boiling in him, and he wished to treat her as a Viking would have treated his mate.

As it was, he could do nothing but hold out his arm again. 'We had better return to the drawing room. I suspect that they are awaiting us in order to announce dinner. We shall, I am certain, have been placed next to one another. Let us speak as friends or not at all, I beg of you.'

'Oh, certainly, m'lord. I am your friend, and will so converse with you. After all, lovers may be friends, I trust.'

She had wrong-footed him again. He gave a little helpless sigh. Emma heard it and said slyly, 'It would be so much simpler to surrender to me, m'lord. You have so much to gain and so little to lose—and you will be able to sleep at night.'

Now, how did she know that? That he could not sleep for thinking of her. But he knew—he knew. For she could not sleep for thinking of him. They were quits in that, as well as in everything else.

Of all the possibilities which he had considered

in the long days and nights since he had parted
from Emma at Lady Cowper's, he could not have
imagined that she would not only follow him north
but would also challenge him to marry her at every
turn. This alone made her stand apart from other
women. He could not help thinking of the small,
shy inarticulate girl she had once been and marvel
at how much she had altered.

As they walked back to the drawing room he
told her so, and asked her what had changed her.
Her answer was both short and simple. 'Why, you
did, m'lord, at Lady Corbridge's when I overheard
you. I am your creation—Galatea to your
Pygmalion—as to some extent you are mine as a
result of my refusal of you.'

These self-evident truths struck so shrewedly at
the core of m'lord's being that they silenced him.

He spoke little at dinner, which did not surprise
the other guests. He had always been a silent man
in the North—his earlier ebullience dampened by
the destruction of all his youthful hopes and
wishes. It surprised Emma a little, because he had
always been a ready speaker with her. But she
knew him well enough to know that he was
thinking hard about what she had said to him.

To distract him she asked after Tish, and begged
that she might be able to meet her again soon.
'Perhaps at the trial,' she added. 'She would like
that.'

M'lord unbent and softened enough to agree to
her request. Miss Whately asked after Mrs

Morton, whom she had met on several occasions, and Sir Thomas, to keep the conversational pot boiling, informed the company that Lord Lufton had said that he had sworn off marriage, and by her conduct it looked as though Lady Clara was following suit.

'I gather,' he added, 'that Blackburn, in an effort to recoup his fortunes, offered marriage to her and was sent away with a flea in his ear. And the consequence of that was, Miss Lincoln, that the bailiffs, whom the moneylenders had been holding off in case his suit was successful, were sent in to turn him out of his home.'

Emma could not, in all politeness, express her pleasure that her old adversary had come to grief, so she offered Sir Thomas some suitable noises instead. She was not to know that, m'lord's and Lord Lufton's social support having been withdrawn from him, the rest of the county had followed suit—with the result that the London moneylenders who had held off whilst he was accepted had gone in for the kill.

'He was always a fool,' offered Sir Thomas uncharitably. 'Knew it for sure when he wouldn't join the Grand Allies. Lufton, too. But Lufton is rich enough not to mind losing what he might have gained from signing up with us.'

Well, at least by the sound of it she would not have to meet either of them again. Nursing that happy thought, Emma spent the rest of the evening being charming to everyone—particularly m'lord, into whose arms Sir Thomas and Miss Whately seemed determined to throw her. She was told to be his partner at whist, and when the teaboard came in Miss Whately asked m'lord to take Miss Lincoln her tea, and practically pushed him into the armchair next to her.

'Tell me,' queried m'lord, 'how did you manage to suborn Sir Thomas and Miss Whately so quickly that they have entered into such a determined cabal to pair us off? I am all agog.'

Emma sipped her tea with such grace that m'lord wished to wrench the teacup from her hand and shower her expressive mouth with kisses.

'Oh,' she said, 'I have done nothing. But from something Sir Thomas said I gather that they are both convinced that you ought to marry, and that they think that the rich Miss Emilia Lincoln, so interested in steam engines, would make you an ideal wife. After all, we should always have Geordie Stephenson as a subject for conversation, if nothing else. Which is more than most husbands and wives have, I suppose.'

This sally had m'lord choking over his tea.

'What in the world has madam been saying, Chard,' cried Sir Thomas, 'to have such an effect on you?'

M'lord being unable to answer, Emma did so for him. 'Nothing out of the ordinary, Sir Thomas. I was merely discussing steam engines.'

'Steam engines, hey?' Sir Thomas was highly entertained. 'Never knew them have such an effect on a feller before. Drink some brandy, Chard. Medicinal, I'm told. Should cure the splutters.' He walked over to Miss Whately's sideboard with all the aplomb of a frequent guest and poured m'lord a giant draught of her best cognac.

M'lord, who rarely drank these days, could not refuse. He took the brandy, trying to avoid Emma's amused eyes. Now look what you have got me into, he wanted to reproach her, but it was his own fault. He should have fled the field the moment he had entered Miss Whately's drawing room and seen her.

The worst of it was that he could imagine the delightful life that they would have together, both in bed and out of it. He had never imagined that he would enjoy talking to a woman so much. Particularly one who had such an original turn of phrase, so that he never knew what was coming next. The only thing to do was to avoid her. But this made him feel so melancholy that even the brandy could not help him.

Later he was bearded again by Sir Thomas, who roared jovially at him, 'The ladies will excuse us for a second, Chard, I'm sure. Need to talk business with you a little. Drawing room not the place, m'dear.' This last to Miss Whately.

'By all means, use the library, Sir Thomas,' she returned, amused as always at his tactless attempt to be tactful and smiling a little as he walked Chard out of the room, an arm flung around his shoulders.

M'lord assumed that it was more about Stephenson that was coming, but he was wrong. Sir Thomas dropped his jolly mask and was a man of power showing his power for once; he usually cloaked it under a mask of light-heartedness. 'Thought I ought to warn you, m'boy—' everyone under forty was 'm'boy' to him, although he was barely forty himself '—that that madhead, Ben Blackburn, is running around the North howling that one way or another he will see you off for ruining him. Dangerous feller, Blackburn. There's not much I'd put beyond him. All the Blackburn men have savage tempers. Known for it.'

'Ruining him?' echoed m'lord, genuinely bewildered. 'He ruined himself, so far as I am aware.'

'Well, not entirely,' granted Sir Thomas. 'Lufton put it about that you turned him out of Loudwater and made him *persona non grata* for some reason or other, which ruined him socially. That and Lady Clara refusing him. Some unsavoury tale about his behaviour to Miss Lincoln when she was Lady Letty's governess, apparently. Claimed it ruined him financially as well as socially. Don't normally listen to such gossip m'self, but forewarned is forearmed where such a loose screw as Master Ben is concerned. Watch out on a dark night and all that. Keep an eye on your lady too.'

The smile m'lord gave was a wry one. Like it or not, he and Miss Emilia Lincoln were seen as a couple. Half the county were determined that one way or another they ought to be married.

And so Sir Thomas told him—his next bit of business, he said.

'I'm an older man than you are, and you may call me a busybody,' he galloped on, 'but you need a wife, Lady Letty needs a mother and Loudwater needs a mistress—and one who would bring a mort of money with her. Any rich woman would do—but Miss Lincoln is more than that. She's a pretty filly and a clever one—just the thing for you, Chard. Wonder you're standin' about and not gettin' on with it.'

'There are problems. . .' began m'lord a trifle stiffly, but Sir Thomas would have none of it.

'Gammon, m'boy. Dotes on you, so she does, and you've more than half an eye for her, that's plain. Do your duty and thank God that it's a pleasure, I say.'

This came out in such congratulatory tones that m'lord could scarce restrain a snort of laughter. Were he and Emma so easy to read, then? He supposed that they were. Like it or not, Sir Thomas's bluff words of advice were widening the crack in his determination not to marry her—a crack which had begun to appear from the moment he had seen her again.

All his splendid resolutions to preserve his honour by renouncing her and her magnificent fortune were apparently only capable of being sustained if he never set eyes on her again. The minx must have known that when she pursued him northwards. A clever filly, Sir Thomas had said, and so she was—now and ten years ago, when she had refused him.

But was he such a weathercock that the slightest breeze could swing him round, make him forswear himself? All that evening and the next day, as he made himself pleasant at The Dovecote m'lord felt that he was being blown by contrary winds.

He had been solitary by choice for so long, but now he was enjoying company again—showing his fellow guests quite a different man from the one they thought they had known. He was the young Dominic Hastings with a difference: time, suffering and responsibility had made him fundamentally serious after a fashion which would never change. But this seriousness gave the charm which he was unconsciously beginning to display again a deeper, truer note.

To Emma it was as though the years had rolled back. M'lord had turned into the man she had at first thought him when they were both young and untried. It was as though then she had imagined him, and had had to wait for the years to bring him to her.

On the second afternoon the company strolled out of Miss Whately's small but pleasant home park towards the rougher ground through which the North Tyne ran. Sir Thomas and Miss Whately manoeuvred things so that m'lord and

Emma were paired off—not that either of them demurred when matters were so arranged.

'Tell me, Miss Lincoln—' she was never Emma to him, for to give way on that meant that he was on the road to giving way over everything to do with her '—what is there about me which is exciting the company so? Display all your noted candour in answering me, I beg of you.' He could not avoid noticing that he was the subject of some uncommon interest.

'Why,' she answered him playfully, 'I believe that they thought you a very bear, and they are surprised to find you so tamed, so civilised a domestic animal rather than a wild one.'

He had been unselfconscious enough for the last ten years neither to know nor care what others thought of him—having been only too careful always to try to please others when he had been a very young man.

'I suppose,' he said slowly, 'that that is what you meant when you said that I was greatly changed from what I had been when you first knew me. I think that the change was so gradual that I was scarce aware that it had happened.'

Emma doubted whether the change had been very gradual, but did not say so. That he was beginning to question himself a little was, she considered, a very good thing—for then he might begin to question his decision not to marry her! His will had always been strong, and so she told him—strong in the wrong way when he was young, but in the right way after he had inherited.

'If no man is a hero to his valet,' he said, a little wryly, 'then I am also no hero to the woman who claims to love me.'

'I could not love a hero,' pronounced Emma solemnly, 'for heroes are perfect. And if I married one I would be unable to live up to his perfection, which would not make for happiness since I would constantly be disappointing him. Now, you, on the other hand—'

'Being imperfect, would love you for your imperfections! A novel doctrine, I must say! Did you know that Sir Thomas thinks you clever, and since he is a very clever man himself, though he tries to pretend that he is not, that is a great compliment. I am glad that being a fool is not one of your imperfections.'

'True,' sighed Emma, accepting the compliment and the bow that came with it, 'but one of my imperfections is not suffering fools gladly.'

'Why, as to that,' said m'lord, frowning a little, 'I have to tell you that you should be careful if you run across Ben Blackburn again—for he, being a fool, is making threatening noises about being revenged on us. Sir Thomas is a little troubled over the matter, and since he takes Blackburn's threats seriously, then so do I.'

'It is difficult to imagine what mischief he can do,' Emma said. 'Miss Whately told me that he is a ruined man, living in lodgings in Newcastle these days. But I will be careful.'

They had reached the banks of the North Tyne, and their close conversation had been watched with approval by their two patrons.

Sir Thomas had received word that morning that the trials of the modified *Blutcher* were to take place within the sennight, and now he invited the whole party to them.

'Another historic occasion to tell your grand-children of.' He beamed at m'lord and Emma as though they had already announced the wed-ding—or the nuptials, as he chose to call them privately to Miss Whately.

'So,' remarked m'lord as Sir Thomas walked ahead of them, 'I must congratulate you, Miss Lincoln. It seems you are to acquire grand-children.' Then he added, a little slyly, 'Not at once, one supposes, but in some distant future.'

'Indeed?' replied Emma, answering him as lightly as he had spoken to her. 'You are sure of that, m'lord? I am to marry, then?' The smile she gave him was a bewitching one. 'I wonder who their grandfather will be? Is it possible that you are able to enlighten me? If so, pray tell me who he is. I usually like surprises, but I would prefer not to be *too* surprised when I discover who my future husband might be!'

M'lord did not yet want to enlighten Miss Emilia Lincoln. At least not in the sense that she meant. He wanted, rather, to enjoy her in the fullest possible way—a desire quite impossible of accomplishment seeing that they were walking in the open surrounded by Miss Whately's guests. Now, if they were alone, and the folly was near. . . or some other secluded spot. . .they might play nymphs and shepherds on the grass to their heart's content.

Of course, if he were to forget his honour, change his mind and marry her, then all these obstacles to his—and her—pleasure would disappear, and the grandchildren would appear in due course.

He looked down at her. The expression on Emma's face was one of such grave delight that m'lord was quite undone. He put his hand over hers. Never mind that to do so was to rouse him even further—a man had the right to enjoy himself.

His love seemed uncommonly quiet. He wondered whither her thoughts were taking her, and unconsciously his hand tightened on hers. Emma felt the loving pressure and was reassured. All would be well, she was sure.

And so, her hand on m'lord's arm, where she thought it ought to be for life, they strolled along the banks of the silvery Tyne—she dreaming of doing so with a clutch of little ones trotting behind them while m'lord wondered how much longer he could hold out against all the lures with which his determined love thought to trap him!

# CHAPTER SIXTEEN

'THE devil take the lot of them,' growled Ben Blackburn into his ale. He was drinking in a low den in Newcastle-upon-Tyne. He had just been informed by one of his hangers-on there that Killingworth was to be the scene of yet another famous event. The much improved *Blutcher*, so changed that it hardly resembled its original self, was due to have another trial run, and everyone from Killingworth and district was determined to go along to celebrate another of 'wor Geordie's' successes.

'Hope the damned thing blows itself up with its own steam,' Ben finished, 'and takes the lot of them to hell together. Particularly Chard,' he added morosely, holding out his tankard for another refill, 'and his damned lightskirt as well.'

He blamed all his troubles on that cursed visit to Loudwater. Chard turning him out because of that damned governess had, he believed, started the chain reaction which had brought him to a pair of filthy rooms in a Newcastle backstreet. He might have been one of those investing money in the hope of being in the forefront of the development of locomotives on rails, instead of which he was so strapped for cash that his landlady had begun to dun him and was threatening to turn him into the

328

street if he failed to pay her the three months back rent which he owed her.

Ideas of vengeance chased one another through his muddled brain. Later than night, sitting on his dirty bed, he took out one of the few possessions which he had salvaged from the general ruin of his life: a pair of pistols which he caressed lovingly, his eyes shut, whilst he determined what he would do with them.

Yes, he would go to Killingworth, and he would give the devil a hand in disposing of Chard—he was sure to be there. And if he weren't then he would find another occasion to finish him off, as surely as he had finished off poor Ben Blackburn and turned him, homeless and penniless, into an unkind world.

The news that a new locomotive, *Wellington*, was to be run at Killingworth again spread throughout Northumbria and County Durham. The word was that it was better than *Blutcher*. Sir Thomas and the other lessees of the collieries around Killingworth, including Chard of Loudwater, were sure to be there to see the fun. Some said that a lady had come from London and was putting money not only into promoting the locomotive, but also into the miners' safety lamp which 'wor Geordie' had developed.

A lady interested in locomotives! That did seem a bit steep, but sure enough, there were ladies present on that afternoon, and one of them was pointed out as 'the Lunnon lass'.

Emma had been worried that m'lord would not be present. They had spent a happy week together at The Dovecote, but merely as friends, and, as m'lord had constantly emphasised, 'nothing else'.

She did not believe him. Or rather, they were friends, but that did not, in her book, ultimately preclude them from becoming lovers. But after the first day m'lord had put his armour on again, which left her with the task of removing it.

Why, she did not know, nor for what reason either, but Emma had a firm presentiment that the run at Killingworth would bring them together. It was stupid to believe such a thing, she knew, but there it was. One could not always be sensible. A sensible woman would not have run after m'lord, but would have accepted the offers of the titled and the famous which were sure to arrive now that she was rich again, as her aunt was fond of telling her.

In any case she would be at Killingworth, and she thought that m'lord would be there as well. He would not wish to offend Sir Thomas, who had been a good friend to him.

'Chard's pullin' things round at Loudwater,' Sir Thomas had said to her after m'lord had left The Dovecote without actually promising to go to Killingworth. 'Sterlin' feller, Chard. Needs a good wife, though.'

Which was, Emma had supposed amusedly, his

notion of telling her tactfully that she ought to be that good wife.

'I think that m'lord would like to choose his wife himself,' she had replied demurely.

'Oh, aye,' he had grunted back. 'But some fellers need a helpin' hand in the mind-makin'-up department, Miss Lincoln.'

There had been no useful answer which Emma could have made to that, and she was thinking about Sir Thomas and his desire to see his protégé settled now, as she stood between Miss Whately and Miss Dacre among the crowd of great folk and small who had come to see Stephenson's new locomotive show off its paces.

M'lord, alas, did not appear to be one of the many standing at the back of Mr Stephenson's small cottage. Sir Thomas was there, with several of the Grand Allies and a Mr Dodds, who had helped Stephenson to take out his patent for his new engine.

Whilst there was not quite the excitement that there had been on *Blutcher*'s first run, there was still sufficient novelty in seeing a machine run on wheels to have attracted a large crowd—even larger than that of just over a year ago. Emma could not help remembering that happy day: the day on which she had first realised how much she still loved m'lord—and that he loved her.

It was almost as though thinking of him had conjured him up. For there he was on the edge of the crowd, descending from his carriage, John

Bassett with him—but without a damaged wrist this time. He had come!

He had seen her, and she had eyes only for him and he for her as he made his way to where she and Miss Whately stood. M'lord was all the Earl of Creation today—to show his appreciation of Mr Stephenson's latest triumph, Emma assumed. He was impressive in a bottle green coat, skin-tight cream breeches and highly polished boots.

What was more important to her was that he was back to resembling the handsome hero of her youth. The grimness which had been such a major part of his make-up since he had inherited Loudwater had finally disappeared. He was easy again, at one with himself, and his eyes shone at the sight of her—as did John Bassett's. But Emma's returning smile was only for m'lord.

Friends, indeed! Oh, no. They were meant to be lovers. The week which they had spent apart had told m'lord how much he missed her, how much he wanted her by him to tease him with her ready tongue and to turn those great dark eyes on him to enslave him permanently. To live without her was a nightmare which he did not wish to face, and the time away from her had merely served to confirm what he had known from the first moment that he had seen her in the hall at Loudwater. They were not two but one, and the split halves of them were burning to be joined.

Behind him, unseen by Emma, since m'lord was

the magnet which drew her sole attention, walked Mrs Morton, Mr Cross and Tish.

'Oh, Papa! Look, Papa, there's Miss Lawrence.' Casting off Mrs Morton's hand, Tish ran towards Emma, crying, 'Oh, why ever did you leave us, Miss Lawrence? And now you are back you must visit Loudwater. Mustn't she, Papa, mustn't she?'

M'lord, whom Tish had left behind in her mad rush towards Emma—she was clinging to her as though she meant never to let her go—was now face to face with his love.

'So you came,' was all that Emma could manage.

'Yes,' he replied simply. 'Although I should not have done. Much though I wish to see Stephenson's new locomotive.'

'Is this one called *Blutcher* too?' demanded Tish, quite unaware of the conflicting passions in the breasts of her papa and her late governess. 'Papa says that you have a new name now. Or rather, that you are being called now by the name you were originally given. I must remember to address you as Miss Lincoln, he says, and not Miss Lawrence. I forgot that earlier when I first saw you and called you Miss Lawrence. Oh, and I am not to bully you, he says. But I never bullied you, did I? Even when you were my governess.'

'No,' agreed Emma, smiling. 'You never bullied me—although I think that I bullied you a little.'

'If I thought that by bullying you you would come back to Loudwater with Papa and me, then I would bully you.' Tish sounded a little sorrowful. 'Papa seems so much happier when you are with us.'

M'lord's eyes met Emma's in a rueful acknowledgement of the truth so naïvely offered.

Sir Thomas interrupted the prospect of any further revelations from Tish by coming up to them, taking m'lord on one side and saying, a trifle conspiratorially, 'My men tell me that Ben Blackburn is in the neighbourhood, still making vague threats against you and Lufton. As to Lufton, Blackburn may do as he pleases, but we had best keep careful watch that he does not have a go at you. I'll have some of the colliers remove him if he does dare to show his face. I'm glad there is a large crowd present to see Stephenson's latest achievement, but it means that it will be easier for Blackburn to lose himself in it than if it were small.'

It was almost last year all over again, Emma thought. John Bassett came up to her to congratulate her on her good fortune, as did Mr Cross and Mrs Morton. Miss Whately and Miss Dacre were introduced to them, and the three women immediately began a conversation on matters more interesting to them than Mr Stephenson's locomotive. Sir Thomas, too, wandered off, taking John Bassett with him quite deliberately, so as to leave Emma and m'lord alone and a little apart from the crowd, which was growing impatient in its desire to see the new engine at work.

They stood silent for a moment—words no longer being needed, each other's presence being enough for them. Emma thought exultantly, Ah, my dearest love, by the softness of your look, by your very stance you betray that your feelings for me have changed and deepened. I shall yet gain my heart's delight. Aloud she said, 'It does not seem a year since we stood together on this very spot, waiting for *Blutcher* to begin his run.'

'Last year,' said m'lord softly, 'I took a cinder out of your eye which *Blutcher* put there. I wonder if this year *Wellington* will be a little more kind to you.'

'Since it allowed you to do me a service, I would hardly have called *Blutcher* unkind, but I would expect any engine named after Britain's latest hero to be kinder to me,' returned Emma, remembering that it had been m'lord removing the cinder from her eye which had betrayed their passion to the world. She wondered what the world was thinking now, as transformed governess and transformed Chard faced one another again.

She had no time to think further on the matter. Tish was calling her over—'There is a better view over here, Miss Lincoln!'—and John Bassett was trying to catch m'lord's attention with a message from Sir Thomas, who had rejoined George Stephenson at the beginning of the run, having given his two protégés time to exchange pleasantries.

'I will go to Tish,' Emma offered. 'Sir Thomas

would no doubt prefer to talk business to you with me out of the way.'

M'lord thought that that statement might not be entirely true, but agreed nevertheless, saying softly, 'I will return to you later. You do not need an escort?' This last was more of a question than a command, and Emma shook her head.

'I have only a few yards to walk before I join her,' she returned. 'I do not need an escort in such a public place, I am sure.'

At any other time such a statement would have been an uncontrovertible truth, but fate had other designs for Emma. She had scarcely gone more than a dozen paces through the crowd before she was caught round the waist from behind, and a harsh voice was whispering in her ear, 'Stay still, my fine doxy, or I'll shoot you instead of your lover.'

It was Ben Blackburn who was holding her so cruelly. She opened her mouth to scream a warning to m'lord, but Ben was before her.

'Chard, hey, Chard!' he called. 'See what a fine fish I have caught! If you want me to leave go of her, you must do what I ask you. Without argument.'

At the sound of his name shouted so peremptorily m'lord swung round, to see Emma in Ben Blackburn's grip.

'What—?' he began. 'Free her at once, Blackburn, and I promise that no harm will come to you.'

'Aye, and no harm will come to her if you do as I ask of you.' Ben grinned back at him. 'It's your skin I want to hang out to dry, not hers. She's merely bait, Chard.'

By now the crowd had turned its attention from Stephenson's locomotive, about to start its run, to the other drama enfolding before them.

M'lord, his face white, began to walk towards Ben.

At the same time a warning growl from the crowd threatened Ben, if he did not release the lady.

He made a half-turn towards them, put his pistol to Emma's head and shouted hoarsely, 'If any of you try to stop me, I'll put a ball in her where it will do the most damage. You, too, Chard. Come closer, man, and when you are level with me I'll let her go. Then I'll settle my reckoning with you.'

Putting Emma and Chard between himself and the crowd, he began to walk backwards, parallel with the tramway. Unaware of the drama being played out at the end of the incline, Stephenson had given the order for the locomotive to begin its run. Several of the men in the crowd in front of Ben moved forward to attack him, but he put the pistol to Emma's head again, threatening her if they came any nearer.

They hesitated, and m'lord called out, 'Don't try to stop him, men. He's a mad dog—not responsible for his actions.'

Enraged by this, Ben backed still further away from the crowd, shouting, 'One more insult like that, Chard, and I'll kill your doxy instead of you.'

'Release her at once,' commanded m'lord as steadily as he could. He was near to them now, and could plainly see Emma's stricken face—and Ben Blackburn's fell one.

Although she had not spoken since Ben had attacked her, on seeing m'lord continue to approach them steadily, Emma cried to him, 'Stop, m'lord. Stop where you are. I'll take the risk of being killed rather than have you come any nearer. If he has to kill anyone, let it be me.'

'Oh, brave,' snarled Ben, 'but it's Chard's blood I want, not his doxy's.' And then, as m'lord disobeyed his dearest love's last wish by walking right up to him, he flung Emma from him with such force that she fell on to her hands and knees. Now! Now was the time to dispose of the man who had ruined him. He brought up his pistol to fire point-blank at his enemy. What matter if then, his pistol empty, the crowd fell on him? He would not mind swinging if he had succeeded in killing Chard.

For a moment m'lord looked death in the face, and then, as the pistol was levelled at him for the kill, he flung himself forward to catch Ben low down, round the thighs, and so bear him to the ground. So fierce was this unexpected assault that as he lost his balance Ben's finger involuntarily tightened on the hair-trigger and he fired a wasted shot into the air, the pistol flying out of his hand.

By the time they reached the ground and finished rolling over and over, m'lord found that Ben was on top of him. Ben took full advantage of his good luck by striking m'lord hard in the face, momentarily stunning him. He rose, triumphant, staring wildly about him, to see that Emma, recovered from the shock of her fall, was running towards where m'lord, his head spinning, was trying to rise to his feet. The crowd was streaming after her.

Baffled, weaponless, thwarted of his revenge, lost to everything but self-preservation now that he had failed, Ben Blackburn gave a hoarse cry and turned and ran from the avenging crowd. His only hope of escaping their anger was to try to cross the tramway in front of the oncoming locomotive, so that they were held up by its passage, giving him a chance to get away before they could reach him.

He might have succeeded had he not misjudged the engine's speed, thinking that it was as slow as *Blutcher* had been. Alas for him, *Wellington*, with its extra power, was upon him in an instant. Instead of escaping he ran straight into its path. . .

His pursuers, stunned by the sight of Ben Blackburn hurling himself to what seemed like certain death on the tramway, started back as the locomotive struck him, lest they, too, were mown down. Neither Emma nor most of the crowd saw

Ben's accident, although those near enough to witness it began to scream and shout.

Emma heard the dreadful noise as she knelt down to help m'lord, who, his head still swimming, was sitting up and ruefully holding his bruised jaw. She flung her arms around him and at last broke down, alternately sobbing and kissing him at the sheer joy of finding him alive. Nothing mattered to either of them except that the other was safe.

Those further up the slight incline, including Sir Thomas's party, had witnessed everything from a distance, not entirely certain of what was happening. It was only when Jem Stephenson had brought *Wellington* to a shuddering stop that they all ran to where Ben Blackburn lay in his blood. Sir Thomas shouted to those around him to look after the ladies and one of the colliers, bolder than the rest, began to tell him of Ben Blackburn's attack on Miss Lincoln and m'lord, and how he had come to run onto the track.

John Bassett, his face drawn and shocked, hurried to where m'lord, who had been helped to his feet by some of the shocked spectators of the attempted murder, was standing, Emma by his side. They were looking towards the stationary locomotive, wondering what all the commotion was about.

'No, don't go,' John said to them, shaking a little himself. 'It is not a fit sight for a lady—or for you either, m'lord.' Then, on seeing their bewildered faces, he said, 'You are not aware of what has happened?'

Briefly, he told them of Ben Blackburn's fate. 'He is still alive, they say—which is most surprising. But he will lose his arm and stand trial for attempted murder—if they can stanch the bleeding, that is, and save him.'

Emma hid her face in m'lord's chest whilst he put a protective arm around her. He was still a little dazed.

'I would not have wished that on him,' he said slowly. 'But he was behaving so wickedly that such an outcome was inevitable. Indeed, I think that I would have killed him myself in order to save Emma.'

'I thought that he was going to kill *you*,' sobbed Emma into his waistcoat. 'I cannot feel sorry for him—no, not at all.' More soberly she went on, 'I might later. But now I can only think that he ran upon his fate when he decided to try to kill you.' She shuddered. 'I thought that he *had* killed when you pulled him down and he struck you so cruelly!'

'Damn killing me!' exclaimed m'lord. 'I thought that he was going to kill *you*.' And he tightened his arm around her, ignoring what the world might think of such a public display of affection. He was having a little difficulty in coming to terms with the fact that he was still alive.

More than that, his world having turned upside down when he had seen Emma in Ben Blackburn's cruel grip, he was finding it hard to turn it right way up again. All that he could think of was that he had been the most unutterable fool to allow anything to stand in the way of his marrige to her. They had already lost ten years together, and for several dreadful minutes it had looked as though fate was determined to part them for ever, their love unfulfilled.

Something must be done about that, he decided. And quickly!

Nothing was going to stop him—not even the exclamations and congratulations of the crowd around them, excited by his escape from what had seemed certain death. Tish was hanging onto him, happy to discover that Papa was still alive.

Miss Dacre gently tried to detach Emma from m'lord. In vain! Neither of them would let go of the other. Like m'lord, Emma had decided that all this foolery about not marrying had gone on long enough, and so she would tell him. But she did not need to, for now that she had stopped sobbing and shaking m'lord took her hand and kissed it.

Regardless of all the curious onlookers, he cried impetuously, 'This may not be the best of times to say it, but I delayed once before, my darling, and I have just made up my mind that I shall never delay again. To think that I might have died without ever asking you what I ought—and all because of some cloudy notion that my honour was involved!

'Miss Emilia Lincoln, I have the honour to ask for your hand in marriage. Pray accept your humble servant, who finds that he does not wish to live without you.'

'Oh, yes, yes,' breathed Emma. 'You know that I will marry you. Ever and always.'

'Excellent,' said m'lord, kissing her rapturously, to the delight of all the spectators. 'Exactly what I wished to hear. Now let us go home and set about the business of making my wish come true.'

For a moment they stood, arms around one another, in a moment out of time, until, blushing, Emma looked around her—at Tish, who was jumping for joy, at a smiling Miss Whately and at Sir Thomas and Mr Stephenson, who had arrived in time to hear m'lord's declaration and Emma's acceptance of it.

They had just finished comforting Jem Stephenson, telling him—truthfully—that at the speed he had been travelling he had had no chance of avoiding Ben when he had run into his path without warning.

'So,' announced Sir Thomas, beaming benevolently on everyone, but particularly on Emma and m'lord, 'that rogue brought about some good, after all. Although he did not mean to. Threw you into each other's arms, did he? And about time too. Man must have been mad, though, to attack you here, so publicly.'

This last sentence was the only epitaph which Ben Blackburn ever received!

All excitements, including the triumphant run of Mr Stephenson's new engine, now being over, the crowd had begun to return home, walking behind the carriages of all the great folk. Some of them were sobered a little by what had happened; others were elated.

Ben Blackburn had been a harsh master, and more than one man privately said that he had brought his doom upon himself by his intemperate behaviour. He had been carried to a nearby house, and a doctor who had been present was tending his wounds, not sure whether he would live or die. A constable had been sent for and was guarding the house.

The wedding was a quiet one. Neither bride nor groom wished to make it a grand occasion. They were married in Loudwater's small chapel with only a few friends present, including Aunt Fontaine and her family, and as many servants as the chapel would hold. The rest were assembled in the kitchen, waiting for the return of the lucky ones so that they might begin to eat the feast which m'lord had ordered.

Louis collected his money for winning his bet after the ceremony was over. 'Always knew she'd nab him, and quickly too,' he announced gleefully. 'Determined madam, the new Lady Chard, and rich enough to save Loudwater, they say.'

'Quite a fairy tale,' was the sentimental comment of the housekeeper, who was wearing a new gown made specially for the wedding.

Comment above stairs was similar, but more

restrained. Not that m'lord or Emma cared one jot or iota for what anyone was saying about them. They had found one another and that was enough for them.

Perhaps the happiest person after the bride and groom was Tish, the only fly in whose ointment was that her new mama would not be able to give her lessons every day—she would be too busy being papa's wife.

'I do believe,' said m'lord with a smile—he was given to smiling again since Emma had accepted him—'that if we gave her half a chance, Tish would have insisted on spending the wedding night with us.' They were alone at last, in his bedroom, when he said this. He was gently lifting from Emma's head the small wreath of white carnations which had held her bridal veil.

Outside, the carriages of the visitors were streaming away down the drive—Emma's aunt's among them. Tish was sitting in the carriage beside Emma's young cousin, Caroline, with whom she had struck up a rapid friendship. She had protested a little at having to leave Papa and her new mama behind, but had been assured that it would only be a few weeks before she saw them again.

'You're lucky,' Caroline told her, from the superior position given to her by her eleven years. 'My uncle and aunt Pomfret spent two years abroad on their honeymoon, and left Uncle Pomfret's two children by his first wife behind.'

Emma had given Tish her little bouquet of white carnations, and she was still holding it as she turned for a last look at Loudwater before driving to the Fontaines' home in North Yorkshire.

'Poor Tish,' said Emma gently. 'But. . .'

'But we deserve a little time to ourselves, I think,' said m'lord. He was now unbuttoning Emma's light gauze overjacket, adding as he did so, 'I'd no idea that a woman had to put on so many clothes in order to get married. It will be quite a feat to find my Emma beneath them.'

'I might say the same of yours,' retorted Emma, pulling his cravat undone so that she might begin to relieve him of his shirt. One thing about having made love to your husband before the wedding night was that it took away a great deal of the worry about how one ought to behave on that momentous occasion.

'Forward little minx, aren't you?' said m'lord with a grin. 'One might almost think that you had done this before.' And his smile was wicked as he bore her to the great bed. 'I hope you don't mind making love again in the daylight, but, having waited ten years to get you to bed, I really can't be expected to wait any longer.'

Emma was on her back now, smiling up at him, murmuring, 'I like your impatience, m'lord.'

He had just enough sanity left to whisper to her before he began to kiss her all over—even in places where Emma had never thought to be kissed.

'Dominic. Call me Dominic, my love. M'lord is meant for the governess, not m'lord's wife.'

'But I always. . .' began Emma, and then, as her senses began to swoon under his ministrations, the last reservation, the last remnant of the resentment she had felt on that long ago night fell away, and she groaned, 'Oh, Dominic, do *that* again, please.'

And so he did. And again. Until even the pleasure which Emma had experienced in the folly was surpassed. She, who had always been so controlled, writhed and twisted beneath him until they both reached a shuddering climax together.

Silence fell. Even Emma's ready tongue was rendered mute by the power of their shared pleasure. The rays of the setting sun fell across the bed, found them sleeping, twined together.

It was some time before they woke—m'lord first, to waken Emma by stroking her until she turned into his arms saying sleepily, 'Don't stop.'

So he didn't. But this time, after they had made love more slowly, but just as deeply, and she was lying in the crook of his arm, he propped himself against the pillows and said, 'You called me Dominic at the last, just now. It is years since anyone used my name. My mother always called me Dominic, but after she died I was always Hastings or Chard. I feel myself again.'

There was such quiet happiness on his face that Emma gave him an impulsive kiss. He said in some wonderment, 'If I had known all those years ago what you could do—to and for me—I would have picked you up and run with you to the nearest altar, demanding to be married!'

At first this set Emma laughing, only for her to stop when he added, in a puzzled voice, 'Why did I not recognise what you were when I first knew you? The gypsy was right when she said that when I met my true love I would not know her—nor did I.'

She lay silent for a little, thinking, then said solwly, 'I think that we both needed to grow up. I did not know myself, so how could you know me? Because. . .because. . .I had spent my life being given things—everything I wanted—and I had never had to earn them or do anything in return for them. I thought that they were mine by right, because I deserved them.

'And you were the biggest present of all. I never asked myself whether I deserved you, or why you might want me for any other reason than because I was personally such a prize. I never thought of you at all. Oh, I knew my defects—I always wanted to be slim and beautiful, not to be fat, not to have a stammer—but it never occurred to me that I ought to do something to cure them myself. I simply took it as my due that you were kind to me and wanted to marry me.

'That was why overhearing your opinion of me came as such a shock. Later, much later, I understood what men and women meant when they said that they had experienced a revelation which changed their lives. That revelation certainly changed mine. My first wish was to hurt you as much as you had hurt me, and I did just that. It was not until I was penniless myself, and struggling to survive, that I began to understand what poverty had done to you. That it had made you desperate to marry money, but also that you might resent what you felt compelled to do to gain it—as I resented my servitude in other people's houses.'

She fell silent. M'lord's arms tightened about her as she added in a lower voice, 'I suppose that is why I shall always think of you first as m'lord—because he was so different from that selfish boy, as I hope I am now different from that selfish girl. It is why I still wish to be Emma, not Emilia. But rest assured, if I call you Dominic it is because I love you, and the past cannot hurt either of us any more. Or so I hope. It lies behind us, and the future is ours to enjoy.'

He kissed her again. 'My love, my only love. Let me say this. Your spirit is such a generous one that I am in awe of it. I still wonder that you have been able to love me again after—'

Emma put a hand on his mouth. 'Shush. It is forgotten. Over.'

'There is something which I must tell you, though,' he said gravely. 'When we first made love I told you that my marriage had been most unhappy. That my wife was not faithful to me. Letitia—Tish—is not my child. It was quite impossible for me to have been her father. Before she was born I had made up my mind to send both the child and her mother away. And then my wife died in childbirth. They took me to see her. . .and there, in a cot beside her bed, crying bitterly, was Tish—another man's child.

'I remember staring down at her. She was so small and helpless, and her cries were so anguished. I don't know why I did so, but I picked her up—and she quietened in my arms. She sucked on my finger when I lifted my hand to touch her face.

'You spoke of a moment of revelation. I had one then. I found that the thought of sending her away, of disowning her—for I could easily have proved that she was not mine—horrified me. I found that I could not abandon something so small and helpless.

'I gave her to the wet-nurse, and said, quite deliberately, "Look after my daughter." And she has been my daughter ever since. She must not know otherwise. I was twitted once about her parentage, and I fought my only duel over it. She is mine, so acknowledged, and is therefore legally mine.

'Like you, I had always taken the good things which came my way as my due, and they had turned into dust and ashes. But Tish was something different. You said that your revelation changed you; I think mine changed me. I had to forget all feelings of false pride and self to keep her. And now she is truly mine, my daughter—as I hope that she will be yours.'

Emma did not tell him that she already knew that Tish was not his. He had freely told her the truth, and in doing so had added to her respect for the man he had become.

'Yes, Tish shall be my daughter too, and will, I hope, be joined by future brothers and sisters. You do want Tish to have some brothers and sisters, I trust?'

'Indeed—as I want the pleasure of giving them to you.' He turned her in his arms again. 'M'lady—for you are m'lady, as I am m'lord—let us begin our life together by trying to create a new one. You agree?'

'Oh, most willingly.' Emma lifted her face for his kiss, the past behind them, the present a delight and the future a land which they would explore together.

Later, as night fell and sleep began at last to claim them, m'lord murmured into her ear, 'I suppose that you might say that in the end we have each had our revenge on the other.'

'True,' replied Emma, settling herself more comfortably in his arms. 'But a sweet revenge, surely.'

# BETRAYED HEARTS
*Elizabeth Henshall*

### CHESHIRE 1080

Lady Ghislaine de Launay had little choice where she married, but she objected to being a pawn between the Earl of Chester and Guy de Courcy...she would rather enter the convent. As far as Guy was concerned the convent was welcome to her—*after* he had cleared his name of murder. A propitious start to their marriage! However, despite all the uncertainty, their mutual attraction was undeniable—but how could she love a possible murderer with all the evidence seemingly against him?

# THE WOLF'S PROMISE
*Alice Thornton*

### SUSSEX COAST 1809

Lady Angelica Lennard took matters into her own hands. Her brother needed bringing out of France and Benoît Faulkener owed a debt to her father. In view of her father's blindness, she would go herself to persuade Benoît to rescue Harry. Fully expecting a piratical smuggler, Angelica was mortified to discover a respectable shipowner—or was he? Some things didn't add up, but somehow Benoît didn't seem a stranger. Was she imagining the warmth and intimacy? When she fell into danger and Benoît's steely will showed through, she was sure of it!

*Available in February*